What the critics are saying...

"Altogether, these stories are perfect for this anthology and no one will be disappointed in reading this book." ~ *Coffee Time Romance*

"If you love books that give you lots of action, sex and romance with a paranormal twist, then pick up this book ASAP." ~ *Romance Junkies*

"This story is downright hot!" ~ *Romance Reviews Today*

"*Blue Moon* is a totally intense werewolf story with the perfect balance of sex and romance." ~ *Angel Brewer with Fallen Angel Reviews*

"*Lorie O'Clare* delights her reader with the high-voltage paranormal tale, *Blue Moon*." ~ *Tracey West with Road To Romance Reviews.*

"This story was a beautiful recount of finding love again after losing someone who meant the world to you." ~ *Coffee Time Romance*

"*Wilder's 'Shadow Hunter'* explodes with vampires, were-cats and love." ~ *Romantic Times*

"This triple collection of electric tales will appeal to women who are brave enough to fantasize." ~ *Romantic Times*

"A downpour of *'Raine'* sensuality and masterful storytelling can be found aplenty in *Ashleigh Raine's Twofold Desires*...Readers must make note to read this one, they might just find that they are pleasantly satisfied not a mere twofold-- but tenfold!" ~ *Tracey West for Road to Romance*

"...*Ms. Raine* has stirred up another fascinating tale between shape-shifters, protectors and a woman who holds the key to happiness." ~ *J.B. DuBose for Just Erotic Romance Reviews*

"...a stimulating romance where myth and legend play important roles. Fascinating characters, sex that's off the charts, and an intriguing plotline..." ~ *Sinclair Reid for Romance Reviews Today*

"The writing duo of *Ashleigh Raine* once again surpasses themselves with this paranormal romance of two tormented shape-shifters looking for the love they need to complete them...a great story..." ~ *Melissa, Enchanted in Romance*

Things That Go BUMP In The Night IV

ASHLEIGH RAINE. J.C. WILDER.
LORIE O'CLARE

ELLORA'S CAVE
ROMANTICA PUBLISHING

An Ellora's Cave Romantica Publication

www.ellorascave.com

Things that Go Bump in the Night IV

ISBN # 1419951262
ALL RIGHTS RESERVED.
Blue Moon Copyright © 2004 Lorie O'Clare
Shadow Hunter Copyright © 2004 J.C. Wilder
Twofold Desires Copyright© 2004 Ashleigh Raine
Edited by: Sue-Ellen Gower and Briana St. James
Cover art by: Darrell King

Electronic book Publication: September, 2004
Trade paperback Publication: September, 2005

Warning:

Contents

Blue Moon

Lorie O'Clare

Chapter One

Wind blew through her coat, the icy chill exciting her. It had been a long time since Sandy Parks had felt so alive. Her pack had relocated and times had been tough for a while. But tonight, something about the way the moonlight lit up the trees, the stars sparkled a bit brighter against the unblemished black sky, everything smelled more alive.

The second full moon this month. And it would wane just in time for Halloween. Her pack worked with some of the humans in town, making arrangements to make the holiday festive. Sandy hadn't warmed to the idea, the thought of mingling with humans still new to her. But after tonight's run, something inside her wanted to embrace life, take on all it had to offer.

Her heart beat with anticipation. The clean night air filled with rich fragrances of spruce, dew covered grass, and the rich smell of the earth. A run through their endless new hunting land filled her with more energy than she'd had in years, reminding her of her youth, filling her with life, with lust, with yearning.

Usually this time of night brought on a melancholy sensation. Individual dens parted ways, everyone heading home for the evening. Couples would saunter off to where they had parked, change to their human form, and dress while whispering contentedly to each other.

Maybe she had grown accustomed to her widowed status. Maybe her empty den no longer bothered her. Her cubs grown, successful in their jobs, Sandy might have reached a point of acceptance with her life as it was now. Quiet and just her.

But something about tonight. Her body craved more, ached to be touched, to be explored. Damnit to hell. She needed a werewolf. And not just any werewolf would do. Images of strength, overwhelming power capable of taking her places she couldn't take herself ransacked her over-exhilarated mind. Sometimes she cursed how picky she was.

She slowed her pace, taking her time reaching her car where she'd left her clothes. Others around her mingled, some of the younger werewolves sparring playfully, enjoying the beautiful night. Those who had changed pulled sweaters over their head, laughing and taking advantage of the isolated hunting ground they now had with their new location.

Glancing over toward her pack leader, Ethan Masterson, she let her gaze stroll over the other werewolves with him. Dear Lord. She acted worse than a young bitch in heat.

Her small car, a cute red Volkswagen, a gift from her daughter, was the only car left on the side of the field when she finally reached it. The tightening of muscles, while her bones popped and extended, gave her a quickening sensation in her belly. Her vision changed, shadows growing more vague, the sounds of the night fading together, while individual conversations became harder to hear.

Stretching, the cold air wrapping around her naked skin, she shivered, feeling so much more alone in her human form than as a werewolf.

"Are you headed home?" There hadn't been anyone behind her a minute ago.

Sandra jumped, startled, and turned around to stare at the pack leader's security man.

"I must be getting old." She giggled, suddenly feeling nervous under the tall man's scrutinizing gaze. The way he appeared to be taking in her naked body made her feel anything but old though. "I didn't hear you come up."

Ralph Hipp cocked his head, making a show of enjoying the view. "You don't look old to me. In fact, not many women can brag that they look better naked than with clothes on."

Sandra couldn't stop the piercing heat that flogged her senses from his praise. Ralph had always been a flirt, his chivalrous manner attracting her attention more than once. But the way he looked at her now, his dark eyes focused on her breasts, had her thinking he had more than flirting on his mind.

She smiled, turning to open her car door to get her clothes. Ralph placed his hand over hers. His rich male scent wrapped around her, the heat inside her swarming to her pussy, her heart creating a pulse there that distracted her.

"Don't get dressed yet." His hand gripped hers, willing her to turn around again.

"Why not?" She couldn't turn around all the way. And the sudden shyness that took over her made her feel silly, embarrassed in the presence of this magnificent man.

She'd admired him more than once in the past, his large stature making him hard not to notice during pack meetings. Ralph kept his head shaved, his body in incredible shape. Unlike so many other werewolves their age, nothing on him appeared to be sagging. She guessed working as a sheriff for so many years, he'd kept in shape. But right now, with his shirt unbuttoned, the thick spread of gray curly hair across his chest sprinkled with black, made her want to drool.

Ralph Hipp was sexy as hell.

"You know I watch you, keep an eye on you." He'd lowered his voice, and she glanced around them, surprised to realize they were alone in the field.

A lone truck, parked not too far away, was the only other vehicle left. She guessed it was his, although she wasn't sure.

"Yes. And I appreciate it." Her mouth had gone from dry to too wet. She wasn't accustomed to feeling awkward around him.

"Appreciate it?" He chuckled, his thick baritone sending chills through her. Although even in the chilly night air, she felt anything but cold. "If you knew the thoughts going through my head, I'm not sure you would appreciate it."

Sandra turned, looking up into that well-chiseled face. He had few wrinkles, but then she seldom saw him smile. His line of work probably helped prevent wrinkles too. An investigator didn't smile a lot. His scent gave her little clue of what he was thinking at the moment, another trait he'd probably learned doing years of investigative work.

"What thoughts are going through your head?" Her pussy throbbed as she asked.

Ralph took her hand, turning her so that she faced him. "I think you know."

He let go of her hand, running his fingers up her arm, cupping her shoulder with his rough palm. Her insides tightened, anticipation clamping down on her pussy, her breath catching, forcing her heart to pound faster.

She couldn't help herself. Reaching out, she touched his bare chest, the soft spread of hair feeling downy against her fingers. His body was warm, his muscles hard and corded against her flesh.

"I'm not sure what you are thinking." It took all of her strength to quit staring at his perfect chest and glance up at him. She attempted a flirtatious smile. "Other than you prefer me naked."

Ralph pulled her to him. His hands ran over her body, powerful and controlling, molding her to him, willing her to relax in his embrace.

A growl escaped his lips. And she felt it rumble inside him, his thick round chest muscles twitching under her hand. "You are a smart bitch." His unshaved face tickled her skin when he lowered his mouth to hers.

Sandra gasped, wondering why she hadn't expected him to kiss her. But up until now, Ralph had simply watched her, kept an eye on her, been around when she needed him. She wondered why it hadn't occurred to her that his intentions went beyond the duties of pack security.

For such a large man, his touch was surprisingly gentle. Most men pecked at her, hurried kisses in hopes they would be able to get a quick fuck. At her age, she'd learned men didn't want a relationship. Either they were no good at being a mate, or their lives were full enough that they didn't have time for anything other than a fling on the side.

Sandra wouldn't be a piece of tail for any werewolf. Just because she was widowed, her cubs grown, she didn't have to settle for some man coming around when the mood hit him. And so she had kept a clear path of the male werewolves in her pack.

But something about Ralph, also widowed, so dynamic with his strong presence, his large build, and the calm confidence that radiated around him whenever he was near. Ralph had always made her feel protected, pretty, like his attention toward her was a quiet statement that she was safe in his hands.

Ralph's hand moved over her bare back, while his fingers combed through her hair, adjusting her head, angling her so that he could deepen the kiss.

Sandra had no fight in her against him. So strong, so tall, so calm in his actions, it was as if this was meant to happen and now Ralph guided her into his warm security, where she belonged.

His strong fingers glided over her rear end, gripping her, spreading her so that cold air drifted over the fire burning in her cunt. Moisture, thick and creamy, soaked her inner thighs, the sensual scent rising in the air around them.

Ralph groaned, tightening his grip, deepening the kiss.

She opened to him, spreading her fingers as far as she could over those corded chest muscles of his, enjoying the thick curls that tickled her skin.

"Woman," Ralph breathed, breaking the kiss with as much authority as he had started it with. "Kissing you isn't enough."

His hands brushed up and down her back, stroking her with a sensual caress. Rushes of excitement built a painful pressure deep inside her pussy. She wasn't some young twit, incapable of controlling her actions. But the urge to reach down, press her hand against his jeans, just so she could feel how big his cock was, overwhelmed her.

She blinked, focused on her breathing for just a second, while she fought to keep her urges at bay. Maybe it was because she hadn't been with a werewolf in such a long time, but Ralph was making it real hard to think straight.

"But I'm not sure what you can handle." His words caught her off guard.

"What do you mean?" She leaned into him, letting one of her legs slide between his. Even through the jean material, she could feel the hard muscle tone, his solid stance what she expected from this pack protector.

"It's been a while since you've been with a werewolf." His calm statement made her want to challenge him, ask him how he would know what she did with her private life.

But the fact was true. And she had a feeling Ralph Hipp could know anything that he wanted to know. Questioning how he knew would get her nowhere. She doubted Ralph would tell her how he knew the details of her life.

"You would rather have a female who sleeps with half the pack?" She decided a coy approach might be her best bet. Anything to calm the fire burning deep inside her.

"If I wanted one of them, I would have them." Ralph's hands moved to her hips, squeezing her soft flesh, centering her, pressing her to him.

The heat from his body scourged through her. His cock pressed through his jeans, throbbing against her naked flesh. The heat as his thick shaft pulsed against her made her dizzy. She imagined a cock that could fill her and satisfy her deepest aches.

"Why are you worried about what I can handle then?" She had a hard time talking, her body one overcharged nerve ending, aching for him to touch her everywhere.

"Because I want so much from you." His growl almost made her come.

Looking up she tried to respond, but her mouth had gone dry. She shivered, not so much from the cold, but more from the promise as to what his statement might mean.

He grabbed her rear end, smashing her against the throbbing length of his cock. "I want to claim every inch of you," he whispered into the sensitive part of her neck.

Sandra thought she would pass out if he didn't hurry and stop the throbbing pain that threatened to take over her entire body.

"What are you waiting for?" She couldn't believe the brazen suggestion had just escaped her lips.

Chapter Two

Ralph could tell her what he was waiting for. But he knew she wasn't ready to hear it. He would have to show her. And that would take time.

Sandy tried to be bold with him. But he saw through her, saw her nervousness, her untamed lust. No. She wasn't ready to hear the answer.

"I'm not waiting." He had waited long enough. She was here in his arms, where she belonged. "But I will take my time."

Her sigh about undid him, the pain in his throbbing cock making it hard to focus.

"If I didn't know better I would say you have a plan." Her delicate fingers ran over his shoulders, her touch sizzling his skin.

"Yes. I do." He wouldn't lie to her.

And that trusting gaze that looked up at him, searching for more answers but not questioning him, told him that he'd judged Sandy accurately. She was aching to be taken, molded, offered what she'd never experienced before.

Her green eyes widened, wondering. But she didn't say anything else. He didn't doubt his comments made her a bit nervous. He'd anticipated that. For months he'd watched Sandy, made sure she was safe, and that none of the strays bothered her. He made especially sure of that last one.

Ethan, his pack leader, had told him a bit about her. Sandy's grown daughter, Beth, who was mouthy and needed a tight leash, proved a challenge Ethan seemed to enjoy. How Sandy had managed to raise her, he wasn't sure. Sandy wasn't a thing like her daughter. Petite and thin were the only traits mother and daughter had in common.

Sandy didn't want to run the show. She kept to herself, managed her own affairs and helped out when the pack needed her. But when approached by anyone personally, to attend pack functions, socialize, Sandy stayed home in her den. Being told he had plans for her put her on edge.

"You have my curiosity piqued," she said, a bit quieter, no longer leaning into him.

"I'll follow you home." He guessed she was ready to go.

Just letting her know that he'd created a strategy to make her his own was enough for this evening. If she even figured out that was his plan. If not, she would know soon enough. Ralph had waited long enough to make Sandy his.

Sandy ran her tongue over her lips, the small movement making his cock dance in his jeans. A pressure that bordered on pain would have to be suppressed for tonight. He would have her, but only when she asked for him. He didn't anticipate that happening this evening.

She took a step backward, nodding, and ran her fingers through her shoulder-length brown hair. Usually she pulled it back in a small ponytail, giving her a girlish look. But after running with the pack it fell free around her face, adding to her sultry air.

Her car had a new smell to it when he opened her door for her. He stood watch while she slipped into her jeans and T-shirt. When she bent over to slip her shoes on her feet, the curve of her ass made him wish he could enjoy the view without her jeans. What a perfectly rounded ass. Her legs were thin, muscular, and her jeans clung to her. He looked forward to gripping her, spreading her wide so he could see her sweet pussy and ass, exposed to him, ready to be fucked.

Sandy straightened, turning toward him to walk around her car. He noticed her hand shook when she put her keys in her ignition. Ralph waited until she had her car started before heading toward his truck.

Her sweet natural scent, something similar to honeysuckle with a touch of something more earthy, more untamed and sensual, clung to him, saturating through his skin. But he detected her nervousness, her fear. She didn't know what to expect from him.

But he knew he had to stop once he saw her pull inside her garage, her garage door sliding down silently behind her car. Sandy's smells clung to him, danced through his bloodstream. All he'd done was kiss her, touch her skin, but she'd kindled the fire already smoldering within him. And he couldn't leave her alone.

"I knew you would knock." She smiled when she answered her door, stepping to the side to allow him to enter.

Ralph sauntered into her den, closing the door behind him. Her place was simple. She hadn't lived here long enough to put her mark on it. The pack was still getting settled, and Sandy had been helping the older members get their dens in order. Her own place still lacked order and her own personal touch.

Her living room was nicely furnished. He could tell she'd moved the contents of a larger home into her smaller duplex where she lived now. The walls were bare though, and a box of pictures sat in the corner.

Walking through her place, he flipped on lights, glancing into each of the rooms. Their pack leader had given her a two-bedroom duplex, more than likely so she would be able to put her daughter up when she came to visit.

"Are you looking for bad guys?" Sandy asked, a smirk on her face.

Ralph ran his hand over her bed, glancing at the pictures on her wall. Her bedroom seemed to be the only room she had completely decorated. Imagining what she did here alone every night caused a painful throb in his cock.

"A den says a lot about a werewolf." He turned to face her, noting how relaxed she was in his presence. She didn't fear him. That was a good thing.

"And what does my place say about me?" Her teasing expression didn't change. She crossed her arms, pressing her breasts together. He loved the view.

"You spend most of your time in your bedroom." He watched her color flood her cheeks and approached her slowly. "What do you do alone in here?"

Sandy glanced past him, her scent changing along with her expression. "I'm sure I do the same things most people do in their bedrooms."

She couldn't look at him, her naturally sweet scent changing to something a bit more tart, like lemons.

"Show me your toys, Sandy." He ran his hand over her shoulder, down her arm and then brushed over her breast, unable to keep himself from feeling her ripe nipple through her shirt, so hard it begged for his touch.

Sandy stepped away from him quickly, turning, leaving him alone in her room.

"It's getting late," she told him. "And I really appreciate your making sure that I'm safe."

Ralph smiled, taking one last look around her bedroom before following her out, shutting the light off in her room as he left. He found her in her living room, looking around it with an almost desperate look while she rubbed her hands together.

"You will learn not to be shy around me," he whispered into her hair.

She shivered. Her scent turned sensual, making him crave her, drawing the beast in him to the surface. Something primal rushed through him.

"I'm far from shy." She laughed and turned to him, her eyes aglow when she smiled. "If I was, I wouldn't have let you in."

"I want more than invited into your den." He couldn't keep his hands off of her. For so long, he'd waited to touch her, learn her body, learn her mind. "I want to know you, what you like, what you enjoy."

He cupped her face in his hands, running his fingers through her hair.

"That's the impression that I got." She made a nervous sound, almost a giggle, and her cheeks flushed an adorable rose color.

Her lips were moist, her mouth so hot. He kissed her, relishing how sweet she tasted. She responded, leaning into him while a mewling sound escaped her. His carnal side, darker than she imagined, aching to surface, forced a pressure through him making his cock throb painfully.

Wrapping his arms around her, he crushed her to him, letting her feel what she did to him. A shudder ran through her when he brushed his hand across her back, and then gripped her ass. She was in perfect shape, not an ounce of fat on her.

And he loved the taste of her. Releasing her mouth, he traced his tongue over her skin, nipping at the sensitive flesh on her neck.

"Ralph. Shit." She dug into his shoulders with her hands, while her head fell back, offering herself to him.

If only she knew how much of her that he needed.

Blood rushed through his veins. His heart pumped so quickly a ringing started in his ears. The urge to growl, allow the more primal side of him to surface sent a surge of electricity through him.

"Do you know how badly I want you?" he growled, barely able to prevent the change from taking over his body.

"I think so," she gasped, clinging to him, her breasts smashed against his chest.

She teased him with her body more than she knew. Her reactions to him were natural, not trained. He loved how she hadn't become immune to her feelings, jaded from too many relationships.

"I am going to make you want me that bad, too." He needed her craving him, begging him to do what he would.

And he would enjoy bringing her to that point.

"Oh." The one word came out on an exhale, sultry and willing.

He sensed her desire to learn, her eagerness to be molded. Sandy was everything he had known she would be while watching her. Untainted, almost like a fresh flower. He could make himself believe she had saved herself over the years for him.

But he wasn't a fool. And he'd never been hung up on too many emotions. Sandy had hidden from the world ever since her mate died. He didn't know the details. But her reason for not dating had nothing to do with him.

He caressed her ass, savored how soft and round it was, ran his fingers over the place he craved to run his tongue. That special spot where her ass curved right before her legs.

"Ralph," she whispered, and leaned into him, stretching against him so that she could press her lips to his face. "It's getting late."

"It's never too late, my dear." He wanted to caress the tender skin at the bottom of her rear end just a bit longer.

And he ached to explore the rest of her, learn those special spots on her body that would make her melt. He wanted her to scream his name, beg him to do anything he wanted to her. But more than anything, he wanted to see the look in her eyes when she reached the edge, right before she toppled over and exploded for him.

"Ralph." She said his name again, adjusting herself in his arms.

He knew she fought her own urges, that she had tried to push him away just now and failed.

She leaned against his arm while he caressed her. Her expression was so flushed, the need building in her. He could see it in her eyes, the way her mouth formed an adorable circle as she struggled to keep from breathing too quickly. Running his fingers over her lips, the heat from her almost burned through him. Her jawline was firm, her neck so slender and fragile.

Instructing her right now would make her balk. So he didn't speak, just let her get accustomed to his touch. He ran his hands over her breasts, loving how firm they were. Her nipples were so hard, so sensitive. She quivered, gasping when he pinched one of them through her shirt. His heart pulsed so hard in his cock he wasn't sure how much longer he could stand the pain.

"Lift your shirt for me, Sandy." He had to see her breasts. He loved large nipples on a lady and he was sure Sandy's would be a perfect mouthful.

"We shouldn't." She nibbled at her lip, searching his face while she hesitated.

"If I lift it I might tear it from your body." He didn't want to scare her, knew she wasn't ready for everything he needed to give her. But with her in his arms like this, he could only hold back so much.

Sandy looked down, moving slightly backward while her hands moved to her shirt. She moved so slowly he thought he would explode. More than anything he wanted to grab her hands, pin them behind her, and yank the material away from her, exposing her to him.

She raised her shirt, revealing her soft mounds. She didn't wear a bra, but he had known that already. He guessed she had dressed simply in preparation for running with the pack tonight. Most of the times when he saw her, her attire was modest. Bra included.

"So perfect," he murmured, knowing they would be.

Full and round, her breasts were more than a handful. And her nipples, a soft brown, large and puckered into hardened nubs. He cupped her breasts, her soft skin so warm against his touch. She cried out when he rubbed her nipples, the rich scent of her desire filling the air around them, mixing with his own lust, bringing a fever into his already tortured senses.

"Okay." She backed away from him, pulling her shirt down quickly, and crossing her arms. A shield against him. "You need to leave now. It's late."

She didn't look at him, but turned toward her front door.

He followed her. "I'll stop by tomorrow. And when I do, I want to see your toys."

She looked up at him quickly, a protest on her lips. But he gripped her jaw, preventing her from answering by kissing her. She didn't stop him, didn't try to push away. He knew he pushed her, but that was the only way he could get her to open up and give him everything he needed from her. And it was the only way she would be able to offer all to him she had suppressed for so many years.

"I...I don't have anything too exciting."

He smiled, acknowledging her acceptance of what would happen when he saw her again. "Then maybe I will bring you a gift."

Chapter Three

Ralph didn't tell Sandy what time he would be by that day. And she would not sit around waiting for him to show up. In fact, she wasn't even sure she wanted him to come over. He'd been so demanding the night before, so sure of himself, and very confident in how she would react to him.

"I think that is all of the Halloween decorations." She brushed her hands off on her jeans, squinting against the brightness as she walked out of the storage shed.

"Looks to me like it's more than enough." Beth Parks, Sandy's daughter, made a face while staring at the boxes on the ground. Her cell phone rang, and she looked almost relieved.

Sandy hated her daughter's phone. It never quit ringing. "Halloween is a wonderful holiday. I don't understand why you don't like it."

"I never said I didn't," her daughter said and then answered her phone.

"We have a big gym to decorate." Olson Full, the principal of the pack's new school, looked proud over the fact.

Sandy smiled at the young werewolf. He should be proud. They had one of the largest packs in the Midwest, and one of the few who could boast they had their own school.

"Well if you don't need me anymore." Beth had hung up her phone. "Duty calls."

"Of course." Olson smiled at her daughter.

And Sandy didn't miss the hidden glance he gave her while he looked her over. But all the werewolves noticed Beth. She was so pretty. Her daughter had eyes only for her mate, though. And Sandy couldn't be more proud of the fact that Beth was now queen bitch. She took on the responsibility as easily as she ran her private law office.

"I guess I should be going too." Sandy didn't know why she wanted to hurry off too.

Olson nodded, turning to walk the two of them to their cars. She had no reason to hurry off. Just because Ralph said he would see her today, she shouldn't go home and sit and wait for him to make an appearance. She wasn't really looking forward to him showing up anyway.

I want to see your toys.

Her heart skipped a beat at the thought. No matter what she'd done all day, she couldn't get his comments out of her head. As she drove home, her hands moist on the steering wheel, she couldn't stop herself from glancing around, checking to see if he was anywhere near.

"Good grief. Stop it," she scolded herself while she pulled into her garage.

The werewolf wouldn't control her like this. She had done nicely over the years, raising her daughter and helping the pack when she was needed. Her life was full. She was happy. Stressing over this over-pompous werewolf would only bring her grief.

Her house was quiet, peaceful and clean. Just the tranquility needed to soothe her frazzled nerves. Her heart raced faster than it had before she got home, anticipation forming a ball in her stomach. She kept glancing toward the windows every time a car passed down her street.

She was more nervous than a schoolgirl. This was ridiculous.

"He shows up, or he doesn't." Talking to herself didn't calm her. But maybe a hot shower would. And no, she wasn't showering for Ralph. She'd been working outside all day, sorting through decorations for Halloween. She would have taken a shower even if she weren't expecting company.

She hummed one of the songs the cubs had been singing in school that day while she showered. Her pussy was so soaked that she hardly needed soap while she shaved, her thick cream making it easy to run her razor over the most sensitive parts of her pussy. And afterwards, some of her special oil that her daughter had given her for Christmas one year made her feel especially sexy. She rubbed the scented liquid over her body before toweling dry, and then slipped into her favorite robe.

None of the pampering calmed her in the least. At this rate, if Ralph didn't show up soon, she would be a frazzled bundle of nerves before the sun went down. She tied the belt that came with her thick terrycloth robe, more than aware of how the material brushed against her nipples.

The way Ralph had pinched them last night had kept them oversensitive all day. They ached, craved more of his attention. In fact, who was she kidding? Every inch of her craved his touch.

"This will not do." There was nothing worse than a female who fell all over a man, flirting with him, begging him to do whatever he wanted to her.

All that did was spoil a werewolf. Ralph would think he could just stop by on a moment's notice and get a piece of tail without asking. And that was not going to happen. The man was aggressive. And she admitted that turned her on. But his pushiness needed curbing. There needed to be rules.

Her nightstand caught her attention, the doors not quite closed on it from the night before. This was what she needed. No werewolf would control her body, be her only means of satisfaction.

She stood, facing the small wooden cabinet where her reading lamp and alarm clock sat. Kneeling before it, she opened the double doors and searched through the contents inside. Her vibrator had to be her favorite toy. Quick and effective. After a long day she knew she could bring herself to a satisfying climax with it.

But it wouldn't take care of the growing ache, the pressure that built deep inside her pussy. She needed something larger, something more thorough. Pulling out the soft gelatin rubber designed to sheath the vibrator, she slid it over her hard plastic toy. The cover was the color of skin, giving her toy a lifelike look.

"You are what I need tonight." She ran her fingers over the cock-shaped sex toy, wondering how it compared to Ralph.

Her pussy moistened in anticipation, the throbbing matching the pounding of her heart. After making sure the gelatin cover was secure over her vibrator, she moved to her bed. The ache inside her pussy intensified while she stroked her toy, imagining a real cock in her hands.

She moved her fingers down to her pussy, the heat and thick musky smell growing stronger the second she moved her bathrobe to the side. Exposing herself, she smoothed her cream over her freshly shaven skin, the smoothness turning her on, making her excited, anxious to feel the hard cock she held in her hand deep inside her.

Her heavy breathing made her mouth dry. She licked her lips, staring at her toy, and then brought it to her mouth, licking its hard round edge. Dipping into the source of her heat, feeling the thick cream wrap around her fingers, she soothed the inner walls of her pussy with her fingers. She felt her inner muscles contract while moist heat soaked her hand. The toy cock was hard against her mouth and she sucked it in, closing her eyes, imagining that she gave head while fucking herself.

She moved on the bed, gyrating her hips while sucking the toy into her mouth, lubricating it so she could fuck herself. It would have to go deep, reaching that spot inside her pussy that she couldn't reach with her fingers.

Pulling the toy from her mouth, the first wave of her lust rushed through her, the pressure inside her pussy building, bringing her to the edge. The ache grew, intensifying while she arched into her hand, forcing her fingers deep inside her cunt.

"Please." She wanted just a little bit more. Needed to be brought over the edge just a bit further.

But her hand wasn't enough.

Placing the toy at the entrance of her soaked pussy, the heat from deep inside her made her burn. The fire reaching past her cunt, surging through her body, had her arching, willing her orgasm to come. She was so close. Heavy throbbing in her pussy ransacked her senses, her breathing coming hard and heavy.

"I've got to..." she urged her body, wanting so desperately to feel that wave of relief.

Her toy cock slid inside her, filling her, stretching the tender pussy muscles that grabbed it eagerly. Pressure shifted, building, forcing her to stop just for a moment. She took slow, long breaths, trying to calm her body just for a moment so that she could ride out her orgasm.

Rolling over with her toy inside her, she flung her robe off of her, too hot now to have it wrapped around her. On all fours, she reached between her legs, pushing her toy deep inside her, fucking herself in her favorite position—doggy style.

Gripping the edge of her toy, she began pushing it inside her and then pulling it out, slowly at first. The sensations rippled through her, filling her body with a need for more. Her fingers were moist against the gelatin, her grip against the smooth surface sliding. Moisture from her pussy saturated her toy, her fingers, her hand.

She plunged the vibrator deep inside, striving to reach the source of her pent-up pressure. That one spot that needed attention, begged to be caressed, fondled, continued to be just out of her reach.

Still the pressure built, the agony of her orgasm bordering on pain. She needed to come so bad.

"Damnit." Nothing irritated her more than not being able to get off.

Sliding off of the bed, she pulled her vibrator out of her, her white cream covering the toy, filling the air in her bedroom with the rich scent of her lust. Almost drunk from need, from the intoxicating fragrance, she pulled her chair out from under her desk.

"You are going to get me off," she instructed her toy, staring at it as if it might answer.

Centering it on her chair, she straddled it, holding on to it until it nudged against the entrance of her pussy.

"Do what you're supposed to do. Now." She forced herself down on her vibrator.

It filled her, pressed through her soaked cunt, stroked her inner muscles. The fire inside her burst into flames, heat rushing through her with more intensity than she could control.

Her toy forced its way deep within her, hitting the most sensitive muscles that craved the penetration. The toy rubbed against that one spot that demanded satisfaction.

Pressure inside of her erupted, the dam exploding, her orgasm flooding through her with wave after wave of molten heat.

She rode her toy, holding on to the back of the chair, her leg muscles burning while she moved faster and faster, riding through her orgasm like it was the eye of a storm.

"Dear Lord. Thank you." Her breathing came hard, her damp hair stuck to the side of her face while she relaxed against the back of the chair, working to catch her breath.

When her phone rang, she jumped, her muscles clamping down on the toy still lodged deep inside her.

She chuckled. "Nothing like getting caught in the act."

At the same moment someone knocked on her door. Sandy looked up, panic rushing through her. She glanced at her disheveled appearance in the mirror over her desk. "Oh shit." She looked a wreck.

Chapter Four

"Hello?" Sandy knew she sounded out of breath when she grabbed the phone, and at the same time tried frantically to figure out what to do with her vibrator.

She never put her toys away without thoroughly cleaning them beforehand. It was a ritual, her caring for the precious objects that brought her so much pleasure.

Whoever was at the door knocked a second time.

"Mom. You sound out of breath." Her daughter, Beth, sounded a bit rushed herself. But that was normal for her.

"I'm fine, dear." In fact, her body still tingled, her pussy throbbed, and other than the growing frantic feeling she couldn't subside, she really did feel fine. "Is everything okay with you?"

There was no other choice. She stuffed her vibrator, her thick cream still covering it, into her nightstand cabinet, silently promising the inanimate object a thorough cleaning later.

"Yeah. Ethan and I thought it would be nice if you could come for dinner tomorrow night. Does that work for you?"

"Sure, honey. What time should I be over?" Sandy grabbed her bathrobe, glancing at her tousled hair in the mirror with disgust.

She struggled into her robe while heading toward the front door.

"Is six okay?"

If she had more time she would have questioned her daughter. She never was invited over for dinner. Both Beth and her mate were so busy she wondered if they ever sat down to a meal together.

"Yes. I'll bring a dessert." She wasn't too sure about her daughter's cooking. At least this way she wouldn't starve.

She tied her robe and opened the door.

Ralph Hipp stared at her. "One more minute and I was going to come in and make sure you were okay."

"Don't bother, Mom," Beth said at the same time. "Jan Price is helping out at the house now. She's a good cook."

"Okay." Sandy stared at Ralph, stepping back to allow him in only when he moved toward her.

"Great. Well I've got to run. Ethan can't handle a committee meeting without me there." Her daughter laughed, blowing kisses into the phone. "Bye, Mom. Love you."

Any other time Sandy might have made a comment on how he'd managed to lead the pack for several years quite well before meeting her. But she simply nodded, her mouth suddenly too dry to speak, and watched Ralph saunter into her living room. The click in her ear reminded her to pull the phone away and push the button to hang it up.

Ralph took in her disheveled appearance, a grin threatening his lips.

She ran her hand through her hair, knowing she couldn't look worse if she had planned it. Her hair was almost dry yet she hadn't combed it. She didn't have any makeup on, and she could only imagine what she smelled like.

No. She knew how she smelled. Heat rushed over her cheeks.

"Who were you talking to?" Ralph nodded at the phone in her hand.

Sandy moved past him to the bedroom, putting the phone on the cradle. "My daughter. I'm supposed to go to dinner over there tomorrow night."

Ralph didn't say anything but she heard him move in behind her. She closed her eyes, anticipating his touch. Warmth spread through her when his hands rested on her shoulders. The urge to arch back into him swept over her when his fingers gripped her, caressing her. Her robe did nothing to prevent how her body reacted to his hands on her. She might as well have been naked.

"And what have you been doing?" he asked, his breath sending fire through her at a dangerous pace.

"I just got out of the shower." There was no way she could tell him she'd just fucked her vibrator.

Her heart raced in her chest when he ran his fingers through her almost dry hair. He tugged, pulling her head to the side. She looked up at him, his expression dark, powerful, all-knowing. That relaxed expression of his, the slight movement of his jaw, and his scrutinizing gaze made it hard for her to swallow, to think.

"You smell like a well-fucked woman." The way he gripped her hair, turning her head to the side so he could see her face, made her feel exposed, vulnerable.

"Thank you. I think." She did her best to hide how he made her feel. What she did on her own time was her own business.

Ralph smiled, turning her the rest of the way toward him. He pulled her to him, his hands sliding inside her robe.

She should stop him. His large rough hands on her flesh stole her breath. She gasped, and his mouth covered hers. Ralph kissed her differently than other werewolves had. He didn't hurry. There was no hesitation. His possessive behavior encouraged her to relax in his arms, allow him the free rein he demanded on having.

After a very long minute, he allowed her up for air. "Show me what you were doing," he breathed into her mouth, his teeth brushing over her lip.

Fire burned straight through to her pussy. His hands glided over her already overheated body, gripping her ass, caressing her back.

"I would rather not." She barely got the words out, his actions doing a number on her already too raw senses.

Ralph turned her around, controlling her actions before she could organize her thoughts and stop him. He moved with her, his hands still under her robe. He'd managed to loosen her tie and move the material to the side so that she almost moved naked in front of him.

"Ralph. Please." She managed to pull away from him, needing his hands off of her just so she could think straight.

"Don't be ashamed." He moved in on her but she put her hand up, wanting more than anything to be in his arms again but needing distance to clear her head.

"I'm not ashamed." She took a deep breath and wrapped her robe around her. "What I do in here is private."

"Then maybe next time you should close your blinds." He walked around her, moving to her windows. He twisted the knobs on each of the blinds, closing them. "Almost anyone could stand outside and watch you," he told her. "If someone were to come to the door they might be able to enjoy a show before knocking."

He had seen her fuck herself. Embarrassment prickled through her. Its sour smell made her wrinkle her nose.

"You were out there watching me." She should be outraged and ignore the bubbling excitement in her stomach that she'd had an audience. "Ralph Hipp. You had no right."

He walked up to her, not hesitating, moving quickly enough that she barely had time to step backward. His hand cupped her jaw, lifted her face so that she stared into his penetrating gaze. She almost forgot to breathe, his predatory nature so strong it was overwhelming.

"The way you lay there. So focused. So in tune with what excites you. I couldn't look away." His bare honesty left her speechless.

She licked her dry lips, his words, his touch, drawing something to life within her. Something she didn't recognize, and wasn't sure she wanted to surface. No one had ever watched her play with herself before. And she shouldn't be so turned on by the fact that Ralph had, that he admitted to it, and wanted to talk about it.

"You invaded my privacy. What you did was wrong." She knew by his expression that her words didn't faze him. "It's against the law," she added for good measure.

He raised an eyebrow. "Shall we call the pack leader?"

Dear Lord. No. The last thing in the world she could do was tell her brand-new son-in-law that their pack security man had stood outside her bedroom window and watched her masturbate.

The expression on her face must have been answer enough for him. "Sandy." The way he whispered her name made her insides melt. "You will learn not to be embarrassed around me."

She wasn't embarrassed. She was annoyed. She had to be upset with him. Ralph was too much werewolf to allow to get out of control. He would manipulate her, control her, get her to do things she wouldn't normally do. That last thought sent a rush of excitement through her so fast it took her breath away.

Her pussy throbbed, making her more than aware of how wet she still was. His hand stroked her neck, feeding the fire growing inside her. She wasn't ready for so much domination.

"I don't think I am the kind of werewolf that you think I am." She had no idea how to get him to see this wasn't her style. But somehow, she had to try.

"I know exactly how you are. You need to see how you are, too. You will open up, relax, learn to be the sexual creature that already exists within you." He had managed to loosen her robe again.

When had he done that?

His hands moved down her front, cupping her breasts. Molten lava flooded through her, the heat more than she could handle.

He would take over, take her independence. His fingers scorched her swollen breasts, offering what she ached so desperately to have. His touch soaked her, filling her pussy with come. Her body ignored her mind. A raw, more primal side of her, buried deeper than the beast within her, threatened to surface.

"Ralph. I can't do this." She fought the desires growing in her, the cravings to have him continue to stroke her, bring her to the edge.

"Yes. You can." His mouth nestled against her neck, his teeth brushing over her feverish skin.

His hand pressed against her belly, caressed her skin while he worked his way down to the source of her heat. A fever surged through her, drawing its strength deep within her. Something untamed, uninhibited, threatened to break loose. His fingers pressed against her pussy, stroking the freshly shaven skin, spreading her come over her tender flesh.

The air around her grew thick with her scent, his lust, and that carnal edge that seeped from both of them. He worked his way toward her hole, so recently fucked with her precious toy. A toy that had been safe, familiar and comforting. But now her body craved more, her mind exposed to a darker side of her, one that would accept being watched, being exposed. She wasn't sure she could handle it.

"This is too much." She would have to be the one to stop this.

Ralph's fingers slid inside her, filling her, able to move quickly since she was so soaked. He plunged deep into her pussy, caressing the inner muscles in a way her toy hadn't been able to.

"Oh. Shit." Sandy collapsed into him.

She could barely focus on the muscles in his arm as they flexed when he drove deep into her cunt with his fingers. He kept one arm wrapped around her, supporting her, while the heat and strength of his body consumed her, taking care of her. His fingers plowed her pussy, building friction, fueling a fire she had tried to appease on her own.

Unable to stop the intense pressure, she rode it out, experiencing an orgasm more intense than her toys had ever offered.

"Ralph." She cried out, clinging to him, digging her nails into his shirt, feeling the powerful muscles underneath.

"That's it, baby. Come for me." His voice turned gravelly, his beast surfacing. "You are going to experience more than you ever thought possible."

Sandy crumpled in Ralph's arms. Her orgasm, so much stronger than the one she'd just experienced before he arrived, left her spent, trembling. That and the tremor of fear that rode through her with nervous excitement. His promises thrilled and terrified her all at the same time.

Chapter Five

Ralph listened to the humans. Their emotions filled the air, billowing off of them like a strong breeze after a good rain. Clean and easy to read, he smelled their fears, their curiosity, their concerns.

"They say a blue moon only happens once every twenty years or so." Danny Richards, owner of the local lumberyard, watched Ethan while he chugged on his beer.

"That's what I heard." Ethan held his spatula in midair over the ribs and steaks on the grill. He looked over toward the driveway when another car pulled in.

"They're saying with it being a second full moon this Halloween, the partiers will be out in droves." Danny had been one of the first humans Ethan had befriended after the pack took over this territory.

Ralph watched the red Volkswagen park behind the other cars in the long, wide gravel drive that ran alongside Ethan Masterson's home. Sandy didn't get out of her car at first. He guessed she was overwhelmed by the amount of people. Ralph had no idea Ethan had planned such a turnout either. He'd been looking forward to spending time with Sandy socially. But apparently Ethan's new mate had turned their little gathering into quite the party.

"Excuse me." He ignored the curious look his pack leader gave him, and headed toward Sandy.

She had her hands full when he reached her car, and he opened her car door for her.

"Thank you." She smiled at him politely, and got out of the car, carrying an apple pie. The pie looked almost as good as she did.

Sandy wore jeans like she always did. They were faded, and hugged her trim figure and thin legs. Her pullover blouse also clung to her, and she wasn't wearing a bra. His protector instincts kicked in full force. She was stunning. Every werewolf, and human, would be tripping over themselves at the sight of her.

She hadn't put her hair back in a ponytail, but instead had curled it so that it turned under around her neck. And with a dab of makeup and perfume, she looked so damned good he almost couldn't speak.

Aware of the fact that the men in the backyard were watching, Ralph took the pie from Sandy, and then put his arm around her. She stiffened immediately, and didn't move.

"You're putting your mark on me, werewolf." Her tone was hushed, but her body language was loud and clear.

She didn't like it.

"I thought I already had." He turned into her, blocking her view of the house and the yard. He wanted all of her attention.

Her pretty green eyes sparkled in the sunlight. And her skin was aglow with life. More than likely the amount of times she had come the night before had done her some good. He was more than ready for it to be his turn. He needed to fuck her bad.

"I don't recall agreeing to anything." She took the pie, and then walked around him. "I take it my daughter is in the house."

Ralph nodded once, watching her, searching her expression for any sign of why she was suddenly so cold toward him. She appeared a bit on the nervous side. Whatever the reason, he would find out soon enough.

The discussion lingered around Halloween throughout most of the evening. Ralph paid attention to the concerns of the humans and Ethan's assurances that any werewolf parties would be well monitored.

Sandy distracted him though. For the most part, she ignored him, spending time with her daughter and the other women there.

The party had moved inside, the night chill sending them into the warmth of the Masterson den. He'd had about enough of socializing. Ethan had given him the small cottage next door that had belonged to the previous pack leader's cousin, and it would take nothing to slip out the back door and call it a night.

He stood in the kitchen, pondering his next move, when Sandy walked in from the living room. Her smile faded when she saw him. "Enjoying yourself?" She sounded too polite.

He turned to face her, noticing her friendly tone didn't meet her eyes. She looked tired.

"I didn't expect so many people to be here." Her confession was spoken quietly, in confidence, letting him know that in spite of her actions throughout the evening, she did feel she could confide in him.

"Your daughter likes to throw a party."

She made a snorting sound and moved to put her glass on the counter. Her shirt hugged her body, showing off her trim waist. The way her jeans hugged her ass made him want to haul her out the back door and next door.

Ralph moved in behind her, needing to touch her. "You should be proud of her," he whispered into her hair, drowning in her scent.

"I am." Sandy's scent changed immediately. Desire swarmed around her. It faded slowly. She was fighting it.

"You've done a good job of raising her." He wrapped his fingers around her waist, enjoying how narrow it was, the softness of her body, the sweet scent that was hers alone.

"We went through some hard times." She wasn't relaxed. Far from it.

Ralph conceded that she didn't push him away. He would accept that for the moment.

She glanced over her shoulder, not quite meeting his gaze. He turned her, wanting to hold her, to feel her relax in his arms. She wanted him. Her emotions didn't lie.

"You've done well with your den by yourself." Over the years he'd watched her, she had never shown any sign of complaining. "And now that Beth is grown and in her own den, you can focus on yourself."

"I am thinking of me." She placed her hands on his chest, the gentle touch of her fingers through his shirt sent fire shooting through him. "And my reputation."

He didn't mean to tighten his grip on her waist as hard as he did. Her eyes widened, not with fear, but surprise. No one had ever questioned his impeccable reputation before.

"Are you implying you would rather not be seen with me in front of the pack?" He would not allow this pretty little bitch to suggest he wasn't a proper date.

"No. No." She shook her head.

"Good." He didn't need to hear anymore.

Lowering his head so that his mouth hovered over hers, her body heat swarmed around him. "You couldn't ask for a better escort."

Her mouth was so hot, her lips so moist. She tasted sweet, a mixture of brownies and coffee on her breath. Her hands pressed against his shirt, her touch branding him. She tried to push away, but he couldn't let her go. The feel of her mouth, the way her tongue dashed around his, he needed more of her.

He wrapped his arms around her and she relaxed, moaning into his mouth.

Finally, she relaxed completely, offering him all of her, while her arms snaked up around his neck. Her breasts pressed against his chest, their full roundness a distraction that sent a fever through him. Thoughts of lifting her into his arms and making a mad dash for the door consumed him. He needed her more than he needed to breathe. Never had a bitch preoccupied him like Sandy did.

He ran his hands over her back, feeling the soft ridge of her ribs, the incline at her waist, the tempting curve of her hips. The beast in him surfaced, the need to claim and protect growing so strong that containing his animalistic side became almost impossible.

The scent of another werewolf entering the kitchen alerted him. They cleared their throat, demanding attention. He fought the impulse to turn and growl at the intruder.

Mine. His instincts consumed his ability to think straight.

Sandy jumped, pushing hard against his chest.

"Is everything okay in here?" Ethan looked at Sandy, watching her actions and then turned his attention on Ralph.

"I'm fine," Sandy said, gasping for air.

She slipped out of Ralph's arms and dashed out of the back door. Ralph hurried after her.

"Ralph." Ethan didn't move, but his tone, even for a younger werewolf, demanded his attention.

He turned on his leader, glaring at him, primal emotions warring with his rational thoughts.

"What are your intentions with Beth's mother?"

Ralph didn't hesitate in answering. "I plan on mating with her."

"And when did you plan on discussing this with me?" Ethan crossed his arms over his massive chest. A werewolf to be reckoned with, even at his young age, Ethan had Ralph's respect.

And that was the only reason he didn't lunge and knock the pompous look off of his face.

"I just did." Ralph turned and left his pack leader's den, heading out into the night to find Sandy.

Chapter Six

Sandy's scent faded as Ralph headed around the side of the house. He ignored the back door opening and closing behind him. Walking among the parked cars in his pack leader's driveway, he watched Sandy back up, and then head down the street. She didn't look his way.

"Do you want to tell me what just happened?" Ethan spoke from behind him.

Ralph didn't turn around. His pack leader would protect his pack, and especially his single females. It was his job. Ralph wouldn't counter that responsibility.

"She's not in any danger." That was all Ethan needed to know.

He turned slowly, meeting the dark gaze of the leader of his pack. Ethan stared him down, his expression dark and alert.

Ralph gave him only a minute of his attention, then turned toward his truck, needing to go after Sandy. Ethan stood in the driveway, watching him, letting Ralph know that his actions were now under scrutiny. Ralph expected nothing less.

There were no lights on at Sandy's house. He parked anyway and walked around her house, allowing his senses to guide him. He didn't smell her. The house was quiet. She wasn't there.

Driving through the small town didn't take much time, and her small Volkswagen wasn't parked at any of the locations frequented by the pack.

There were several locations the pack would meet outside of town for group runs. He'd reached the third one when he noticed her car, isolated in the small field where they often parked. Parking next to hers, he walked around her car. Enough time had passed that she was long gone, running in her fur somewhere. He would wait. Being in law enforcement for over twenty years, sitting and waiting for long periods of time were par for the course.

Several hours later, the moonlight caught a figure moving through the trees on the edge of the field. Ralph got out of his car, allowing the change enough to heighten his senses. His muscles bulged against his clothing while shadows disappeared around him. His vision altered, allowing him to better see the werewolf approaching him warily.

Sandy's ears perked, a snarl on her lips while she circled around him. Ralph didn't back away from the deadly creature even though in his human form he was no match to her. And he knew her instincts controlled her at the moment.

"You are safe with me," he told her, moving toward her slowly.

Sandy lunged at him, growling viciously. She stopped within feet of his boots. Ralph didn't move. He didn't back away. Once again she walked around him, moving toward her car.

Ralph followed her, his own body in a state of flux. Still human but with his beast's blood surging through him, his reaction to her was hard to control. Her scent called to him, pulled the werewolf in him forward. A raw and untamed need surged through him, his cock throbbing as it grew almost too hard. Walking became an effort, his cock pressing painfully against his jeans.

"Change," he ordered her. "Change now. Or I will change."

Sandy straightened. No longer slinking. No longer ready to pounce. She looked at him, understanding his words. And his meaning.

He could change before she would be able to outrun him. Instinct would take over. He would take her without question.

He would fuck her without asking. Werewolves existed on instinct.

Or she could return to her human form. He would allow her that. As a man he would respect her wishes. He would not take what she didn't willingly offer.

Slowly, Sandy began to stand, her front paws altering while the fur disappeared on her body. Her face transformed, lips appearing while her eyes altered, the color changing from brown to green.

He closed the distance between them immediately. "Don't run from me again."

Wrapping his arm around her, he could feel her heart pounding still too fast for her human body.

"I had to." Her voice sounded husky, her werewolf blood still pumping through her.

Ralph gripped her hair, forcing her to arch back so that she looked up at him. Her panting excited him as much as her perky breasts, damp from the night air, her skin shining under the strong moonlight. Her nipples so hard they were beacons, calling to him, begging for his attention.

She stared up at him, searching his face. After a moment, he felt her body relax, sensed her desires peak. The smooth roundness of her ass pressed against his cock, teasing him. Blood drained through his body, settling in his groin, the pressure building to a boiling point.

She adjusted herself in his arms, continuing to watch him. Slowly, her tongue moved over her lips. It took more power than he knew he possessed not to lunge at it. His muscles shook from the amount of concentration it took not to force himself on her, to bend her over her car and plow deep inside that tight little cunt of hers.

When he knew she should be more afraid of him than ever, her small hands slid up his chest. Fire scourged through him where she touched him, her gentle touch enough to undo him.

"I wasn't ready for Ethan to see me as more than the mother of his mate." She whispered, leaning into him, stretching her naked body against his.

"You are much more than just her mother." He knew she saw that.

She was a woman with so much sexual power. In that tiny little body of hers, she had the ability to disarm him, bring the dangerous werewolf quivering to his knees.

"I know." She looked down, her soft brown hair fluttering in damp strands around her face.

Focusing on her hands, she ran them over his chest, driving him mad with her touch. He held on to her hair, barely able to contain himself. Pulling her head to the side, he tasted her neck. The saltiness of her body was a feast to a starving man.

Her hands moved down his chest, toward his belt, dangerously close to his cock. She would know what he had for her. No longer could he wait. Taking her hand, he pressed it over his hard shaft, her warm touch taking his breath away.

Sandy gasped, her body quivering against his. She wanted him. Her reaction, her scent, her willingness to be guided. Ralph was no cub. He knew women, knew the signs.

Reaching for her pussy, feeling her heat absorb into his skin before he even touched her, he knew he wasn't mistaken.

"Do you know how wet you are?" He parted her velvet skin, her cream clinging to his fingers.

Her rich lust drifted to his nose. He inhaled her, allowing her scent to consume him. His craving for her soared to a dangerous level.

"Yes," she said on a breath, grinding her muscles down on his fingers, sucking him in.

He wanted his cock in her more than he wanted to breathe. "You need to be fucked."

She stared at him, her green eyes larger than life in the darkness. But he saw her trust, saw that she believed in him, had faith in him. She ran her teeth over her lower lip. "Yes," she said quietly.

Ralph undid his jeans, releasing his cock. His swollen flesh jabbed forward, reaching without mercy to touch her, experience her flesh touching him.

"Can you get pregnant?" He didn't have a condom with him, but he would accept the fact if she could. Neither one of them were at a point in their lives where they wanted more cubs.

Sandy shook her head. "Not anymore."

Relief swept over him. More than anything he wanted to enjoy the closeness of her pussy wrapped around him.

He would turn her around, bend her over her car, except that he wanted to see her face. She hadn't stopped looking at him, and he wouldn't let go of her gaze.

Lifting her like a child into his arms, her legs caressed his hips as she wrapped them around him, spreading her pussy open over his inflamed cock.

He drowned in her heat, knew passion like he'd never experienced it before. Without hesitating, she relaxed into him, sliding his swollen flesh deep inside her.

Immediately she arched, threw her head back, her mouth opening. "Ralph," she cried out. "Yes. Damn."

The moonlight danced over her skin, accenting her curves. Her hot moist muscles gripped his cock, sucking him deep inside her. Her heat burning through him out of control like a wildfire.

"You're so hot." He buried his face in her chest, drinking her in.

She was so tight, her pussy clamping down on him while he sank deep inside her. He'd reached her deepest point, raging heat almost suffocating him, and still he could go further. It had been a while since Sandy had fucked and he barely fit inside her.

Grabbing her ass, he lifted her, giving her inner muscles a chance to grow accustomed to his size, his shape. He would mold her, make her his own, but he wouldn't rush her. He didn't want to scare her with his size.

Sandy brought her head forward, a wild look in her eyes. "You're too big," she told him, her voice husky, thick with her lust.

Ralph couldn't help but smile. What werewolf didn't love hearing those words?

"And you are perfect." Perfect hardly described the incredible pussy that wrapped around his cock.

She bit her lower lip, gripping him, while her arms tightened around his neck. He allowed her to lift herself up, raise herself off of him. His cock slid through her pussy like hot velvet.

Her eyes widened, her mouth forming a luscious circle when she slid back down on him. "Damn. That's good." Her words came out on a breath, so hot it matched the heat absorbing into his groin.

Cradling her ass, he spread her open. She molded to him, her soaked cunt forming a perfect glove, designed just for him. Filling her, taking all she offered and then showing her how to give him more, he fucked her.

The moonlight spread over her glistening skin. When she arched into him, the curves of her breasts caught the light, round and beautiful, absolutely perfect. She almost panted, her breath coming quickly as he built the momentum.

He would prefer to fuck her for hours, to taste and experience everything she had to offer. But he knew he filled her more than she'd been filled before. He reached depths within her never touched by a werewolf before. Her petite body would grow accustomed to him, but for now he would have to hold back.

Not to mention the pressure building inside him was unbearable. It had been a long time since he'd been with a female. He'd had opportunities, willing widows in the pack over the years. But Sandy had caught his eye a while back, and keeping an eye on her had made the other women dim in comparison.

He lifted her ass as he built momentum. Harder and deeper he drove into her soft folds. Her fingernails dug through his shirt, pinching the flesh on his shoulders. The sweet pain drove the beast within him wild. His heart raced, blood pumping through him with a fierce velocity. Muscles tensed while he thrust again and again, the friction against his cock burning through him, feeding his need to push her over the edge. He wanted to experience her explode around him, feel her muscles contract while she let go of the sweet passion he could smell growing within her.

"Come for me." He watched her breasts bounce between them. She leaned away from him, her head falling back, arching her neck, completely vulnerable to his manipulations.

Her fingers dug mercilessly into his shoulders. She gritted her teeth, slowly raising her head to look at him. Her face was flushed, her body glowing as her passion dripped from her.

"Fuck me harder, wolf man." She growled the words, her mouth barely moving.

Chills brushed over his skin, his muscles bulging and hardening as her words, so raw, so sensual, about made him come.

"I don't want to hurt you." He could barely speak.

He gripped her ass so hard it would leave marks. Already he pounded her tender flesh, stretching her further each time he impaled her. The friction between them burnt his skin. And yet this sweet, adorable little bitch asked for more.

"Fuck me." She contracted over him, her orgasm right there.

Diving into her, bearing down on the primal side she stirred within him, he fought his beast from surfacing with what little coherent thought he could master. And that wasn't much. Muscles throughout him strained against his clothing. His cock grew inside her. She sucked in her breath, feeling the change, and that drove him even closer to the edge.

Her weight shifted in his hands. He knew she battled the beast within her also. Her legs clamped against him hard enough to steal his breath. She clung to him with strengthened muscles. And her pussy changed as well. She thickened, molding to his engorged cock. He closed his eyes, realizing she would suck the life out of him.

"I'm going to come." He could barely speak.

The heat surrounding them grew so intense he could barely breathe. Her flesh burned through him, branding him. Her muscles pulsated, quivering, while her hot juices began to flow.

"Damn." She cried out as her body began quaking against his.

And as she collapsed into him, he exploded, filling her, soaking both of them with liquid passion. The way her muscles wrapped around him, clinging to him, while she draped her body over his, he lived and breathed his adorable bitch.

"Are you okay?" he whispered, cradling her to him, praying he hadn't hurt her.

"Uh-huh." She didn't move, completely sated in his arms.

And for the moment, he couldn't move either. But holding her like this, the moonlight making her body glisten, he had no desire to go anywhere.

Chapter Seven

Sandy helped Greta Hothmeyer out of her car, and then grabbed the packages out of the back seat.

"Did you hear?" the old werewolf asked her. "With the birth of the Millers' grand-cub, we now outnumber the humans in the territory."

"I'm sure the humans will be thrilled to hear that." Sandy followed the pack healer up to her house, the array of aromas from the herbs in the grocery sack tickling her nose.

"When will you be a grandmother?" Greta pushed open her front door, left unlocked, a habit the old woman refused to break no matter how many pack members begged her to lock her door when she left. "You would think that pack leader and your daughter would have an announcement for the pack soon."

Sandy had accepted the fact long ago that with her daughter's busy schedule she would be more than lucky if she ever became a grandmother.

"I haven't heard anything yet." She placed Greta's groceries on her kitchen counter, feeling the sore muscles tighten throughout her.

She reached for her lower back, hating to admit she wasn't as young as she used to be, and hot wild sex could take its toll on her.

"We'll get some ointment rubbed into you here in a bit." Greta never missed a thing.

She reached for the phone on the wall just as it rang. It was an unnerving quality in the old woman that Sandy had grown to accept. To this day she'd never looked fast enough to see if Greta actually moved for the phone before it rang, or if she just had good reflexes.

"I'll be fine." She knew Greta ignored her. The old healer picked up the phone, answering it and then listening to an excited voice that tickled Sandy's ears.

She began putting away the groceries, having helped Greta long enough that she knew the woman's kitchen as well as her own. But with every turn, every twist, another muscle inside her cried out.

What a fool she'd made out of herself the night before. Imagine a werewolf her age, fucking outside next to her car. In her younger years, steamy sex in a field after a pack run had been wonderful. But that had been with her mate. And ever since he'd died, so many years ago when Beth had still been a young cub, she'd not given thought to such activity.

Of course Ralph was pure alpha male. She didn't view him as a male slut, but she wouldn't doubt he'd enjoyed a good romp with a willing bitch from time to time. She worried she'd simply added herself to that list. Ralph was in better shape than some of the werewolves half his age. That body of his didn't have an ounce of flab on it anywhere.

Her pussy instantly began throbbing with thoughts of how she'd enjoyed being in his arms, his cock buried so deep inside her she was sure he'd hit some internal organs.

And he'd been so gallant afterwards, completely at ease. It hadn't surprised her that he'd followed her home and made sure she was secure and locked in her den before leaving her. She'd been taken by a master.

What worried her was that she wasn't sure that he'd taken just her body. Granted, she hadn't had sex in ages, at least not with anything other than her toys and her imagination. Ralph Hipp had come along and moved right into her thoughts. And with every move, and every muscle in her body reminding her, she couldn't get him out of her head today.

"Who is hurt?" Greta's question pulled Sandy out of her thoughts.

The old woman clutched the phone to her ear, her expression impossible to read. After a moment, she nodded and hung up the phone without saying goodbye to whoever was on the other end.

"That was your werewolf." The healer moved around her, digging through her grocery sacks and pulling out herbs.

"My werewolf?" Sandy asked.

"You have Ralph Hipp's scent all over you." Greta didn't look up while she transferred some of the herbs into her cloth medicine bag. "You think because I'm old that I have forgotten about sex?"

Sandy opened her mouth to respond but embarrassment made her temporarily dumb. Greta ignored her awkward moment and walked out of the kitchen.

"I need you to take me over to the diner. Some of the pack got in a tumble with a few humans." Greta left her front door open and headed toward Sandy's car.

Sandy hurried after her, pulling the door closed but not locking it. She wasn't sure if Greta knew where her house key was.

"Who got hurt?" Sandy caught up with Greta in time to open the car door for her.

Greta waved her skinny hand in the air. "More than likely it's just some scrapes and bruises." She took her time sitting in the car seat then situated her bag on her lap. "That pack leader and his ideas of exposing us to humans. This will happen every time."

She pursed her lips together, jutting her chin out. Sandy knew the look to mean that Greta had no more to say on the subject. She shut the car door and hurried around to the driver's side.

They drove in silence to the diner but Sandy's thoughts were anything but quiet. Greta smelled Ralph's scent all over her. She didn't smell him on her. And she'd showered, last night and this morning. She had put lotion on and a dab of perfume.

Not that she cared if she looked good for anyone today. But she was the queen bitch's mother. And her duties for the day entailed running the pack healer around. It was important to look nice.

Greta had stronger senses then most werewolves. Sandy knew that. She also knew the old healer seldom joked. It had been a long time since she'd had sex, but no one had ever commented that they smelled the werewolf on her the next day. Greta implied what Sandy and Ralph did last night was more than fucking. They'd made love, marked each other without even realizing it. Or at least, she hadn't realized it. She had no idea how she felt about that. It made her nervous and excited all at once. And the more she thought about the damned werewolf, the more she ached to have him inside her again. She needed to get a grip on herself.

Sandy pulled into the gravel parking lot of the diner at the same time Ralph exited in his truck on to the street. She met his gaze, captivated by his dark brooding look. But then he looked away, leaving her and driving off.

He was working, she told herself. And besides. Did she want to see him right now anyway?

Sandy parked and then helped Greta out of the car. Several werewolves talked in excited tones outside the diner, but parted ways and nodded to the two women while holding the door open for them.

Her pack had always shown her respect. Since Beth had mated with Ethan Masterson that respect had only grown. Of course, she knew Ralph was held in high esteem with the pack also. But would everyone approve if they knew what she'd done last night?

Werewolves her age just didn't go around fucking under the moonlight, did they?

She almost stumbled over a chair at one of the tables while she followed Greta. The old healer turned and gave her a reprimanding look.

Pay attention to your day. There was nothing she could do about Ralph Hipp at the moment so she wouldn't think about him.

"I don't think it's anything serious." Matty Crock stood at the end of the counter, wiping her hands on her apron. She gestured to her oldest cub, who was busy clearing one of the tables. "Paul. Take Greta back to the men."

The teenage werewolf, sporting some facial hair he hadn't had the last time Sandy had seen him, carried the dishes behind the counter. He glanced at the pack healer.

"They are back here." He walked slowly, and glanced at his mom when Greta took his arm.

The smell of blood and body sweat filled the small room that was used as a break area for the Crock family between rushes. Frustration and anger lingered in the air as well, and Sandy rubbed her nose to keep from being rude and sneezing from the harsh smells.

"Well, well. What has happened here?" Greta set her bag on the round table in the middle of the room that several pack members sat around.

One of the werewolves hunched over at the table, nursing what looked like a broken hand. "Humans trying to tell us where we can take our cubs trick-or-treating." he said filling the air with a fresh spurt of outrage.

"The matter will be handled." Ethan spoke from behind her, and Sandy turned to acknowledge their pack leader.

The others in the room straightened as well.

Ethan filled the doorway with his massive frame, his dark features glowering at his pack members in the room. His gaze barely softened when he looked at her.

"You need to go talk to your daughter," he told her.

If she hadn't been watching him, she might not have known he was talking to her. He moved around her, taking slow strides around the table while eyeing each of his werewolves. The room grew respectfully silent while he moved quietly and slowly. Ethan had a way of grabbing a room's attention by not speaking. Sandy had credited that trait with one of the many reasons he had such a successful pack. But right now, she wanted to speak. She wanted to know what was going on with her daughter.

"Go on." Greta broke the silence, looking up at her while she worked. "One of these gentlemen will give me a ride home."

"Yes." Ethan nodded and reached for his cell phone at the same time. "Tell her I sent you. She was upset this morning, and I want you to talk to her."

"Upset?" Sandy wanted to know immediately what had upset her daughter. "Beth is upset?"

Ethan answered his phone, turning away from her. The only way she would get answers was to go see her daughter.

The news reporter speaking on the TV over the counter reported something about local legislation being passed to prevent werewolves and humans from trick-or-treating together. She'd hardly had time to keep up with current events. No wonder her daughter was upset.

She hurried out of the diner, glancing at her watch. In the middle of the afternoon she knew it might be hard to get in to see Beth.

"Excuse me." A young woman she didn't recognize walked toward her.

Sandy froze when she realized the woman was human, and a man walked behind her carrying a large black camera. The woman stuck a microphone in Sandy's face.

"Where will you be taking your children trick-or-treating this year?" The woman turned around before Sandy could answer. "Cut that," she told her cameraman, and then turned to Sandy again. "I meant, where will you take your cubs trick-or-treating this year?"

A hard knot formed in Sandy's stomach. She stared at the red light on the camera, and then at the young human woman who reeked of nervousness.

Suddenly her mouth seemed too dry to speak. She licked her lips. The pack would want her to be friendly to the human. The last thing needed was to start a fright over Halloween. But she was no spokesperson for her pack. No one had ever mentioned to her anything about where or where not to take the cubs.

"Mine are all grown." She did her best to sound friendly, ease the woman's nerves. "And since I've just moved here, I couldn't say where the safest places are."

"And there you have it." The reporter turned away from Sandy, staring into the camera. "The werewolves admit just moving here. And they are searching for *safe* places for their cubs to trick-or-treat. Looks like we better keep a close eye on our children this year."

She slid her finger across her throat and the camera guy lowered his camera.

"Wait a minute." Sandy tried to reach for the human.

But the lady moved away quickly, barely glancing over her shoulder while she hurried to a running van parked in the corner of the lot.

Sandy thought about chasing her down but didn't. She worried though that she had just made trouble for her pack. Maybe it would be a good idea to seek out her daughter. She might need a lawyer.

Chapter Eight

Ralph hated leaving Sandy alone amidst all the turmoil taking place at the diner. He didn't like the mood there. The humans had learned it was a werewolf-owned establishment and were descending in curious hordes. Sandy needed protection.

And to make matters worse, his pack leader was on edge today. It didn't make his job any easier protecting everyone when Ethan was glowering at him with suspicion. If the werewolf was suddenly going to get overprotective about his mother-in-law, then Ralph and Ethan needed to have a talk.

Ralph glanced at the dark sky overhead after parking in the city parking lot. He smelled rain in the air, and the cold chill suggested the weather could turn nasty. He buttoned up his coat and hurried toward the courthouse.

Voices and people moving around echoed throughout the old building. Ralph climbed the stairs to the main floor and headed toward the meeting room.

"Good afternoon, Ralph." A pretty young werewolf who worked in the mayor's office grinned flirtatiously at him.

He couldn't remember her name but winked, which produced a broad smile on her face.

"They're expecting you." She sauntered in front of him, shaking her ass nicely in what he might assume was an invitation.

"Thank you, sweetheart." He smiled again and opened the large door where a handful of officials had already gathered.

He noticed Beth Parks behind him, her secretary in tow, and held the door for the two ladies. Beth scowled at him and he got a strong whiff of irritation when she walked past.

"This shouldn't take too long." The mayor glanced at his two armed security guards and Ralph did the same. "I think from what I've heard we all want the same thing."

Ralph didn't sit but stood behind Beth, his ears tickled by her whispers with her secretary.

"We're asking for an ordinance to be passed that states where werewolf children will be allowed to trick-or-treat." Frank Hoffman, who Ralph knew had recently been voted on to the city commission, passed papers around the table while he spoke. The young human's hands shook slightly while he spoke. "I think we've split the town equally so that both human and werewolf children can enjoy the holiday."

He smiled at Beth. Ralph guessed the nervousness in the room came from him. Beth took the papers, glancing over them quickly.

"Most of our pack lives in the same area." She addressed the mayor. "I don't want to see any child shipped out of their own neighborhood in order to trick-or-treat. We need to keep in mind that this holiday is for their enjoyment."

"Exactly." Hoffman cut her off, and Ralph smelled her annoyance immediately. "And it's imperative our children be safe."

"Your children have been trick-or-treating alongside werewolf children as long as the holiday has existed, Mr. Hoffman." Beth stood abruptly, tossing the papers Hoffman had given her on to the table. "Mr. Mayor, I will advise you of the neighborhoods the werewolf children will be trick-or-treating. But I won't have any child segregated over the holiday."

She turned to leave while her secretary hurried to gather together papers. "I'll have something to your office later today." She glanced at the proposal that Hoffman had suggested. Her secretary slid it into the file along with other papers. "That is unacceptable. And if your office passes any similar ordinance without consulting me, you won't like the legal mess I'll create for you."

She left the room, her shoes clicking against the tiled floor as she hurried toward the hallway that led to her office. Ralph heard immediate whispering but didn't stay to hear what was being said. He left when Beth did, closing the door silently behind him.

"It was nice to see you again." The secretary who had given him the eye before, sounded a bit too flirty this time. More than likely she tried to make the other women in the office believe she had something going with him.

He nodded and smiled. She didn't hold a flame to Sandy.

"Mr. Hipp." Beth's sharp tone wasn't missed by anyone listening.

Two people walking across the foyer area turned to look at him, their looks making it clear they wondered what terrible thing he'd done to earn the wrath of the successful young Beth Parks. He wondered the same thing.

He walked across the open area, more than aware of more than one person watching him. "Call me Ralph," he said, maintaining his smile against her hard gaze.

"I want to speak to you for a moment," she turned and headed down the hallway. "In my office."

He got the overwhelming sensation that he'd just been called to the principal's office.

"What can I do for you, young lady?" Ralph asked, after closing the door to her office behind him.

Beth dropped into her chair behind her desk and glared at him. Her animosity was more than apparent.

"Cut the crap." She leaned forward, giving him a look he was sure had made more than one werewolf quiver in his time.

He imagined Ethan had a time with her when the two of them were alone. She didn't appear to be the type of female that did anything she didn't want to do.

"I want you to keep your paws off of my mother," she hissed.

Ralph raised an eyebrow, realizing he suddenly tread on thin ice. Say something to upset the daughter, and he would have the mother to deal with.

"Has she said something to you?" He hadn't had time to speak with Sandy today. It hadn't crossed his mind that she might be upset after last night. And it sure never entered his mind that she would discuss it with her daughter. He wondered how much Beth knew.

Beth sighed. She stuck her lip out, running it slowly over her top lip. For a brief second, she looked like her mother.

"Mr. Hipp," she began.

"Ralph," he corrected her.

The look she gave him bordered on outright hostility. "We are not establishing a friendship here," she hissed. Anger filled the room with its hot, spicy fumes. "You are a womanizer and you will stay the hell away from my mother. Is that clear?"

Something churned deep inside Ralph. The urge to set this little lady in her place almost got the better of him. His two cubs had been gone from the den now for so many years, and he seldom saw them since both of them had moved to packs back east. He'd forgotten the defiance one's own cubs could show.

And although Beth wasn't his cub, she was Sandy's daughter. He didn't know the young lawyer that well, other than her outstanding reputation that spoke wonders about her. But she would be part of his life if he continued to see Sandy. And he had every intention of doing that.

"I'm afraid that isn't possible." He spoke just as someone tapped on Beth's office door.

"What?" Beth almost yelled while glaring at Ralph.

Sandy opened the door, looking at each of them with curiosity and concern covering her expression. "Am I interrupting something?"

"Not at all, Mom." Beth forced a smile although her anger filled her office. "I think my point is clear, Mr. Hipp. You may go now."

He'd been dismissed. Sandy gave him a rather amused look. He knew she was guessing what had just transpired here. He glanced from mother to daughter and then slowly left the office. But he had every intention of waiting for Sandy.

Chapter Nine

Beth was absolutely outraged. Sandy could only imagine what her daughter and Ralph had been discussing before she'd arrived.

"Ethan told me that you wanted to talk to me." She decided her daughter could fill her in if she wanted.

"Mom." Beth picked up her pen, clicked it open and closed a few times, then dropped it on her desk. "Ethan told me that he saw you and Ralph in our kitchen last night."

Sandy leaned back in her chair, waiting for her daughter to say what she would. Obviously she was upset by the news. Angry—if the encounter she'd just missed with Ralph in here was any indication.

"I take it you don't like Ralph," she said when Beth seemed at a loss as how to continue.

Her daughter shook her head, her anger still simmering. "He's incredible security for the pack. And his investigational skills are outstanding."

Sandy nodded, knowing all of this already. Ralph had a solid reputation with the pack. In fact, he had a solid everything. She blinked, trying to stay focused for her cub. Grown or not, Beth needed her right now. She was upset. And Sandy understood. Beth had never had to share her.

"He's just not right for you, Mom." Suddenly the successful attorney was gone. Her child, trusting and concerned appeared before her.

Sandy stood up and started to walk around Beth's desk. "You shouldn't get yourself so upset about this."

Beth bristled. She held her hand up, stopping Sandy in mid-pace. "I am looking out for your best interests. And if you don't see what those are, then I guess it's my job to open your eyes."

Sandy didn't like her daughter's tone. It was one thing to be concerned. But she wouldn't be reprimanded by Beth.

"I do know what my best interests are, young lady." Sandy didn't try to approach her any longer. Instead she turned toward the door. "You will not speak to me like that."

Beth sighed. "Mom. He is a werewolf on the prowl for a piece of tail. And from what I've seen, he is doing okay without adding you to his list of conquests."

Sandy turned back around. Ralph wasn't playing the field. She was sure of it. "How could you say such a thing? I know it's always just been you and me. But you've got to accept the fact that it is okay for me to date."

Beth took her time coming around her desk. The anger no longer lingered in the air. Something akin to concern surfaced. And Beth's concerned look worried Sandy. Her daughter didn't know something that she didn't, did she?

"Just be careful, Mom. I don't want you hurt." She reached out, taking Sandy's hand. Her warm touch softened Sandy's heart. Beth was really worried about her. "Sometimes we don't see things as they really are. Just don't do anything you might regret later. Please."

"I won't, dear. I promise." Sandy hugged her daughter, and then turned to leave.

Beth's words hit her like a brick though. Maybe her daughter did see something that she didn't. It had been so long since she'd dated. Hell. She never really had dated after her mate died. She'd been too busy raising Beth.

But Beth had started a life of her own. And now her daughter had found a really good werewolf. Her daughter was not only the most successful lawyer in the Midwest, she was queen bitch. Her triumphs were more than commendable.

So where did that leave her? She continued to help the pack when needed. And that was almost every day. Her life was full. Or so she'd thought.

Ralph had woken something up in her. She hadn't known how much she'd missed good sex. And maybe there would be no long-term relationship. She didn't know. But she would prepare herself for the knowledge that being with Ralph might be casual. All she knew for sure was that fucking him had been damned good. Better than good. She couldn't remember sex being so awesome.

Beth's secretary was on her the minute Sandy opened the office door. Calls were holding. There were messages. Her next appointment was waiting. It made it easy to slip out of her office without more drama.

It had grown colder since she'd been inside the courthouse. She should have worn her heavier coat. Leaves blew along the ground and the skies were dark and heavy. This was Halloween weather. She loved this holiday.

Bundling up, she hunched over, hurrying to her car. It dawned on her when she reached the parking lot that she'd been so upset by her conversation with Beth that she'd forgotten to mention the reporter confronting her.

The wind blew in her face, wrapping Ralph's scent around her. Looking up, she saw him coming toward her, his truck idling next to her parked car.

"What did your daughter say to you?" Ralph wrapped his arm around her, pulling her into the warmth of his body.

"That you are a womanizer, and I should leave you alone." She saw him smile at her words and wondered why he found it so amusing. "What did she say to you?"

"That I am a womanizer and I should leave you alone." He opened her car door for her and held it while she hopped in. Immediately she missed the heat from his body.

"Well, are you?" She looked up into his rugged face, those handsome features. Ralph had a body that was in better shape than most twenty-somethings. The fact that he was a bit older only made him more appealing. He reeked of experience and technique.

"Am I what?" He gripped the top of her car door, his biceps bulging when he bent closer to her.

It was suddenly hard to breathe. Just having such a wonderful eyeful of this magnificent werewolf was enough to stop her heart in mid-beat. She forced the lump of excitement back down her throat just so she could speak.

"Are you a womanizer?"

"Nope." He spoke with such confidence, just like he always did. As if that one word would end the conversation, drop the subject as if it merited no further discussion.

He straightened. "Follow me back to the diner. We'll grab a cup of coffee."

Sandy opened her mouth to tell him she would check on Greta, see if she was still there, but she wasn't sure about having coffee with him. She needed time to sort out her daughter's concerns. Not that she would run from him because her over-dominating cub told her to. She would make her own decisions, form her own opinions of the werewolf. She just wanted time to do that.

But Ralph didn't give her the opportunity to say that. He closed her car door and headed back to his truck before she could speak.

She swore his scent had claimed her clothing. All the way to the diner she could smell him. Her skin still tingled from the brief moments he had wrapped his arm around her, shielding her from the chilly breeze.

But what had her worried was how being so close to him had made her want him again. Bad. Her pussy throbbed just thinking about how he'd fucked her the night before. Heat flushed through her with such intensity the chilly wind outside didn't stand a chance in cooling her down.

It wasn't like her daughter to jump to conclusions without facts to back her statements. Beth hadn't become the successful attorney that she was by speculating. That bothered Sandy. Beth had told her to keep her eyes open, that Ralph was a womanizer.

And what if he was? She searched her memory for times when Ralph had been with other women. She couldn't remember any. But then she didn't usually pay attention to the dating scene within the pack.

She stared at the back of Ralph's truck, realizing she was dutifully following him to the diner just as he'd instructed. And as they neared, she noticed Ethan was still parked there. Had Ralph known the pack leader would still be there? More than likely he did.

Ethan would tell Beth that they showed up together minutes after Beth had warned her mother about Ralph. Sandy sighed. More than anything the thought of fucking him again distracted her thoughts. Her body tingled with desire. A craving too intense for any of her toys had started, and she knew only Ralph could ease her growing ache.

Ralph's turn signal began blinking, indicating his intent to turn into the diner parking lot. The blinking light held her gaze. And at the same time a strange realization sunk through her straight to the pit of her stomach.

More than anything she wanted to fuck Ralph again. But she hesitated in reappearing at the diner with him after her daughter's warning. It bothered her how her pack leader might react to her silent statement that she paid little heed to her daughter's words.

If Ralph was a womanizer, what did that make her?

She would willingly fuck him again, but worried about how they might appear being seen in public together. Hell. She was no better than the werewolf her daughter accused Ralph of being.

Suddenly everything was way too confusing. Sandy needed time to think. On an impulse, she waited for Ralph to turn into the diner ahead of her, and then drove on down the street. She didn't look back to see if Ralph watched her.

Chapter Ten

Sandy's phone hadn't rung once. No one had stopped by. She couldn't remember the last time she'd spent an entire day alone in her den. And she would have enjoyed herself, except for the fact that she felt she'd been grounded.

Her daughter had power. And she had rank in the pack. It crossed her mind more than once that Ralph might have been ordered to stay away from her. He would respect the pack's wishes. If her daughter had convinced Ethan to tell Ralph to leave her alone, she would be left alone.

Piddling around in her kitchen, she wished her body would quit tingling, quit craving Ralph's touch again. But for the life of her, she couldn't quit imagining his hard cock pounding the deepest spots in her pussy. He fed her like no toy ever could, like no werewolf had ever done before.

"And he hasn't bothered to come see you at all today," she reminded herself, mumbling while she flipped the steak in the frying pan.

The weatherman on the TV warned of possible snow over the next few days. It would be a cold Halloween. The commentators went on about appropriate ways to dress children while trick-or-treating.

Sandy drowned it all out. Maybe her daughter had been right. Maybe she was nothing more than a fool who had fallen for the oldest trick in the book. She was out of practice, knew nothing about the dating scene. And Ralph Hipp certainly had what it took to be a werewolf on the prowl.

"So now I'm a piece of tail." She stabbed at her steak with her fork while it sizzled in the pan.

Something the news reporters commented on caught her attention. "It will be curious to see how the werewolves dress their children for Halloween."

"They call them cubs, Steve, which makes sense since they are half-wolves." The pretty newscaster laughed at her lack of wit.

Sandy scowled at the television, wishing people wouldn't talk about things they knew nothing about. Half-wolf indeed. Did that make humans half-ape? Or was it jackass? Because that was exactly what the lady on the news report was making out of herself.

"We sent Judy out to do some research on the matter. Let's see what she has for us." The two of them turned to a flat screen next to them and Sandy stared in horror.

There she was. The newslady, who had stopped her yesterday in the parking lot, spoke with one of the younger mothers in the pack.

"We don't have a problem trick-or-treating around humans." The mother adjusted her cub in her arms. "And I think both of my little ones will be ghosts this year."

The scene changed. Sandy recognized the van behind the reporter when the woman spoke into the camera.

"This new pack that has made our town their home seems ready to hit the streets in droves Halloween night." Her expression was grim.

The scene changed again. Sandy watched herself smile at the reporter.

"Where will you take your cubs trick-or-treating this year?" the reporter asked.

"Since I just moved here, I don't know the safest places."

The scene flashed. Once again the reporter faced the camera. "And as you can see, without knowing our town that well, these werewolves could be just about anywhere."

The newscasters thanked the reporter and then began a discussion about how the town planned on zoning areas where the werewolves would be allowed to trick-or-treat.

Sandy's phone rang and she stared at it a minute, her stomach tying in knots. Was she in trouble with the pack now?

She turned the flame off underneath her steak. It looked like she'd cooked it too long, but she wasn't sure she could eat anything now anyway.

"Hello." Her palm grew sweaty holding the receiver.

"Hi, Mom." Beth sounded cheerful. "I just saw the news. Why didn't you tell me a reporter stopped you?"

"I was going to but you distracted me a bit yesterday with your accusations about Ralph." She didn't mind scolding her daughter for the intrusion into her life. It wasn't like she was some old ninny who needed taken care of.

Beth sighed, taking her time before commenting. "I'm worried that you might be harassed further. The humans are just dying to find any werewolf they can get to comment."

And she apparently had gullible written across her forehead.

"Would you mind coming over to our house for a while? I'll be home this evening. We could make Ethan barbecue."

Her daughter had never been the best at apologies, but if this was an attempt, Sandy figured she might as well grab it. The last thing she wanted was friction between her and Beth. Besides, it didn't appear that she had anything better to do.

After a shower, and changing clothes three times, Sandy headed over to her daughter's. She glanced in the mirror before she walked out of her home, running her fingers through her hair. Wrapping a fluffy white twist tie around her hair at the base of her neck, the streaks of gray running through her brown made her cringe.

"You should focus on becoming a grandmother, and not on chasing hot sexy werewolves," she scolded herself, all too aware of the lines that appeared around her eyes when she frowned.

And having grandchildren would be wonderful. She couldn't wait. But she didn't feel old. Her gray hairs hadn't stopped Ralph from seeking her out.

"And that is because you aren't old." She squared her shoulders, knowing damned good and well she told herself the truth.

And after that hot sex she'd had the other night with Ralph, she sure didn't feel old. Other than a sore muscle here and there, she couldn't wait to ride that cock of his again.

"So I'm not old, I'm a nymphomaniac." Somehow that cheered her up. Grabbing her coat, she headed out the door.

The night air was too cold for her human skin. So instead of standing outside, breathing in the wonderful smells from the grill in the backyard at her daughter's house, she sat in the kitchen, enduring the mundane chatter of Patrick Oberhaus, the sixth grade social studies teacher.

"With this new funding, we should be able to buy enough computers so that there will be several at least in each classroom." Patrick rambled on, for the most part about things Sandy already knew.

She nodded and dug into the chips bag for another chip. She dunked it into the dip Beth had set on the table, and glanced toward the back door. Maybe enduring the cold in her human form would be better than listening to this old fart brief her on the financial standing at the pack school.

"You should be careful what you eat." He wagged a finger at her while smiling.

Sandy turned and looked at him, her mouth full of dip.

"We need to keep an eye on our diet, you know." He patted his tummy, which didn't bulge, but certainly didn't have that hard look that Ralph's had. "The days of our youth when we could eat whatever we want are long gone."

"A good run every night and hot sex keep me trim." Sandy enjoyed the wide-eyed look Patrick gave her, his mouth opening and then shutting like a fish trying to breathe out of water.

"Mom!" Beth came in from outside, the chilly night air quickly filling the room.

Sandy turned in time to see her daughter's scolding look. "Mom is such a tease. You'll have to forgive her," she said apologetically to Patrick.

"Oh. I don't mind." Patrick smiled at her, although his tone was much more hushed and he blushed just like the schoolchildren he taught every day. "I like feisty women."

Sandy stood, having about all she could take of the now drooling schoolteacher. She followed her daughter into the other room, hoping Patrick wouldn't tag along.

"You invited him over here to try and set me up with him," she hissed, and then grew silent when she saw Jan Price, the young bitch who helped out with her daughter's busy schedule, walking into the dining room from the living area.

"All I could find was this white linen." She held up the folded material in her hands. "I hope it's okay."

"That's just fine." Beth moved to the opposite side of the dining room table. "Here. I'll help you."

Jan opened the tablecloth and the two of them spread it over the table.

"There is nothing wrong with Patrick Oberhaus." Obviously Beth didn't mind discussing the matter in front of Jan. "He is a very nice werewolf."

"Yes. He is." Sandy also believed him to be an outstanding teacher for the cubs. But that wasn't the point. "But I don't need you trying to set me up with him. Or anyone else for that matter."

Jan finished straightening the cloth at her end of the table, looked at the two of them, and then hurried out of the room, an amused smile on her face. But Sandy wasn't amused.

"I just think that if you want to date," Beth paused for a moment, searching her mom's face. Sandy saw her worry and concern but feared her daughter was more upset about sharing her mom. Beth reached out, taking her hand. "You should find a werewolf who is a bit more...well...tame."

Sandy had to hide a smile, deciding commenting on the wild sex she and Ralph had alongside her car in an open field the other night probably wouldn't help matters at the moment.

"Whether I decide to date or not, and who I date, is up to me." Sandy tried to keep her tone gentle.

Beth chewed her lower lip, the worry still obvious on her pretty face. "You know he told Ethan that he plans on mating with you."

Now that took Sandy by surprise. She stared at her daughter, the impact of her words taking a minute to sink in. "He did?"

Beth nodded. "Now do you see why I'm worried?"

"It doesn't sound like he's after a piece of tail if he wants me for a mate." Sandy's palms grew damp while her heart began racing.

She couldn't believe she was discussing the possibilities of being Ralph's mate so casually.

Beth threw her hands up in the air, her frustration filling the room instantly. "He's not right for you," she snapped.

Sandy turned at the sound of the back door opening. But her heart stopped in mid-beat when she heard Ralph talking to Ethan. The two of them appeared through the doorway in the next moment.

"Come with me." Ralph reached for her, and she found herself taking his hand before she realized her actions.

Chapter Eleven

The atmosphere in the room changed in the next breath. Ralph's strong grip squeezed her fingers together, the heat from his touch sizzling through her skin, sending prickles of anticipation racing through her. Her mouth went dry while her heart began pounding an erratic beat.

She'd never seen him look at her the way he did now. Ralph's features were hard, intense. His presence filled the dining room. And he was angry. She sensed that right away. But the tightness of his body, the rigid outline of his muscles bulging through his shirt, made him appear ready to spring.

He looked from her to Beth and then back at her again. The smoothness of his head, the dark brooding stare that burrowed through her, the firm set of his jawline, all of it showed he wouldn't be crossed right now.

He turned to leave the dining room, her hand clasped in his. Ethan stood behind him in the doorway. Sandy saw the two werewolves stare each other down. Both of them were so large, so powerful-looking. Their gazes locked. Silent communication of two creatures driven by emotions raw and unleashed.

"Wait a minute." Beth cried out from behind her. "You can't just leave. Ethan. We have company."

Ethan took a step toward his mate. Ralph pulled her through the doorway. He moved through the kitchen with more agility than a man his size should be able to. She swore he growled at Patrick Oberhaus. The schoolteacher stepped to the side, muttering something inaudible while he nodded a polite gesture of goodbye. Sandy did all she could not to stumble in tow.

The cold night air slapped her face but did little to stop the fire rushing through her. Ralph dragged her to his truck, opened the passenger door, grabbed her by the waist, lifted her in, and slammed the door shut. She watched him stalk around the front of the cab. Intent. Dominating. Laying claim.

Cold air washed around her when he slid in next to her. The engine of the truck roared to life. She focused on his large hands, gripping the steering wheel while they pulled away from her daughter's house.

"What were you doing over there?" He sounded angry.

She looked over at him, his strong profile, thick solid arms, his broad muscular chest. The entire package was about the deadliest werewolf she'd ever known. And he was upset. No. More like outraged. She should be terrified. But for some reason she wasn't.

"We were getting ready to have dinner."

"The four of you." His fingers tightened and relaxed around the steering wheel. He seemed barely able to contain some storm within him that threatened to explode in all its fury at any moment. "Why were you there with Oberhaus?"

He looked at her then, a quick glance. She studied his face, masked to prevent the strong emotions she smelled and sensed through the tenseness of his body. His dark eyes pierced through her with the intensity of his gaze.

In the next instant, he returned his attention to the road. Her body tingled from the power emanating from him. She responded to his aggressive emotions, her own primal instincts coming forth, aching to lean into him, give herself to him, allow him to do with her what he would.

But he was bullying her. And that wouldn't do. No werewolf would yank her out of her daughter's home and then accuse her of anything. She wouldn't have it.

"I wasn't there with anyone," she snapped at him, letting him know she wouldn't be pushed. "I went on my own and was given no indication of the guest list."

She turned away from him, crossing her arms to show her indignation with his behavior. But in reality, she needed to make sure she wouldn't reach out and touch him. Her body churned with electricity. An ache had spawned and continued to grow the longer she sat so close to him and didn't touch him. Her pussy throbbed, beating a quick little pulse that made her want to reach down and rub her clit to ease the growing pressure.

Ralph turned the corner a bit too fast, causing her to lean to the side. She would have easily fallen into him if she hadn't braced herself. But her jeans rubbing against her pussy, pressing against the pulsating, swollen nub, made her explode. She pressed her hand against his leather seat, not only to keep herself from falling into him, but to brace herself while molten heat surged through her.

"You are not available for other werewolves to date." His words had the finality of a direct order.

She was so taken back by them that she didn't realize until he parked that they were in her driveway. Her heart seemed to have stopped breathing. She licked her lips, her mouth suddenly too dry.

"What do you mean by that?" If he intended to make her his bitch, he would do it properly. And then she would think about it.

Ralph opened his car door, grabbed her hand, and pulled her across the seat. She adjusted herself quickly so she wouldn't hit the steering wheel. He almost crushed her hand while he guided, almost pulled her, to her front door. But he didn't answer her. His silence was almost as dangerous as his aggressive behavior. And she wondered at herself for being so excited by his primitive actions.

It wasn't until they stood there at her front door that she realized she didn't have her purse, or her coat. The cold night air seemed to have no impact on her though. Her body was so charged with raw energy, reacting to his possessive behavior.

"I don't have my keys." She looked up at him.

He looked ready to pounce. He wanted her. Pent-up energy made his muscles taut, his grip on her hand burning with uncontrollable heat. The way he looked at her, almost as if he hadn't heard her, made her insides melt.

She took a deep breath fighting to control the beast within her that wanted to break free, to take on the aggressor, to demand he soothe the fire burning out of control through her body.

"Come on. I can get us inside." He headed around the side of the house, still leading her, still maintaining a tight grip on her hand.

"What are you going to do?" She wondered what skills he possessed. After all, he was a security man and had been in law enforcement for years.

Ralph let go of her hand when they reached the back of the house. Suddenly the night air attacked her, the biting chill ransacking her body, raging with the heat that continued to burn inside her.

She barely noticed what he did. But within less than a minute he'd slid open her bedroom window.

"Remind me to get better locks," she mumbled, watching while her bedroom curtains fluttered through the open space.

"You wouldn't be able to lock me out." It sounded like he chuckled but she couldn't be sure. He turned to her, lifting her up before she could react. "Go inside and unlock the back door."

He held her so she could slide her feet in first. Before she knew it, she stood in her dark bedroom, the warmth of her home feeling good instantly. She didn't hesitate, but hurried through her home and opened the back door for him.

His strong scent wrapped around her. His dark gaze that of a hunter. Muscles seemed to bulge everywhere on him. So much power. So much raw, untamed lust. He didn't smile, didn't offer any expression that gave away what he thought. But the way he approached her, as if he stalked her, moving closer with slow, meditated efforts, made the beast in her awaken.

"You will understand something about me." His voice was a deep growl, almost a whisper.

Chills ran over her body. He looked like he wanted to devour her.

"I have never thought of myself as old. But maybe I am old-fashioned. When I fucked you, it meant something," he told her.

She should have known she wasn't a piece of tail to him. The aggressive way he looked at her, the way he moved in, so powerful and dominating. He believed he had claimed her. Mated with her.

There was only one problem. He'd never asked her.

"Tell me what it meant." She dared to stand up to him, rooted her feet to the ground so that she wouldn't back up.

He reached for her. There was no way she could dodge those large hands. He took a hold of her shirt, pulling her to him. Her feet almost left the ground. The material of her shirt stretched, threads popping, almost tearing.

"It meant," he whispered, his face inches from hers, the heat of his breath melting her, feeding her lust for him. "After years of watching you, I made you mine."

She stared at him, her heart pounding so hard she swore she could hear it. Domination and lust filled the air around them. Her insides sizzled with a craving running so deep she could barely control it. Her breaths seemed staggered. The beast in her growing by the moment, singing through her veins.

His intense size, the way he had her pinned by her shirt, the glow in his eyes, told her he would spring at a moment's notice. It took more effort than she thought it would simply to swallow.

Her body shook with her efforts to control the change that begged to rush through her. And she knew she would have to change to protect herself if he sprang into action. But she would say her mind. He would never intimidate her.

"I don't recall you asking." She was proud of how calm she sounded. She never let her gaze waver, and her voice didn't crack.

The growl that rushed through Ralph's body made her shiver. He pulled her to him. Her shirt ripped. The sound of it made her pussy contract, cream soaking her jeans, her own scent filling the air, consuming his dominating scent.

Sandy saw something go beyond desire in Ralph's face. His look was hard, intent, his expression tight while he looked at her. She knew she pushed him. Knew that she asked more from him than he would offer of his own accord.

He needed to humble himself, risk her declining his offer by asking. She tested his male strength, the strength of his ego. She demanded he take her mind along with her body.

He attacked swiftly, his throaty growl indication that words were difficult for him at the moment. His mouth melded with hers, burning her lips with the intensity of his kiss. Somehow he managed to let go of her shirt, and wrap his arm around her, crushing her against his rock-hard body.

They moved through the kitchen, his mouth devouring her, her senses blurred with his body smashed against hers. When they reached her bedroom, he tossed her onto her bed, leaving her gasping for air when his mouth no longer covered hers.

He closed the window with one swift movement, although the cold air still lingered, helping her to calm her overheated senses somewhat.

Ralph removed his clothes, not rushing, but peeling them off, his penetrating look never leaving her. The smoothness of his muscles, bulging and outlined by the glow of the moonlight from the window, made her fingers itch to touch him.

"Why didn't you want me to ask you the other night when I fucked you?" He was over her in an instant, his powerful arms on either side of her while he knelt on the bed looking down at her.

Sandy licked her lips. He was so close, on top of her, naked, his cock a rock-hard dagger aimed directly at her, but not touching her. Focusing on his answer was almost too much to ask.

"You didn't tell me you were mating with me the other night." She knew her answer made her sound a bit too modern. Traditionally making love meant that the two werewolves agreed to mate. And mating was for life.

"Allow me then to make myself perfectly clear." His muscles rippled and flexed while he lowered his head, and pressed his lips to hers.

Heat surged through her like molten lava erupting with volcanic heat. Her pussy throbbed painfully, her body on fire with need for his touch.

She pressed her fingers against his chest, ran them over his shoulders, brushed them against his bald head. Every inch of him, she wanted to know and touch every inch of his perfect body.

Once again Ralph ended the kiss. Leaning back on his haunches, he grabbed her shirt, pulling it hard enough to send buttons flying everywhere.

"Damn. Ralph." His actions soaked her, her lust so strong in the air around them it was intoxicating.

He pulled again, freeing her of the restrictive clothing. And then his knuckles brushed the swell of her breasts. Her heart pounded too hard against his hand while he gripped her bra. With a quick tug the clasp gave way in the back, and he slid it down her arms.

Her nipples hardened instantly. Stripping her the way he had, so rough, so carnal, excited her more than she imagined it would.

"Are you going to take these off? Or am I?" He'd grabbed her jeans, his hand pressing into the softness of her belly. His flesh so hot it burned right through her, adding to the intense fire already surging through her.

Quickly she lay back on the bed, undoing her pants, sliding them down her legs. Ralph's impatience had her panting. She knew if she didn't move fast enough he would rip them from her body, too.

"You are mighty demanding." And she wasn't sure how to feel about how excited it made her.

"I'm making sure there is no confusion this time." He ran his hand down her body, stroking her from in between her breasts to the soft tender skin shaved smooth between her legs.

"You will not take anything without asking." She wanted, more than anything, to hear him ask her to be his mate. Maybe it was that she too was a bit on the old-fashioned side, but hearing those words from him suddenly meant a lot to her.

Ralph growled, the look he gave her almost fierce. He grabbed her legs, his thumbs pressing deep into her inner thighs. Her rear end left the bed while he lifted her, stretching her legs apart, spreading her wide open. All the while, his gaze was lowered, watching her pussy.

When she was sure if he spread her legs any further she would split in two, he dove down, burying his tongue deep inside her.

"Oh God." She cried out, tossing her head from one side to the other. Her hair broke free of its ponytail holder, long strands sticking to her face.

But she couldn't move them, couldn't do anything but fist her bedspread in her hands, and hold on for dear life.

"More. Give me more." Ralph spoke into her pussy, his hot breath teasing her soaked cunt.

Wave after wave of smoldering passion rippled through her, the intensity of it so strong she feared she would pass out, slip into some other state. Never had she climaxed like this before, and from simply his mouth.

Ralph lapped at her like a starving animal, showing no mercy, feeding from her like she was his lifeline. When she was sure he had consumed everything she could offer, his tongue did a wicked dance around her clit, stroked the inner side of her pussy, and she exploded again.

All of this was more than she could handle. She would lose it, change into her fur, lose her ability to think rationally. Something. Ralph took her to levels she didn't know existed.

"I can't." She feared he would drain her of all moisture. "It's too much."

"No." With measured effort, he placed hot wet kisses against her inner thighs. "It will never be too much, my dear."

He teased her with how slowly he moved, his tongue and lips tracing fiery paths across her skin while he worked his way up her body. He lavished one breast and then the other, sucking in each nipple, teasing them ruthlessly with his teeth and mouth.

"Ralph." She knew she would beg if she said another word. All would be over then. She bit her lip, struggling not to say more.

"Yes?" His hot breath was as torturous as his cock, weighing heavy just above her pussy.

"Please." The word escaped her. She didn't want to say it, hated that she was ready to beg him to enter her, take away the pain, the pressure, the urgent need that throbbed ruthlessly throughout her.

"Please what?" His breath smelled of her rich cream. He looked up at her with so much more than just lust, just passion. She could see so much more.

It was on the tip of her tongue to beg him to fuck her. She took several deep breaths before speaking. "Please ask me," she finally said, more than proud of herself for holding on to a small glint of sanity throughout his torture session.

Ralph slammed his cock deep inside her at that moment. His thick, large shaft spread her, filled her, penetrated so far inside her she thought she would split in two.

"God. Oh. Ralph." She screamed as he fucked her. His cock pulling out and thrusting deep inside of her faster than she was prepared for.

She couldn't catch her breath, couldn't hold on, couldn't think. It was all she could do to see. His chest muscles bulged and contracted above her, his body wound tight while he beat her pussy with his cock harder and with more intensity than she thought she could handle.

Her human form barely had the strength to let go of the bedspread. She reached upward, grabbing his shoulders, feeling his hot moist skin against her hands. Digging into his flesh with her fingers, she held on, wishing somehow she could take the upper hand.

His cock stroked her inner pussy walls, appeasing the fire that burned there while making her burn hotter at the same time. The pressure he'd appeased with his tongue now grew again with more intensity than it had before.

But she wouldn't go over the edge without him. "That's it, wolf man." She forced herself to talk, to at least sound like she held some semblance of control over the situation. "Fuck me. Take care of that itch you created."

His eyes rose to hers, his look either disbelieving of her brazen words, or willing to take on her challenge. She wasn't sure which.

He rose above her, straightening while her hands slipped down his body, feeling the quivering of muscles under his smooth flesh.

His lovemaking slowed only for a moment, long enough for her to move her legs so her heels rested next to his neck. Then he plowed into her again.

The angle had changed. The spot he hit deep inside her different. Her tender pussy grasped his cock, soaking it, easing his path with her thick rich cream.

"Yes. Oh yes." She exploded when he hit that one spot that had craved his touch.

The dam of pressure broke, volcanic heat exploding inside her while wave after wave of liquid heat rushed through her.

"That's it, baby." Ralph choked out the words.

His cock swelled inside her, engorged and ready to explode. She held her hands out, wanting to hold him but not able to bring him down to her. His concentrated expression looked wild as he closed his eyes, his head dropping back, veins bulging from his neck. His release into her burned and soothed all at the same time. The convulsions of his cock made her come again, her body quivering as he filled her with his cum.

"Holy shit." He dropped down, moving to the side just in time before he collapsed with his full weight on top of her. "I'm not as young as I used to be. Damn woman."

He chuckled, pulling her next to him. She cuddled up willingly, stretching along the length of his body.

"You seem pretty damned good to me." And she knew he knew that, but decided he'd earned his ego being stroked a bit.

Ralph pulled her in closer until she rested her head on his chest, listening to his heartbeat until she fell asleep.

Chapter Twelve

It was Halloween. Sandy had always loved this holiday. And waking up snuggled into Ralph's warm body started the day off perfectly.

She showered and then started coffee and stood staring out her front living-room window when Ralph's scent drifted in from behind her. His rich intoxicating all-male smell had her pussy throbbing instantly. Her nipples hardened as if calling out to him on their own, begging for his attention. Every inch of her was like an exposed nerve ending, ultra-sensitive to his mere presence.

"What are you doing today?" His greeting didn't surprise her. His protective nature would always demand to be informed.

"I'm going to help the school take the cubs downtown for trick-or-treating." She looked down at her fingernails, examining them while her stomach twisted in knots of anticipation. "And I want to talk to my daughter."

He stood right behind her. If she leaned back barely an inch his powerful body would be there, comforting, a security blanket. But she wanted more from him than just his security.

She turned around and examined his calm expression. So relaxed, he appeared not to have a care in the world. She knew that made him a good investigator. But she wasn't one of his cases to be solved.

"I asked you for something last night," she began, her mouth suddenly too dry. She licked her lips, taking in a deep breath. "And you didn't give it to me."

His expression didn't change. She thought she saw something dark pass through his eyes, something intent, but then it disappeared.

"I want you to be my mate." His words came quickly, and she supposed that was as close as a proposal for mating that she would ever get out of him.

She sighed, looking down. More than anything she wanted to run her fingers over the bulging muscles that were outlined through his shirt. She could wrap her arms around him, cuddle into him, allow his warmth to soak through her.

But she had to be strong around him. If she leaned on him he would make all of the decisions for them. He needed to see that she would think for herself.

"I'll think about it." Her heart raced in her chest while she waited for his reaction.

He turned from her, heading toward the door. "I'll call you later." And then he was gone.

Ethan dropped off her purse and coat to her shortly after Ralph left. She was grateful the two werewolves didn't cross paths at her house.

"How is Beth doing?" she asked, knowing he understood the question.

"Give her time," was all he said.

She nodded and he left shortly after that.

The day was full of holiday activities, which helped Sandy keep her thoughts off Ralph. By dark, he hadn't called. She hadn't heard from her daughter either. Large snowflakes had just started to fall when she decided to drive over to Beth's house.

Ethan and Ralph stood just inside the doorway when she walked up, a swarm of cubs around her all dressed up for trick-or-treating.

"Trick or treat," they yelled out in unison, and she barely managed to sneak around them while the two large werewolves made a show of dumping candy into their sacks.

She strolled through the house undisturbed until she found her daughter upstairs, sitting at the computer.

"You never did like Halloween." She smiled at her daughter who sat cross-legged in oversized sweats and large fuzzy slippers.

Beth turned, searching her mom's face for a moment before smiling. "I remember you used to bribe me with anything you could think of to get me to put on a costume and go door to door with you."

Sandy grinned, remembering how stubborn her cub had been. Some things never changed. Beth turned back to her computer, pointing to it.

"I was reading through some e-mail. This came in from one of my old college buddies." She laughed and Sandy rested her hand on her daughter's shoulder, deciding to enjoy this moment even if they weren't discussing what bothered her daughter.

And Beth was bothered. Worry and frustration swam in the air around her. Like Ralph, she liked to control situations. But Sandy wouldn't be manipulated by either one of them. It would take time, but they would both come to accept that.

"It's a list of what not to do on Halloween." Beth leaned back, her expression showing she was getting ready to make some point. "Don't howl at the moon unless you want to pick up a werewolf," she read. She looked up at Sandy. "You know there is a blue moon tonight. You plan on doing any howling?"

Sandy looked into her daughter's probing eyes. "That, my dear, is none of your business."

Beth stood up quickly, immediately pacing. "It is too my business. You're my mother. And I have a right..."

"Stop right there." Sandy held up her hand, and Beth stopped in mid-stride, her hands going to her hips. "Yes. I am your mother. But I've raised you. You've moved on, made a wonderful life for yourself. I have a right to do the same."

"So you want Ralph Hipp then? Are you sure about this? He's so...so..." Beth gestured with her hands, while she frowned.

"So demanding? Control-oriented? Bullheaded?" Sandy couldn't keep from smiling, thoughts of Ralph trying to manipulate her just like her daughter did grew suddenly very clear. "He's a lot like someone else I love."

Beth sucked in her lower lip, reminding Sandy of how she looked when she was a little girl, frustrated with something.

"Do you love him?" she whispered.

"Maybe." She thought she might, and maybe she always had. But it was something she would explore and not be rushed, by either of them.

"Then I guess you should go to him." Beth sat back down at her computer, giving her mother one of those dismissive waves she was so good at.

Sandy would give Beth time to digest that much knowledge. She didn't expect her to immediately congratulate her on her newfound happiness. Leaving the room, she wandered back down to the kitchen. The TV was on in the living room, deep male voices speaking quietly as the two werewolves discussed something.

She went to the back door, staring out at patches of clear black sky in between the heavy gray clouds. A blue moon, the second full moon in the month. Just like her. The cycle completed and coming around for another chance.

Stepping outside, she crossed her arms over her chest while her nipples puckered against the cold. It wasn't late but the dark night, and white coat of soft snow on the ground would probably end trick-or-treating before long.

There were two people inside that she cared dearly for. She watched while the full moon, the blue moon, slowly appeared from behind a cloud. A second later its brightness allowed her human eyes to see the surrounding yard more clearly. And that was how it would be with Ralph and Beth. Time would allow them to see clearer, to understand that what she asked of them was what would make her happy.

Turning, she decided that was all she could do for the night.

"You two have a good evening," she told the two werewolves when she walked into the living room. "Ethan, let Beth know I went home for the night."

Ralph stood. "We are going on a run here in a bit."

She knew he expected her to go along. She smiled. "Have fun. Give me a call tomorrow."

An eyebrow shot up, his look penetrating and shrewd while he seemed to search her thoughts, learn what she was about. She turned and left her pack leader's house before her knees began shaking.

A noise woke her later that evening. Glancing at her clock it was the middle of the night. Her heart lurched inside her when she spotted the figure standing in her doorway.

Ralph's massive frame, broad chest, thick torso and long legs, filled the doorway to her bedroom. He smelled earthy, telling her he'd probably just returned from a run.

"You told me to call you tomorrow. It's tomorrow." He moved toward her, approaching slowly.

She couldn't decide whether it had been a good idea to go to bed without her nightgown on or not. He would have just ripped it off of her if she had worn it, and she liked her nightgown. Nonetheless, she gripped her blankets, using them as a shield against him.

"What are you doing here?" Her brain was still foggy from sleep.

"You know I'm not going to leave you alone." He began unbuttoning his shirt, his gaze never leaving her.

And she knew she didn't want him to leave her alone. Her heart pounded in her chest, the same beat making her pussy throb. He undressed in front of her, that incredibly sexy body slowly appearing while he shed his clothes.

"Yes. I know," she whispered, admitting the truth.

He crawled onto the bed, hovering over her, like the predator stalking his prey. His body glistened from the strong ray of moonlight streaming through her bedroom window. Solid muscle, bulging, taut, he moved like he was still in his beast form.

She looked down at the long length of his cock—hard, solid. Her mouth watered. Tingles rushed over her skin, an exciting sense of anticipation making her feel almost giddy.

"And I think you want me here." His voice was low, not a whisper, more like a growl, matching the slinking movement of his body.

Hot cream soaked her pussy, the scent rising through the air, answering his question before she spoke. "Yes," she whispered.

His mouth covered hers, hot and moist, feasting on her. She rose up to him, letting go of the blanket, reaching for him. Her hands brushed over his body, his muscles quivering under her touch. Reaching down, she encircled his thick shaft with her fingers, feeling it pulsate against her palms.

Ralph groaned into her mouth, feeding her while he took from her all she would offer. He empowered her, made her drunk off of his strength. Sitting up, she pushed into him, forcing him to his knees.

For the first time, she ended the kiss, looking up into his lust-filled eyes. She studied the strong jawline, his thick neck, ran her hands along his broad shoulders. His coarse chest hair tickled her hands while she explored the curve of his muscles, the width of his torso.

Then looking down, she ran her hands over his cock. It danced in eagerness, thrusting toward her while her mouth grew so wet she had to swallow just staring at how glorious he looked.

"I think I will have you," she told him, running the tips of her fingers over the swollen curve of his cockhead.

Ralph moaned, reaching for her, trying to push her down on the bed. "Sandy. You've had me for a long time now."

His words soared through her, making her heart dance. He'd wanted her for a long time. How special that made her feel. But he'd watched her, not taken time to get to know her. And now he would know her. And he would know that although petite, a widow with an overbearing daughter, she was also strong.

She pushed back, looking up at him, finding it hard not to grin at the surprised look he gave her. Ignoring his reaction to her defiance, she went down on her hands and knees and ran her tongue over the round smooth surface of the tip of his cock.

"Dear God. Damn." He grabbed her head, his long thick fingers tangling through her hair. "Woman. Yes."

She could hardly open her mouth far enough to suck him in. The rock-hard shaft with skin so soft against her lips, moved in and out of her. Fucking her. Taking all she offered and pushing a bit harder for more. She gagged against him, feeling him stretch her throat, wanting even more of him.

Running her tongue over the satin skin, she tasted his saltiness, smelled his rich scent, and her body rushed with an ache so severe, so full of need, she could barely hold herself up.

Ralph pinned her head, holding her in place while he impaled her mouth, her lips tingling while she drooled with a lusty craving for more.

So carnal. Almost rough. His actions made her wild, wanting more even though she gagged on what he offered.

His hands moved down her, gripping her, turning her while she still had her mouth open, still felt the friction from his cock.

"I need to fuck you." His words rushed through her, her cunt swollen with a fiery ache that craved him. Needed him.

"Yes. Oh. Yes." She gripped her headboard, arching her back so that his cock pressed into the soft mound of her ass.

She felt his hands on her, spreading her, exposing her while his swollen damp cockhead pressed into her skin until it trailed its way to her soaked hole.

And he wasn't gentle. She hadn't expected him to be. Kneeling behind her, he thrust into her craving cunt with a fierceness of possession.

"Who do you belong to?" he demanded to know from behind her.

His cock pressed deep inside her, riding her hard and fast.

She shook her head, letting her hair fly around her, taking all that he offered while holding onto her wooden headboard as if she would float away if she let go.

His words floated toward her, drifting on a sea of unadulterated passion, fiery lust, and a love so solid she knew it was here to stay.

Looking over her shoulder, she saw the darkness of his frame while he gripped her ass, impaling her with a fury that soared through her hotter than a prairie fire.

"You are mine." She cried out while hot cream exploded inside her, flowing with incredible speed through her, soaking her cunt, her inner thighs, his thick cock.

Ralph growled, making one final stab into her fiery hole. His fingers crushed her with his steel grip while he filled her with cum that branded her with its fire.

She almost laughed, the intensity of her orgasm was that good. Quivers rushed over her body. Without looking, she had found a mate, and the second time around would be glorious.

About the author:

All my life, I've wondered at how people fall into the routines of life. The paths we travel seemed to be well-trodden by society. We go to school, fall in love, find a line of work (and hope and pray it is one we like), have children and do our best to mold them into good people who will travel the same path. This is the path so commonly referred to as the "real world".

The characters in my books are destined to stray down a different path other than the one society suggests. Each story leads the reader into a world altered slightly from the one they know. For me, this is what good fiction is about, an opportunity to escape from the daily grind and wander down someone else's path.

Lorie O'Clare lives in Kansas with her three sons.

Lorie O'Clare welcomes mail from readers. You can write to her c/o Ellora's Cave Publishing at 1056 Home Ave. Akron, Oh 44310-3502.

Also by Lorie O'Clare:

Shadow Hunter

J.C. Wilder

Chapter One

As the sun sank in the west, the crowds on Bourbon Street grew rowdier. With each passing hour the average intoxication level per human increased, as did the threat to their lives, not that they knew it. The humans had no clue Death walked among them.

Halloween was one of the prime times for human death at the hands of a preternatural. Until two years ago it had been Rik's job to keep them safe.

But not anymore.

Rik threaded his way through the steady stream of tourists as he headed for the *Chat Noir*, a popular restaurant and jazz club in the heart of the French Quarter.

The fragile peace in the preternatural world was tenuous at best, but everyone was on edge. Until the Council of Elders, the ruling body of the preternatural world, dealt with Mikhail and his unprecedented challenge for control of the Council, anything could happen. The vampire was determined to bring down the Council no matter how many lives he destroyed in the process. For each day that passed, the body count increased and nerves grew more frayed.

Rik seriously doubted that when the Council made a move to pursue Mikhail and his followers that everyone else would fall into line. While most preternaturals supported the Council, a surprising number had adopted a wait-and-see attitude about the whole situation.

He didn't understand the apathy they displayed because the situation was clear to him. If Mikhail succeeded in taking control of the Council, there would only be chaos and the destruction of hundreds of lives. At least while under the control of the Council, the preternaturals could live safer, more ordinary lives. They were governed by a distinct set of laws and everyone was treated the same in the eyes of the Council.

To him the situation was a no-brainer. On one hand was anarchy and on the other was peace. Many of the Shadow Dwellers were too young to remember what life was like before the Council—himself included. He'd heard stories from the Elders of the constant power struggles and the everyday fight for survival. That was no way to live and he would do everything in his power to avoid such a bleak future for his people.

From behind his black Ray-Ban sunglasses, Rik scanned the sea of faces, always on the lookout for trouble. There were a select few who wished him ill or dead, whichever came first.

Old habits died hard.

It was an unseasonably warm Halloween and the majority of the costumed throng had been drinking heavily. A poor imitation of a vampire ran into him and Rik barely managed to conceal a snarl as he was forced to sidestep a large gorilla throwing up in the gutter.

Tourists.

The wide windows of the Chat were a welcome sight and he spotted his ex-boss, Trey, seated in the far corner of the restaurant with his back to the wall. The tall were-cat was leaning back, his chair balanced on two legs. He wore black sunglasses and Rik had no doubt he was aware of everything and everyone around him.

That was Trey; always ready for action.

Rik entered the Chat and waved at Tom, the bartender, before heading toward his friend's table. The restaurant was nearly full with the exception of the tables nearest Trey, but that was no surprise. One look at the Welsh warrior was enough to persuade any mortal to give him a wide berth.

At six foot six, he was all legs, long black hair and attitude. With his sunglasses, a silver ring through his left nostril and a matching one through his left eyebrow, he was an intimidating presence even when sitting in a lighted restaurant drinking steaming hot *café au lait*. Then again, his dark purple leather coat and black leather pants with more buckles and straps than a bondage store would put anyone on edge.

Few realized that Trey was an Elder, a preternatural of unnatural age. It was this extreme age that gave him an aura which made most a little skittish. The very air around the man was charged with his energy and anyone standing close would feel the hair on the back of the neck stand on end. Rik had grown so used to the sensation he barely noticed it anymore.

"You're late," Trey said.

"You're ugly but you don't see me calling the media." Rik grabbed the chair next to his friend then sat down with his back to the wall. He deliberately jarred the other man with his elbow forcing him to sit up. The front legs hit the floor with a thud.

"You can't sit across from me?" Trey muttered. He shifted his chair to the right a few inches.

"Not unless you want me to leave myself open," Rik shot back. "Do you want someone to stick a knife between my ribs?"

Trey's lips quirked. "It has occurred to me a time or two."

"I'll just bet it has." Rik pulled his sunglasses off and dropped them on the table. "This had better be good. I have a buxom blonde with a mouth like you would not believe waiting on me—"

"Get your mind out of your pants for a moment. The werewolf, Weylyn DuLac, arrived in New Orleans this morning and he and his pack-mates are here to do a little damage."

"I'm retired," Rik said flatly. "Log into the *shadowdweller.com* site and find yourself a licensed Hunter to deal with Fido. I'm out of the business and off your payroll."

"Not this time, Rik. You're back on the job whether you like it or not. It appears you're the object of Lyn's hunt." He spoke in a deceptively mild tone and when those black sunglasses turned toward Rik, he wished he hadn't removed his so fast. "Any idea what this might be about?"

"Maybe he has fleas?" Rik shrugged and he could tell Trey was not amused. "Who knows? It could be anything." Like the fact he'd bedded Lyn's human mate before he'd known she was his. It wasn't like she'd thought to share the information before she had her mouth on his cock.

"Ulrik…" There was a note of warning in the way Trey said his full name. "I can't allow trouble in the city tonight. You know as well as I do that the entire preternatural world is in a precarious state and the last thing I need is a pissing contest between a were-cat and a wolf."

Rik scowled. "No one is going to get into a —"

"I want you to go make nice with him."

Rik stared at his friend, shocked he'd even suggested such a thing. Cats did *not* associate with wolves. Ever. Wolves were an ignorant, unkempt lot who were more concerned with fighting anyone who got near them, especially the were-cats. It was rare to see a cat and a wolf in the same room let alone have a conversation. It simply didn't happen if one or the other wished to walk away alive.

He shook his head. "Who are you kidding? I'm not going to apologize for an honest mistake to that butt-sniffer."

Rik started to rise when Trey grabbed his arm in an iron grip that prevented his escape. Pain radiated from his wrist to his shoulder in a harsh wave that took his breath away.

"So you do know what he wants," Trey said.

Irritated, Rik dropped into his chair and the other man released him. The pain faded immediately and he resisted the urge to rub his arm. Damn! He hated that little trick.

"When I was in New York last month I made the acquaintance of a young woman. She made an interesting sexual advance and I took her up on her offer. It wasn't until after the fact that I found out Serena was Lyn's human mate."

Trey frowned. "She didn't wear a brand or carry a medallion?"

"Not a thing."

"So basically, you fell for the oldest trick in the book?" Trey ran a hand over his mouth, trying to disguise a smile. "You wouldn't be the first to fall into bed with a curious human mate of a wolf. Some of the more adventurous ones have been known to bed a were-cat just to compare the lovemaking techniques between the two species."

"So it would seem." Rik braced his arms on the table. "Now you understand how I don't owe him a damn thing, least of all an apology. If anything, his woman owes me one. She had to have known what she was doing when she came after me."

The other man shook his head. "I'm not asking you this time, Rik; I'm telling you. The wolves are restless and are looking for the slightest provocation to justify getting out of line. I don't want this stupid incident to be the beginning of a big free-for-all. It's Halloween and it's a waxing moon. I don't need anything else thrown into the mix."

"Hell," Rik snarled.

"Retired or not," Trey continued, "if you don't do this and all hell breaks out, think about how many innocent humans could be killed."

"I—"

"In this case, it doesn't matter what you think." Trey tipped his chair back and leaned against the wall again. "This is a mandate from the Council and if you go against them, I'll have to put out an order for your apprehension."

Rik's lips tightened and he bit back a growl. The last thing he wanted was one of his friends having to pick him up. Marcus would like nothing more than to put him in handcuffs and conveniently leave him bound for a few hours. He had a sick sense of humor.

"Fine." He swiped Trey's *café au lait* and downed it, knowing this would irritate his friend more than words could. "What do I have to do?"

Trey pulled a square of orange paper from his pocket and handed it to Rik. "Be at The Chamber at 11 p.m. and they will be waiting for you."

"I'll bet they will."

"Make sure you take at least one other ally with you, just in case Weylyn turns out to be a dick."

Rik snorted and stuffed the paper into his jacket pocket. "Too late for that. He was a dick the moment he was whelped." He rose and picked up his sunglasses. "Anything else?"

"Thanks."

Rik looked down at his friend. Trey was a strange one; he guarded his privacy like a cat with a ball of catnip. While he was remarkably tight-lipped about himself, there was no one better to have at your back when it was time to rock and roll. The man wasn't one for wasting emotions, so Rik knew what he'd said was heartfelt. He clapped a hand on his friend's shoulder and gave it a squeeze before leaving the restaurant.

The sun had set and the streetlights had come on but he didn't remove the dark lenses. His cougar senses allowed him to see well in the dark.

He had several hours before it would be time to appear at The Chamber. His previous plans with the voluptuous blonde had been cancelled due to his meeting with Trey and now they would have to be put on hold for the night, thanks to Lyn. This was shaping up to be a great night all around.

His gaze caught on a beautiful redhead across the street. She was dressed in a harem costume and the sheer outfit showed every inch of her drop-dead curves. Her hair licked at her back and her butt gave a friendly little jiggle as she hopped off a curb.

Now *there* was something he'd like to investigate further. This one was so sweet his teeth ached just to look at her. The full moon coupled with the need to mate caused his blood to heat just by watching her walk.

His skin prickled, alerting him to the arrival of another preternatural. Trey stood in the doorway of the Chat, and after a slow pan of the crowds in the street his gaze locked on Rik. His face was expressionless.

Trey gave him a slow nod, then turned and walked in the opposite direction. The mortals crowding the sidewalk parted before him in a wave.

Rik shot one last look at the redhead just as she vanished into a crowded restaurant. First he had to deal with Fido and after that, he would hit one of the local bars with the specific purpose of finding some female companionship. The moon was waxing and the need to mate was strong.

Tamping down his overactive libido, Rik headed down Bourbon Street. It was early but he'd arrange for some backup and head over and scope out The Chamber.

* * * * *

Charlene grinned as she thought about the humorous e-mail she'd sent to her college friends, Jill and Beth, several days earlier. It was finally Halloween and she'd sent a joke e-mail about the Top Ten Things to Avoid on Halloween. Number eight was her personal favorite: Don't date a shapeshifter, as you'll never know what to wear from one minute to the next.

Her grin turned to a wince as Maribel tugged on her corset strings.

"Easy girl, you're killing me."

"Wimp," Maribel muttered as she tied the corset off. "You're all laced in."

Char turned and stared at herself in the full-length mirror. In this outfit, her friends from the New Orleans Public Library wouldn't recognize her at all. Not to mention her family back in Boise.

Sheesh, if she showed up dressed like this they'd lock the doors and call the police.

"Char...girrrllll, you are going to burn down the house." Laurance looked up from where she was crouched at Char's feet. The other woman was lacing up Char's thigh-high vinyl boots.

"Ya think?" Char tilted her head and studied her appearance.

"There isn't a man at The Chamber that won't be panting to take you home," Maribel said. "Meow!"

"I'll second that. I think you're hot and you're not even my type." Raymie, a local drag queen and one of her very best friends, nudged her. "Can I borrow those boots when you're through? They'll look fab with my new leopard-print skirt." He fluttered his impossibly long lashes at her and made a smooching sound.

Char laughed and shook her head. She placed her hands over the exposed tops of her breasts. "I don't know. I think this outfit might be a little risqué for me."

"Honey, this is risqué for half of N'Awlins." Laurance rose. "You're all laced into your boots." The slim blonde stretched and looked in the mirror. Her eyes widened and she gave a low whistle. "Me-ow is right, Char."

Raymie thrust out his skinny stomach then stroked the small bulge. "I think I'm bloated."

Char elbowed him out of the way then turned to examine her backside. She gulped when she saw the indecent amount of thigh that was exposed by her napkin-sized skirt.

"If I sneeze I'll flash everyone," she said.

"And what a bee-you-tiful butt it is." Raymie patted her on the backside then sashayed toward the bathroom.

"I love the costume, Laurance, but I don't know if I can wear this out in public. I mean, I really appreciate all the work you put into it but my butt is hanging out." Char wailed the last few words.

Maribel plunged her hand into her own bodice, plumping them to her best advantage in her tight red dress. "Raymie is right, you do have a lovely bum." She reached over and tweaked one of Char's velvet ears that were fastened on top of her head. "You look hot…almost as hot as I do." She made a kissy face in the mirror.

"Gee, thanks." Char frowned and tugged on the skirt. "I feel like if I move the wrong way something might fall out or I'll stop breathing."

Laurance propped her chin on Char's bare shoulder. "The trick to a corset is to take slow, shallow breaths." She ran her hand over Char's laced-in tummy. "You aren't laced in too tight so you should be okay. Just take it slow and easy."

"Raymie, do you have my shoes?" Maribel bellowed from the bottom of Char's closet.

Raymie's head popped out of the bathroom. "Who are you kidding? I only wear Italian leather on these stems, not that cheap plastic crap you drag out of dumpsters."

"This isn't too tight? I would hate to see what it would feel like if it were any tighter." Char ran her hand over the narrow strip of belly that was visible between her corset and skirt. "Though I must say the cleavage is pretty impressive this evening."

"I still think you should've gotten your belly button pierced as Laurance had suggested." Maribel had located her stiletto heels and she was pushing her feet into the lethal-looking shoes. "That would have been really hot."

"Piercings are very cha cha this year," Raymie called.

"Yeah, that would be sexy. A puffy red welt with a ring through it." Char tugged on the hem of the indecent black vinyl skirt again but it didn't get any longer this time either. She tweaked the cat's tail that was attached to the waistband. "What about this? I'll be poking everyone all night."

"Quit fussing," Laurance slapped her hand then reached for her tiara on the dresser. "You look perfect, Char. Cat Woman never looked better."

"I'll say." Maribel stepped up behind her and all three women were framed in the mirror. "We look like sex incarnate."

"What about me?" Raymie, resplendent in a green sequined evening gown and towering black wig, exited the bathroom and joined them. "Am I not too sexy for words?"

Char tilted her head and studied their images. She was dressed from head to toe in black vinyl as Cat Woman while Maribel looked lethal in blood red as a devil, complete with horns on her head. Laurance was dressed as a fairy in a delicate white tutu and puff sleeves that shimmered as she moved, while Raymie looked like Cher, only with an Adam's apple.

"If we don't get hit on, hard, then all of the men in New Orleans are blind." Laurance picked up her wand and tapped Char on the shoulder. "I think we're ready to go, ladies."

"I'm not too sure I want to get hit on," Char gulped. Her hands were both hot and cold at the same time. "I'm too worried about my butt falling out of this skirt."

"Oh, but it's easy to pick up a man." Raymie slung a miniscule evening bag over his shoulder. "First you find a hot one, then you just wiggle your breasts and flutter those lashes and he'll be panting for you."

Maribel tossed an arm around Char's shoulder. "Weren't you just saying last week that you were determined to take charge of your life? You tossed that worthless Brad out of your bed over seven months ago and there is no better time than tonight to find a new boy toy. It's Halloween and the moon is full..."

"And its time to let your inner animal loose," Laurance chimed in. "Claim your sexuality and your life at the same time."

"But..." Char laid her hands over her breasts, which bulged from the top of the corset. "I feel so exposed. I still think I need"

Raymie shook his head. "The twins are fine. They look good snuggled in their corset like two little troopers." He reached past Laurance and picked up a round compact. "This might help, though." He dabbed some of the sparkly powder over the exposed tops of Char's breasts and shoulders.

"Perfect." Laurance clapped her hands. "You're a fashion genius, Raymie."

"Now, let's go." He tossed the compact onto the vanity and linked arms with Maribel. "The men of New Orleans await our pleasure."

Char looked down at her exposed breasts that now gleamed with the shimmery powder. "Yeah, that helped," she muttered. Picking up her coat, she followed her friends out the door.

Chapter Two

The Chamber was a popular nightclub that catered to the ever-present tourist crowd. Bondage gear decorated the walls and the bartenders were clad in various forms of leather and chains. Cages were suspended over the dance floor and half-naked women gyrated to the loud music.

When Rik had arrived, he'd done a slow tour of the building and learned where all the exits and possible ambush spots were located. He didn't like having this forced meeting in such a public place, but since he wasn't in the driver's seat he didn't have any say in the matter.

He leaned against the bar and sipped his cranberry juice, while watching the crowds. There were several other preternaturals close by, mostly young vampires and a few revenants—no one he needed to worry about. Then again, there were very few predators a full-grown were-cat needed to be concerned about.

A jolt of awareness shot across his skin, alerting him to the approach of another were-cat. Marcus entered the main door and moved through the crowds like a machine, his movements easy and economical. Dressed in worn blue jeans and a black leather jacket, he looked deadly capable of handling anything that might come his way, which was why Rik had called him for backup.

"You're early," Rik said.

"So are you." Marcus' dark eyes moved over the crowd. "I thought I would pop in and check out the action." He smiled as a petite blonde dressed in dominatrix gear squeezed past them, her ample breasts coming into contact with Marcus' chest.

"Lively crowd." He winked at the woman.

Rik's gaze moved over her curves. "Well, it is Halloween." While she was well-endowed in the chest, he preferred a little more flesh on his women. It was much easier to hang onto a woman in bed if she had real hips.

"Yes, it is." Already Marcus' attention was focused on the woman and he was slowly moving away. "I think I'll prowl until it's time to play with the dogs."

"Stay alert," Rik said.

"You too, bro."

Marcus vanished into the crowd and Rik continued his survey of the room. The music was blistering; the dance floor was a colorful sea of gyrating bodies and, in the center, was a raised platform. That, too, was crowded with dancers. He noted a small group of young male vampires near the platform. He made note of their faces and was thinking about ordering another drink when a flash of black vinyl against pale skin caught his attention.

On the edge of the platform near the railing was a curvaceous woman dressed in a skin-tight black vinyl skirt, what little there was of it, and matching thigh-high boots. A wicked-looking corset with miles of laces embraced her ample breasts and little cat ears were perched amid her rumpled, reddish-brown curls. A long black tail was attached to the waistband of her skirt and it swished from side to side as she danced.

While most of the dancers bounced around the dance floor as if they'd drank too much coffee, she moved like a cat, slow and sensual. A soft smile curved her pink lips and her eyes were half-closed. That dreamy smile let him know that she heard the music on a whole other level than those around her.

Cat Woman raised her arms over her head and he held his breath, waiting to see if her abundant breasts would spill from the corset. They didn't, though he could have sworn he glimpsed the slightest edge of a rosy areola.

He set his empty glass on the bar. There was something about the woman in black vinyl that made him both hungry and aroused. It could be the sensual dancing or the fact she seemed to be completely unaware of the crush around her. She could have been dancing alone in her bedroom for all the attention she paid to anyone else. Even in the midst of hundreds of people there was a sense of serenity and innate sensuality that surrounded her, and it set his senses on full alert.

He pushed away from the bar and started toward her. Lust curled in his belly and the need to mate burned hot. He lifted his head and inhaled. Through the crowd his cougar senses allowed him to discern her scent. Feminine and sweet, it drove a bolt of heat through his gut that threatened to steal his breath.

He wove through the crowd until he stood at the bottom of the steps, just feet away from her. Up close, his Cat Woman was even more exquisite. Her face was heart-shaped, her pink mouth was slick with gloss and her eyes were a deep, emerald green.

A tall woman dressed in red leaned over and said something to his Cat Woman. She tilted her head back and the musical laughter that poured forth transfixed him. He adored women who laughed, and this one had a full body laugh. She wrapped her arms around her belly and held herself upright, her eyes dancing with amusement.

This was his kind of woman. Lush, curvy, and she knew how to laugh. She had a mouth made for kissing, a body created for sin and he wanted to sample both.

He wondered how she liked to be bedded. Would she be energetic and vocal, or did she expect him to do all the work?

Once he had this unpleasant business out of the way, he'd have to make her acquaintance. They'd laugh, flirt, maybe have a few cocktails and before dawn, he'd have her in his bed.

Already he could imagine taking her, sinking into her slick flesh and feeling her tighten around him as she took her pleasure. His cock hardened. Without speaking to her, he knew it would be good between them. Just watching her dance was making him hard as a pike; he could only imagine how he'd feel once he got her clothing off.

A man jostled Rik from his reverie and a slim blond man walked up the steps toward the woman. Rik frowned when the blond caught the long tail that was attached to her skirt. He tugged on it to get the woman's attention.

She turned and her eyes widened when she saw the person who held her tail. She grabbed the padded vinyl appendage and shook her head but the man didn't relinquish his grip. She was smiling but it was a forced expression.

Judging from her body language, she didn't want her tail manhandled by this man. It looked like Rik would have to make her acquaintance sooner rather than later. He started up the steps.

How he loved a damsel in distress.

* * * * *

"No, really, I'm flattered but I don't want to dance with you. I'm already dancing with my friend—" Char broke off when she realized Maribel was nowhere to be seen.

"Come on, Cat-babe. I'm the best dancer here." The man shook his hips in a lewd movement that made her nose wrinkle. "Let's give it a shot."

Char retained her grip on the troublesome appendage and rued the day she'd decided to dress as Cat Woman. At the library, most men had a tendency to overlook her, even on her good hair days. Maribel claimed that her clothing choices enabled her to blend in with the woodwork, but that certainly wasn't the story tonight.

In the past hour, more men had accosted her tail then had ever asked her out on a date. While it was funny the first few times, now it was just downright tedious. Did these men really think if they tugged on her tail she'd jump right into their arms?

Because it had been manhandled so much this evening, she was afraid that if she let go of the tail, this fool would pull it free and destroy her pitiful excuse for a skirt.

"Look, I'm sure you're a fabulous—" She gave the tail another tug.

"Darling, did you miss me?"

A deep, purring voice drew her attention away from her tormenter and she looked up to see a giant walking up the steps.

Her mouth went dry.

The stranger was huge, well over six feet of hard-muscled bad-boy fantasy. Dressed like a biker in a black leather jacket and worn jeans, he looked tough with his tousled, streaky blond hair and chiseled jaw. His dark, golden gaze flicked over her face and she felt as if he'd touched her with his hand. He moved with an easy predatory grace that set every feminine instinct within her on alert.

The new arrival took her wrist, and the grip on her tail loosened. He raised her hand to his lips and his deep golden eyes twinkled with amusement. His mouth brushed the back of her hand and shivers raced up her arm.

"The kids are fine and they're tucked into their little beds. Your mother says hello and hopes we're having a good time."

She gulped.

"Do you know this guy?" the tail-tugger asked in an arrogant voice.

Char blinked. She wasn't sure she could even form a coherent sentence as the stranger's scent, leather and warm male, surrounded her. Her tongue felt thick and uncoordinated while her body felt unexpectedly loose. He released her and the stranger propped his hands on his hips. His jacket parted to reveal a sculpted chest along with a six-pack of abs that she'd only seen on magazine covers.

Yowza! He wasn't even wearing a shirt.

Their gazes met and a slow tingle began in her belly. His smile widened and her toes curled in response. He was hot.

Red hot.

Volcanic.

Mute, she couldn't break her gaze from the newcomer's so she settled for a jerky nod.

"Of course she knows me; she's my wife," the stranger said. "Doesn't she look great for someone who gave birth less than a month ago?" He slid his arm around her waist and pulled her close. Her hand landed on his bare chest and his skin seared her palm. "This is our first night out since the newest arrival."

Char felt the other man release her tail but she paid him no mind. Instead, she fell headlong into the depths of her "husband's" eyes. Thickly lashed, they were twin pools of molten gold surrounded by a ring of darker gold. The depth of blatant male appreciation would have rocked her off her heels if he hadn't held her so closely. She'd never had a man look at her with such desire, and she longed to wrap herself in his arms.

To taste his lips…

His skin…

His cock…

An overly exuberant dancer slammed her elbow into Char's ribs and his arm tightened around her waist. Jolted from her sensual trace, she was horrifyingly aware that she'd been staring at him like a love-starved dimwit. She looked away and cleared her throat.

"So how many children do we have?" she asked when she found her voice.

He made a tutting noise and shook his shaggy head. "How soon you forget. We have four children." He slid his other arm around her and they began to sway to the music. "The twins, Jessica and Frank, are five, Michael is three and little Hermantrude, just a month old. We call her Herman because she looks like your mother."

She wrinkled her nose. "I'm pretty sure she looks more like your mother."

"Hmm," he pretended to consider her statement, "I guess you're right. They do have the same moustache."

Char felt the laughter bubble up in her throat and she shook her head at the stranger's nonsense. "Sounds like we have a beautiful family." She couldn't help but stroke the hard planes of his chest. She'd never seen one so well-sculpted and yummy-licious in her life. She wanted to treat him like an ice cream cone and lick him from head to toe.

"We do, and we'll have more children in the next few years." His smile grew. "I think we decided on twelve when we married."

"Indeed." She tipped her head back and smiled. "That sounds like a litter to me."

He chuckled. "Exactly."

Dazzled by his smile and the sensuality he exuded from every pore, she could barely keep her mind on their conversation when her attention wanted to venture lower...much lower. He moved well, and judging from the hard length pressed into her belly, it would be well worth the trip.

"And what, pray tell, is the name of the father of my children?" she asked.

"You can call me Rik."

"Rik." She rolled the name over her tongue. The name suited him—short and to the point. It was a strong name, the name of a warrior or a rogue lover.

"And I would know the name of my lovely wife," he said.

She grinned. "Charlene, but you can call me Char; everyone does."

"Well, Char, I think we'll make beautiful babies together."

She couldn't help but laugh. Whoever this man was, she found herself in serious danger of being completely charmed by him. He might look tough but he had a quirky sense of humor that was appealing, not to mention the fact she could eat dessert off his flat stomach.

Meow!

"Don't you think you're forgetting something?" she asked.

His brow arched. "What would that be?"

"Asking me out might be good for a start," she said. "It's hard to get to first base if you don't step up to the plate."

His big hands slid down to her hips and her eyes widened as he insinuated his knee between hers and pressed even closer. She felt the warm slide of his jeans-clad cock against her stomach.

Yowza!

"But, we're already out," he said.

"Some more than others," she whispered.

He laughed. "A man can't hide when he's interested."

Her cheeks warmed and she could have sworn the dance floor tilted. This man was like no other that had paid attention to her. Handsome, funny, and he packed a strong sexual punch. If she wasn't mistaken, he was definitely flirting with her.

Was he trying to pick her up? If he was…then hurray for her!

"I think you should kiss me first. I've been here a while and it's just possible that I've received other offers to father my future children." She ran her tongue over her lips, and a thrill snaked down her spine when his gaze dropped to her mouth. "I think it's prudent to make a comparison study."

He laughed again and she enjoyed the play of muscles in his throat. She liked a man who knew how to laugh and this one did, in spades.

"Do you kiss every man you meet?" he teased.

She gulped. "Actually, no. I can't remember the last time I kissed a complete stranger." She paused when his head dipped toward hers. "In fact, I don't think I've ever done so."

His eyes heated and his breath was warm against her lips. "Let's make an exception then." He took possession of her mouth in an intense kiss that made her head swim and her body melt.

She moaned when he swept into her mouth and his taste hit her already overloaded senses. His tongue was nimble and surprisingly rough as it tangled with hers. That added roughness sent her nerves into overdrive, and she moaned again. His grip tightened, aligning her to his brawny frame.

The raw, heated scent of his body invaded her senses and she gave herself over to his mastery. With each sensual movement of his hands and his mouth, he proclaimed himself very knowledgeable about how a woman needed to be touched, caressed.

Her body burned and she clutched at his leather jacket, desperate to remain upright. She'd never experienced anything like this, this raw need for the touch of a man. It was as if she were starving for him, and only him. Only his hands, his body, could assuage the need that had come to life the moment he'd spoken to her.

When he pulled away she realized she'd pressed against him as if she were trying to scale his big frame like a tree. With her cheeks burning, she lowered her leg from where she'd wrapped it around his.

He ran his thumb over her lower lip and she shivered at the tender caress. His other hand landed on the small of her back; his agile fingers slid over the narrow strip of bare flesh above her waistband, sending chills of delight up her spine.

"That was some kiss." His voice was low and rumbling, and she quite liked the sound of it.

"It was." Her gaze fixed on his mouth and she leaned toward him until her aching breasts were pressed against his chest. Even through the corset she could feel his strength, his heat.

"Kiss me again," she whispered.

His lips quirked and he captured her mouth. She opened for him, moaning as he moved inside to search out her secrets. She longed for him to press closer, to spread her thighs and touch her where she ached for him most. To caress her breasts and free them from the torturous confines of the corset, to take her nipples into his mouth and suckle her until—

"Well, well, what do we have here?"

* * * * *

Rik silently cursed as he set Char away from him. A Shadow Hunter who failed to pay attention to his surroundings was a dead Hunter. Even though he was retired, it had been years since he'd forgotten that lesson.

He turned and placed himself between the newcomers and Char. His gaze raked over the rangy wolf standing only a foot away.

Weylyn was tall and thin, with unruly pelt-like hair that women seemed to find attractive. Behind him was another man who could have been his twin, and beside him was a third man Rik didn't recognize. The one who resembled Weylyn was probably his younger brother, Bo.

Three against one, the odds weren't weighted too heavily in Rik's favor.

"Ulrik," Weylyn spoke first.

"Lyn." Rik felt a spark of satisfaction at the flash of anger in the wolf's eyes. He knew the other man hated it when people shortened his name. Rik crossed his arms over his chest and straightened his stance.

"You were looking for me?" Rik asked.

Lyn gave a pointed look at the crowds around them. "Let's go somewhere a little quieter, where we can talk in peace."

He nodded then turned to Char, careful not to present his back to the wolf. "I'll be back. Will you wait for me in the bar?"

"But I wouldn't dream of separating you two young lovers," Lyn spoke up. "Please, bring her with you. I insist."

Rik shook his head. "She's not involved."

"Oh, but she is now." Lyn made to move past him toward Char and Rik grabbed his arm.

"No, she isn't," Rik ground out. Out of the corner of his eye he caught a movement. It was the brother. His grip tightened. "I just met her with the intention of bedding her. She is nothing to me," he hissed, hoping Char couldn't hear him.

Lyn's eyes narrowed and his lip curled. "You were-cats are such amoral creatures."

"And you would know, wouldn't you, Fido?"

Rik released him and Lyn stepped away. His dark, contemptuous gaze flicked over Char.

"Let's get this over with." The wolf jerked his head toward the back of the club. He said something that sounded like a short series of growls to the third man, who nodded then disappeared into the crowd.

Rik caught Char's arm. "Will you wait here for me?" he asked.

Her troubled gaze met his. "I don't like them."

Rik chuckled. She was a good judge of character and he was liking her more and more. "Not many do, Char. I'll be back in a few minutes. Meet me in the bar?"

Her eyes narrowed. "Are you doing something illegal?"

"No, it's just business."

Her disturbed gaze moved back to Lyn. "Yes, I'll be there. But you watch your back, I don't trust that one at all."

"I've got that covered."

"Oh you do, do you?" She seemed to shake off her dark mood and gave him a saucy smile. "I'll wait for you, but only for about ten minutes. It doesn't do a girl's self-esteem good to be waiting any longer than that."

Rik grinned and dropped a kiss on her soft lips. "I'll make it nine and a half then."

With the sound of her musical laughter following him, he walked down the steps to follow Lyn and the brother. They wound their way through the crowds toward a doorway that exited into an alley behind the club. When they approached the door Marcus materialized beside him.

"Been busy?" Rik asked.

"The same could be said for you," Marcus said. "I don't think that shade of red is quite your color."

Rik rubbed his mouth and grinned when he saw the faint stain of lip-gloss. "Maybe the color isn't, but the woman suits me just fine."

Marcus chuckled and they exited the building. The alley was deserted, and the stench of rotting garbage and spilled alcohol lingered in the air. Rik didn't detect the presence of any other preternaturals lying in wait for them.

"What is it you want, Lyn?" Rik spoke first. He was eager to get this nonsense over with so he could get back to Char and her magical laugh.

"I believe you received your directions from Trey earlier." Lyn smirked. "I'm waiting."

Rik ground his teeth. It was bad enough he had to apologize to the smug bastard but having him know he'd received a direct order from the Council was more humiliation than he wanted to deal with. Apologize he must, but Trey never said he couldn't needle the hell out of the mangy bastard in the meantime.

"You seem to think I owe you an apology." Rik shrugged. "Sorry, dude. I didn't know she was marked as yours." He smiled, and it wasn't a pleasant expression. "She couldn't tell me that while she had my dick in her mouth."

Lyn snarled and started toward Rik when the brother stepped in to block his brother's lunge. He threw a pained look at Rik.

"That wasn't smart, man," he said.

Rik shrugged and he felt Marcus shift beside him, a subtle tension radiated from his friend. "I don't play well with others and I certainly don't always follow directions."

Lyn's eyes glittered and his lips curled in a feral snarl. "Your kind always fall into line sooner or later, pussycat. That's what your precious Council expects of you—mindless loyalty like that of a drone."

Rik refused to rise to the bait. "What would your kind know about loyalty? You eat your dead, not to mention using roadkill for party snacks." He gave a mock shudder. "The Council expects loyalty but they also understand that there are exceptions to be made."

"We stand on our own and live by our rules. The wolves have deliberately chosen not to join the Council," Lyn snapped. "We do not answer to vampires and *cats*."

Rik wasn't bothered by his name-calling. It was long understood that the wolves wanted nothing to do with the Council, and that was their choice. Unfortunately, their inability to police their own people had led to far too many in-fights and the near decimation of their line several hundred years ago. It was only in the last forty years that the number of werewolves had reached the point where they were no longer extinct in the eyes of the preternaturals. It was amazing how many bodies had piled up during their constant struggles for pack leadership.

"Whatever the reason for not following the Council, I couldn't care less," Rik said. "You expect an apology from me and I'm telling you that your woman should be kept on a shorter leash. She picked me up in a bar and she neglected to tell me that she was your woman and that is that. I didn't find out until much later."

The wolf shook his head. "She wouldn't do that to me."

"Well, she did. I'm sorry your woman was unfaithful but I don't owe you anything, not even the time of day."

"You owe me, Ulrik the Fair, you owe me big." Lyn stepped away from his brother. "And I will see to it that your bill is paid."

The door to the club opened. The third werewolf exited and he was pulling someone behind him. It was Char. She'd put on a coat—a floor-length, shiny vinyl duster—and she looked none too happy. The man shoved her toward Rik and he caught her arm as the door slid shut.

"Let go of me, you freak of nature," she snapped. She shook off his touch and her eyes widened then narrowed when she saw it was Rik. "Just what is going on here?"

He ignored her and fixed his gaze on Lyn. "I told you that she has nothing to do with this," he ground out.

"It sure didn't look that way to me." Lyn smirked.

"Then you need some glasses, Fido," Rik said. "You're wrong."

Lyn's lips tightened at the slang name for a werewolf, and judging from his tight expression, he'd try to make Rik pay for calling him names. His gaze flicked to Char and an unpleasant smile crossed his face.

"It grates, doesn't it?" Lyn moved toward her. "Knowing that I'm going to touch her, have her, as you had Serena."

Char's eyes widened when Lyn put his hand on her shoulder. "What is he talking about, Rik?"

"Love, sex." Lyn moved his fingers down her arm then up again. "Betrayal."

Rik felt the beast within him rise. The blue flame that constantly flickered in his mind, the essence of his animal nature grew stronger. If he let it, if he let his beast free, he would tear Lyn to pieces in seconds. Too bad that wasn't an option, as the mental imagery was most satisfying.

He tamped down on the feelings of outrage and forced the flame down. He would control his beast, and no matter what happened, Char would walk away unscathed. He'd protect her with his life if needed.

"What are you doing, Lyn?" Rik's tone was contemptuous. "You would risk all-out warfare over a woman?"

"Warfare?" Char's voice wobbled. "What's this about warfare?"

"She's worth it, isn't she?" Lyn smiled and the tips of his canines flashed. "She's beautiful and she looks like a prime piece of ass." His other hand landed on her shoulder. He pulled her backward until she was just short of leaning into him. "What would you do for her, pussycat? Will you fight for her?"

Rik's gaze landed on Char's beautiful face. She was scared and her breathing was shallow and quick. He tried to give her a reassuring smile.

"What do you want?" Rik's gaze never left hers.

"You, on your knees."

Marcus cracked his knuckles. This was going wrong, horribly so. An apology was one thing, groveling in an alley at the feet of a dog was another. Even the Council would understand that.

His gaze flicked to Lyn. "How about this instead? I promise not to kill you if you release her now." The brother and the stranger shifted toward Lyn. "And you three can walk away."

The stranger laughed. "You seem very sure of yourself, pussy-man."

Rik held his hands out to his sides. "I haven't been wrong yet."

"Unbelievable." Lyn shook his shaggy head. "Even now you don't realize you're beat." He touched Char's pale throat with the back of his fingers. "While that is a very generous offer, I want you on your knees or it's no deal."

Rik crossed his arms over his chest and Marcus aped his movements. "No deal."

Lyn shrugged and his grip on Char tightened. "Then we're at an impasse. I will take your woman and ruin her for any other man—"

"Weylyn..." His brother's voice held a hint of warning.

"Bo," Lyn snarled.

"I really am tired of people just talking around me," Char interrupted. "I want to know what the hell is going on here." She started to move toward Rik but Lyn didn't release her.

"I don't think so, little one. I have great plans for you," Lyn said.

"Oh, yeah? Well, so do I," she snapped.

In a surprise move, Char made a fist and brought her arm up over her shoulder and smacked Lyn directly in the nose. While it probably didn't hurt him, the werewolf's head snapped back and his grip on her shoulders loosened.

She grabbed his wrist then dropped and twisted, her movements stiff in the constricting corset. She landed on her back as she pulled Lyn forward then down with her. Bracing her feet against his belly, she flipped him to land on his back at Rik's feet.

The look of shock on the wolf's face was so amusing that Rik wished he'd had a camera.

"Now who's groveling?" Rik leaned over the wolf.

Char lunged to her feet and stalked toward Rik, her stiletto heels making sharp, angry clicking sounds on the pavement. "You have a lot of explaining to do—" she was cut off when Marcus grabbed her and pushed her toward the wall to safety.

A rough growl sounded from Lyn and his lips pulled back to reveal his sharp canines. The bones of his face began shifting under his skin and his eyes took on a deep, red glow.

Oh shit...

The third wolf tossed a garbage can at Rik's head and he ducked and rolled. He heard Char scream but he didn't spare her a glance, as he knew Marcus would keep her safe.

A detached sense of calm descended over him, a frequent and familiar companion from his Hunter days. He'd been trained to hunt and kill rogue preternaturals and his old persona fit like a pair of comfortable jeans. He was in his element.

God, how he missed this.

Rik moved like a machine, making quick work of the brother by knocking his hard head against the wall and tossed him into a dumpster.

The third wolf made the mistake of running at Marcus, who knocked him out with a single blow to the chin. The man was unconscious before he hit the ground.

Lyn stood in the middle of the alley watching Rik. His face had taken on a definite wolfish look and his long teeth glinted in the darkness. While he was in the midst of a transformation he didn't seem to be in any hurry to complete the task. His arms had lengthened, along with his fingers and claw-like nails. His reddish gaze was locked on his adversary and bloodlust glinted in their depths. Rik could only hope Char couldn't see any of this, as she was behind Marcus.

Rik felt the power of the moon and the call of his animal nature was strong. If it weren't for Char, he'd embrace his animal and they'd rumble but it couldn't happen tonight. Not in front of her.

"You don't want this, Lyn." Rik's voice was deep, thick with the need to shift.

"Fuck you," the wolf snarled in barely intelligible English. He lunged.

Rik darted to the side, but not quite quickly enough. He barely felt the graze of the wolf's claws where they struck his upper arm. He twisted and dropped, rolling to the side, while Lyn's momentum carried him a few feet further.

Rik gained his feet and pulled the knife from his boot as Lyn spun toward him. They began circling. The hilt of the blade felt comfortable, familiar in his palm. He was a patient man and he could wait until Lyn made a mistake, and it would be the one that cost him his life.

"Down here, down here!" someone screamed. "They're fighting."

At the mouth of the alley, several humans had gathered, along with two police officers. The cops started toward them.

Lyn tilted his head back and gave a wild roar that echoed off the brick walls. The humans shrieked and scattered, while the cops paused long enough to pull out their guns.

"This isn't over, Ulrik," Lyn snarled. He fished his brother's unconscious body from the dumpster with one hand. "We'll rumble some other night. Your woman will never be safe until you pay your debt to me, pussycat." He loped down the alley in the opposite direction of the cops.

"Rik." Marcus shoved Char toward Rik, then stopped to pick up the unconscious wolf and toss him over his shoulder. "Run with her; I'll take him."

"Stop right there," one of the cops shouted.

"Stay safe," Rik said to Marcus. He threw open the door to the club and pushed Char toward it.

"We can't just leave," she shrilled. "The cops—"

"Are better off without us. We'll only cause them more paperwork if we stay." He caught her around the waist and tossed her over his shoulder. "We need to boogie, babe."

He ignored the curious patrons who were alerted to their presence by the shrieking bundle of femininity tossed over his shoulder. Who knew such a compact package could make so much noise?

It took a few hairy moments to negotiate his way out of the club, and he breathed a sigh of relief when they made it out the front door. Ignoring Char's squeals of rage, he ran down the street toward the lot where he'd left his car. When he reached the sleek BMW, he set Char down.

In the moonlight her cheeks were flushed, her hair mussed and her little velvet ears were cockeyed. She was so beautiful that she stole his breath away.

She stepped back, straightened her corset then placed her hands on her hips. Her sharp little chin jutted out and she glared up at him.

"Just who the hell are you and what was that all about?"

Chapter Three

She needed to have her head examined.

Char eased Rik's jacket off his broad shoulders, wincing as she did so. This man was a complete and total stranger and—somehow—she'd allowed him to sweet-talk her into bringing him back to her place. She'd be lucky if he didn't murder her in her bed.

New Orleans was one of the most dangerous cities in the U.S., and she knew better than to pick up a stranger. Heck, under normal circumstances she didn't open the front door to someone she didn't recognize, much less invite them in to sit on her bed.

She held up the jacket to examine the destruction. It was ruined. The soft leather had three slash marks across the arm and there was no way it could be repaired. She dropped the garment then flinched when she saw the damage to his tanned flesh.

"You're a mess," she said.

He glanced down at the three slashes then shrugged. "I've had worse."

"Typical." She snorted and stepped into the bathroom to gather some first aid supplies. She'd laughed at her friends when they'd suggested that she find a companion for the evening. She simply wasn't a pick-them-up kind of girl. She'd bet her paycheck that they'd never envisioned anything like this.

She exited the bathroom with her supplies and dumped them on the nightstand. "If your intestines were hanging out, you'd probably say the same thing."

He grinned and her stomach flopped. "I'm a man. I'm not supposed to admit to feeling pain."

"Yeah, well, feel this."

She stepped closer to slide one leg between his. His eyes heated and his warm, masculine scent teased her senses. Her skin tingled at the nearness of him. She wanted to push him back on the bed and kiss every inch of his big body. She longed to lick his amazing six-pack and suckle his flat male nipples. Instead she placed an alcohol-soaked cotton pad over the wounds on his upper arm.

"Sadist," he muttered through clenched teeth.

"Hmm." She held the pad over the wounds to staunch the sluggish blood flow. "Are you going to tell me what that scene in the alley was all about?"

His muscles shifted beneath her hands when he shrugged. "There isn't much to tell. Lyn and I have a sordid past and I guess he's not too happy with me."

Char rolled her eyes. That was an understatement if ever she'd heard one. She'd grown up with three brothers who'd enjoyed pummeling each other every chance they got. In all her life she'd never seen a man in a murderous rage such as the one this Lyn person had experienced.

"Do all of your friends want to beat you to a pulp?" she asked.

"Only the good ones." Rik had a slight smile on his gorgeous mouth.

"Somehow, I believe it." She lifted the pad, pleased to see the bleeding had slowed. She tossed it into the trashcan and picked up a clean pad. "Where did you learn to fight like that?"

He laughed. "Me? Where did you learn to flip a gorilla like that? Lyn has to outweigh you by at least one hundred pounds."

"My older brother is a police officer and he's taught me all sorts of useful moves." She reached for the bottle of Betadine.

"What kind of moves?" Rik asked with a mock-leering grin. "I want to make sure when you use them on me I know what to expect."

She snorted. "If I decide to take you down, you won't see it coming."

"Ah, a little warrior, eh?" His big hands landed on the backs of her thighs and she jumped, almost falling off her heels. She braced her hand on his shoulder and righted herself.

"Careful there, stud." She swiped the reddish-brown liquid over the cuts. "Don't start something you can't finish."

"Who said I couldn't finish?" His warm palms moved up the back of her thighs then down again.

"You're wounded and probably should avoid any strenuous activity." She tossed the stained pad into the trash and grabbed the bandages. "I need to get this covered."

"Yeah, well," his hand slid up her thigh to tease the lower curve of her buttocks, "if you're really worried about me straining myself, I'll let you do all the work."

His dark eyes were lit with a look of desire as old as time. Her gaze dropped to his mouth. He was an amazing kisser and she longed to kiss him again. Her breath caught and arousal reared its head. She exhaled and her nipples chafed against the restrictive corset. She wanted this man, probably more than she'd ever wanted a man in her life.

She forced her gaze away and concentrated on bandaging his arm. Rik was injured and having sex was the last thing he needed to be doing. She'd bandage him up and send him on his way—after she tattooed her phone number on his butt. She definitely wanted to get to know him better...much better.

She shook her head. "I don't think so—"

"This skirt is a bit superfluous, if you ask me." He slipped his hand beneath the thin vinyl and cupped her butt cheek. "It's pretty small and you aren't wearing much underneath it."

Exasperated and more aroused than she wanted to admit, she slapped the last piece of tape into place. "What did you expect, pantaloons? There isn't much room for a lot of clothing under there."

"Which is something to be thankful for."

He cupped both cheeks now and gave them a firm squeeze. Heat ignited between her thighs, and their gazes locked. Her thoughts immediately turned south, even as she shook her head no.

"You're hurt."

"I'll heal."

"We shouldn't—"

"We should." He licked his lips and she stifled a groan. He pulled her closer until she was leaning against him, his face level with her breasts.

"Rik..." It was a half-hearted protest.

"Char." He leaned back, taking her with him. She gasped at the ease of his movement when she landed, sprawled across his big body.

Damn, he was strong.

Their legs tangled and the brush of denim against her inner thighs was both shocking and arousing.

"This is much better." His eyes twinkled. "Less pressure on my arm."

"For you, maybe, but this corset is killing me." Her eyes watered. The metal stays were digging into her ribs and it was increasingly difficult to breathe.

His gaze focused on her breasts that threatened to explode from the corset. He trailed a fingertip along one of the plump curves. "Sexy as this garment might be, it's killing me too."

He toyed with the corset tie and their gazes locked. She knew what he wanted; he was asking her permission to untie it. He wanted to touch her, kiss her, make love with her. Breathless, she gave a faint nod.

He tugged on the lace and the bow dissolved. She braced her hands on the bed and rose up so he could reach the laces more easily. With his gaze locked on hers, he loosened the corset's grip slowly, deliberately. Char felt oddly breathless as he worked his way down the garment until the punishing grip eased. He removed the garment and tossed it to the side.

Shyness washed over her and she bit her lip. It had been seven months since Brad had walked out the door. In her entire life, only two men had ever seen her naked and Rik would be the third. What if he thought she was fat? What if he hated the scar on her thigh from —

"You're thinking too much," Rik said.

His golden gaze moved to her mouth and a surge of female power moved through her. Judging from his expression he was anything but repulsed.

His chest was rock-hard beneath her and all that warm male skin was hers for exploring. She couldn't wait to get started. Char dipped her head and pressed her lips to his. Before she could fully enjoy the sensation of his lips against hers, he quickly took over the kiss. His tongue teased hers and her head spun off her shoulders. His masterful touch awakened nerves she hadn't even known existed.

She ran her fingers over the ends of his tawny hair and found it to be as silky soft as it looked. She gave the locks a gentle tug and he growled, a deep sound that emanated from his chest. It was strangely animalistic and very arousing.

His arms tightened and he surrounded her, overwhelming her with his sexuality and the sheer strength of his well-honed body. His erection pressed into her stomach, turning the flesh between her thighs liquid soft.

He moved his leg higher between hers then swung her over until she was flat on her back on the bed. Braced on his arms, Rik loomed over her, his tawny hair creating a shaggy halo. His lips were damp from her mouth and his eyes glittered with need.

"Your shoulder," she said.

"My arm."

"That too —"

"Will live. But if I don't have you now, I might not." His voice was low, urgent. "I want you, Char, more than my next breath or my next meal. I need to taste you, to kiss every inch of your body until you beg me to stop."

She shivered at his erotic, evocative words. She'd never seen a man display such wanton need. She stroked his cheek, enjoying the prickle of beard stubble against her fingertips.

"You scare me," she whispered.

He shook his head and his silky hair licked at her hand. "You have nothing to fear from me, Char. I would never hurt you." He turned his head and kissed her hand; his tongue flicked out to taste her palm in that curiously rough caress.

Instinctively, she knew she was safe with him. Rik might be a complete stranger — she wasn't even sure what his last name was or what he did for a living — but she knew in her soul that he wouldn't hurt her. This was a man who cherished women; he didn't frighten or abuse them. She gave a lock of his hair a gentle tug and guided his mouth down to hers.

He growled and it was low, deep and filled with need. He nipped at her lip and she sighed his name.

"Say it again," he whispered against her mouth.

"Rik," she sighed.

He laughed and gave her a noisy kiss that scattered her thoughts. He began kissing his way down her throat, then headed for her breasts. As he worked his way over her flesh, he made a soft purring sound reminiscent of a large cat, which was both arousing and soothing at the same time.

He raised his head, ran his hand up her thigh to her hips and unzipped her skirt. The slippery vinyl parted to reveal her black lace thong panties. He urged her hips up before he slid the skirt out from beneath her. Clad only in the thong and killer boots, Rik trailed his hand down her belly then up again.

"Wow," he said. "You're gorgeous."

She tweaked a flat male nipple. "Wow, yourself."

He dipped his fingers under the narrow band of her panties and slid them down.

"Lift your hips."

Char did as he asked and he removed them and tossed them on the floor.

"What about the boots?" She lifted her leg and waggled her foot. It had taken about ten minutes to get her laced into them and she wasn't sure she wanted to wait that long to taste him again.

His smile was dark, hot. "Leave them on. I kind of like how they look on you."

She laughed and let her leg drop. "Good answer."

Rik settled over her, pressing his erection into the apex of her thighs. She wrapped her legs around his waist, enjoying the rough friction of his jeans against her skin.

His hands seemed to be everywhere at once, touching, caressing and increasing her arousal to a near fevered pitch. She was just short of begging him to take her, when he stopped and rose.

"What—" She blinked. Rik was standing over her, rummaging through his damaged jacket. He removed several condoms.

What a boy scout! Lucky for her he was prepared.

He began removing his pants and she sat up. "Allow me." She reached for him.

His hands fell away from the buttons and she took over. She opened his fly and pushed the pants down toward his ankles, when she realized he still wore his boots.

"Your boots are in the way." She leaned back on the bed and gave him a wide smile. "You're on your own there, babe."

He chuckled and made quick work of removing the boots and stepping out of his pants. When he stood, she sat up and wrapped her fingers around the thick shaft of his cock. He sucked in a harsh breath.

"You have a tattoo." She ran her hand over a black paw print on his hip.

He chuckled then gave his straining cock a pained look. "That's the best thing you can think of to say at a time like this? 'You have a tattoo'? Maybe you'd like to exchange recipes while we're at it?"

She grinned. "Oh, I'm sorry. I forgot my part." She gently cupped his balls and made a soft cooing noise that made him laugh again. "You have the biggest cock I've ever seen." She stroked the long, hard shaft and cupped the broad head. "It's just enormous…the biggest in the city, I'm sure of it. Wait, let me get my camera and I'll take a picture of this bad boy. I think I should call Ripley's…"

She shrieked when he pushed her backward onto the bed and covered her again.

"You're headed for a spanking," he laughed and blew a raspberry on her shoulder. "You're rotten."

She snickered. "You have no idea…"

"Not yet, but I will." His gaze dropped to her breasts. "For now, let's see how good you taste."

She moaned when he took an erect nipple into his mouth and began suckling her. Her fingers tangled in his hair and she luxuriated in the feel of his mouth on her skin. His rough tongue lapped at her flesh and she shivered at the added sensation. She'd been right, this man knew his way around a woman's body.

He slid his hand up the inside of her thigh and through the moist tangle of curls until he parted her damp flesh and touched her intimately. She shivered and spread her legs to give him better access. She ached and burned as he stroked her, her hips following every movement to drag out the sensations. She'd never experienced such intense need, such heat.

Her eyes slid shut and her nails dug into his chest when he plunged his fingers into her. Her hips arched toward him, and throaty noises like she'd never heard were coming from her mouth. Too aroused to care how animalistic she sounded, Char threw herself into the maelstrom of heat and need he'd created.

With a few deft strokes she peaked and release coursed over her. Screaming out her satisfaction, she was vaguely aware of Rik speaking to her in a low whisper. His warm mouth trailed down her throat while she fought to catch her breath.

Wow!

Feeling boneless and lazy, she forced her eyes open. Rik was propped on one elbow, watching her with a satisfied smile on his handsome face.

"Feeling good?" he asked.

She felt so scattered and relaxed she wasn't sure she could even form a coherent sentence. She licked her lips.

"I think you know the answer to that." She reached for his erect cock and ran her fingers around the broad head. "But we're not done yet." She reached for a condom with her free hand.

"True."

She made quick work of sliding the thin sheath over his cock. While she longed to linger, she wanted him too much to take her time. He moved between her thighs and she guided him to her. He sank his cock into her throbbing flesh in a slow, delicious movement that left them both reeling. In unison, they groaned.

She arched her back, relishing the feel of his cock stretching and filling her. She laced her legs around his hips and he began to move, a soft rolling motion of his hips that made her eyes roll back into her head at the delicious friction.

She clutched his hips and their gazes locked. His eyes were dark with an almost feral look of lust that made her melt. It was the look of a man losing himself in the pleasure afforded by his lover's body. The look of someone taking the ride of his life.

She twined her legs around his hips and he began thrusting in earnest. The room echoed with the squeak of bedsprings and the slap of slick skin against skin. Time receded and she lost count of the times he'd brought her to release. It was as if she'd become a vessel for Rik, to be filled and possessed by him and him alone.

Her head thrashed on the pillows and she sobbed as he pulled her tighter, thrust harder, his fingers digging into her flesh.

She came again, spirals of release moving through her system, when she felt him tense. She blinked to clear her vision of the lust-inspired glaze. His head was thrown back and his body was magnificent, every muscle tense in anticipation of release.

She tightened around him and that was enough to send him over the edge. His arms went rigid and he came with an animal-like roar that caused every hair to stand on end. His skin gleamed with sweat and she wrapped her arms around his shoulders until he fell forward to rest on her.

Her tongue snaked out to taste his shoulder, reveling in the warm, salty flesh. Never had she had a sexual encounter that even came close to what she'd experienced with Rik. It was more than sex; it was making love on a level so primitive, so animal, that she couldn't even begin to fully contemplate it.

She stroked his tangled hair. Just who was this amazing man?

* * * * *

Rik snagged his cell phone from his pants pocket before it rang for a second time. He glanced at the lighted display as he rolled out of bed.

Trey.

He hit the 'talk' button then slipped from the bedroom into the miniscule living room so he wouldn't wake Char.

"What's up?"

"Just what the hell did you do this evening?" Trey snarled.

"Hmm, let's see. Had dinner, met up with Marcus, fended off a rabid werewolf who wanted my head on a platter... Maybe that's what you wanted to know?" Rik stalked toward the wide windows as Trey swore in his ear.

"Yeah, well, it kind of pisses me off when someone demands I grovel at his feet then comes at me with his claws out," Rik hissed.

"Lyn is out for blood."

"No shit."

There was a moment of silence before Trey spoke. "Marcus told me there was a woman involved."

Rik glanced at the darkened bedroom doorway. "Yes."

"Can't you keep your dick under control for a few hours?"

"Screw you, Trey. You don't know anything about this."

"Just what the hell were you thinking, or were you thinking at all—"

"Fuck you," Rik snapped. "I've never let you down before and you'd better keep that in mind."

"Who is she? Some brainless bimbo from the bar?"

"Back the fuck off, Trey. I don't work for you anymore, remember?" Rik tilted his head back and forth, trying to loosen up his tense muscles. This conversation was definitely pissing him off. It was all he could do to keep from hanging up. "It's none of your business who she is and she has nothing to do with this."

"So you'd like to think," the other man said. "Lyn wants her bad and, thanks to you, he views this woman as a way to get back at you."

Rik cursed under his breath.

"She's in it up to her neck, whether you like it or not."

He stared out the window into the darkness. The pitch-black paint of his BMW gleamed under the streetlights. The dark was where he and thousands of other Shadow Dwellers were more at home than in the light of day. The darkness was where the deepest secrets lived and breathed; it had sheltered him for more years than he cared to remember. He felt the inexorable pull of his old Hunter lifestyle.

Honor.

Duty.

Act on the will of the Council and protect life at all costs.

He leaned his forehead against the cool glass. No matter how long he stayed away from the Hunters, their covenant still resonated within him as strong as the day he signed their sacred Covenant.

"I'll take care of her," Rik said.

The other man sighed. "I know you will. Marcus is already looking for Lyn and he's called in Santo and Dirk. Right now they're trying to head off all-out warfare between the cats and the dogs. For now, just keep the woman safe and busy for the next day or so and we'll see what comes up."

Feeling powerless and pissed at the same time, Rik muttered his thanks.

"Yeah, you owe me," Trey said.

The phone went dead.

He propped his arm on the wall and continued staring into the darkness. He never should have approached Char. Before he left the Hunters, he'd never have made such a stupid mistake. Putting a human at risk went against everything he'd fought for and believed in. Meeting her and getting her tangled up in this mess was one of the most colossal mistakes of his life.

The phone rang again and he glanced at the panel, frowning when he didn't recognize the number. He hit the Talk button then held the phone up to his ear. He didn't speak.

"You were set up." The voice held the distinctive twang of the bayou. It was Lyn's brother, Bo.

"How's that?"

"Lyn set you up. He told Serena to seduce you so he could use her infidelity as a reason to pick a fight with you."

Rik snorted. "Did he honestly believe I'd fight him over a one-night stand?"

"Lyn knows you're honorable, for a were-cat at least. He knew you'd defend your actions and that if he tried to grind you into the dust, you'd fight back no matter what the Council had ordered. Your temper is as legendary as is your sense of humanity. Lyn wants to start a war and you just played right into his hands tonight."

Rik closed his eyes and allowed his head to drop forward. He'd been played like a patsy, and by a werewolf at that.

Damn.

He forced his head up. "So what are we going to do about this mess?"

"We?" The other man chuckled. "There is no 'we' here. You're on your own, pussycat."

"Then why did you call? Why are you telling me this if you aren't going to help me fix this mess your brother created?"

Silence. All he could hear was the faint hum of static on the line.

The other man sighed. "You probably won't believe this but there are many of our Clan who do not want warfare. While we choose not to join the Council, we also don't wish to disturb what is already in place for those who decide to abide by their laws. We simply want to be left alone to live in peace."

Rik snorted. "And you're going to try and convince me that your brother is one of them?"

"No. Lyn wants what is best for him and his goals. Mikhail has offered him a seat on the new Council, the one the vampire will command once he brings down the current administration."

Rik swore under his breath. If this were true, then there was no telling what Lyn would do to bring him down.

"My brother wishes to join with Mikhail and destroy the current Council. He's doing his part in aiding the vampire by starting a war and dividing the Shadow Dwellers from their leaders."

Rik whistled under his breath. "That's a pretty serious charge. If this is true, the Council will brand him a traitor and send the Hunters after him."

"I realize this." Bo's voice was heavy. "But I speak the truth, pussycat. Right is right and this isn't. Lyn is bitter and misguided but there is little I can do to sway him from his current path. Watch your back, as he's determined to put a knife into it."

The phone went dead.

Chapter Four

Rik stood in the doorway of the bedroom, watching Char as she slept. She looked like a tumbled angel with her rumpled hair spread out across the pillows. Moonlight filtered in through the blinds to outline her amazing curves.

Humans were such fragile creatures. Their lifespan was brief, and in a blink of an eye, they were gone. It wasn't that way with a were-cat. Blessed with nine long lives and the ability to heal at an accelerated rate, they could live for many centuries without even using up one of those lives.

Their immortality was both a blessing and a curse.

It had been so long since he'd been human, truly mortally human, that he'd forgotten their constant need to be touched, held. The human need for love and companionship were what drove a human. It was those very same needs that had been eradicated from him long ago with his Hunter training.

After Rik had left Trey's employ, he'd done little to change his lifestyle. If he wasn't on the prowl for a sexual partner, he spent most of his time alone, either reading or indulging in his newfound passion for computers and electronics. For him, women were the easy part. The sexual prowess of male were-cats was legendary among the preternaturals and while the humans didn't comprehend what he was, the human females sensed — on at least some level — his sexual mastery.

He'd done as little as possible to bed them and had enjoyed their company in spades. He loved women, their soft curves, the secrets in their eyes, and if they had a good sense of humor, that was even better. But he'd never allowed himself to want them — to really want them — on anything more than the primitive level of sexual need.

Human females were delicate creatures and they commanded a great deal of attention. Most were high-strung, much more so than a female were-cat, and he'd found none that were worth risking a broken heart over.

But Char was unlike any mortal female he'd ever met. The moment he'd seen her he'd sensed a sort of quiet peace about her, a serenity that came from being confident in herself and her abilities. She didn't appear to be looking for a man to make her whole, she already was.

Her quiet self-assurance and that sense of peace was a powerful draw for him and he found he wanted more from Char than he'd ever desired from another woman. He needed to possess all of her, the entire package, her laughter, her sexuality, her tears, every last delicious inch of her.

He rubbed the center of his forehead where a slight ache threatened. The thought terrified him to his very bones. How had a woman, a human at that, gotten beneath his defenses so quickly and so effortlessly?

She put her life on the line for mine in that alley and she didn't back down. Instead she rose to meet the challenge and defeat it.

She'd been frightened; he'd smelled her fear, had seen it written on her face, but she hadn't hesitated to step in. She'd handled herself well in the face of danger, she danced like a dream, looked hot in a corset and she didn't take herself too seriously. In his opinion, Char was a rarity among human women.

And if you dare to love her, you will lose her in the end.

That thought saddened him. All humans eventually faced their own mortality; while were-cats could become sick, they couldn't be killed very easily. The claw marks Lyn had inflicted upon him would be completely gone within two days and by then he should be long gone from Char's life.

Thanks to his past as a Hunter, he'd be forced to look over his shoulder for the rest of his life. He'd killed hundreds of rogue preternaturals, all with the full consent of the Council. But there were those like the wolves who didn't acknowledge the Council and they had a tendency to get a little testy when one of their own was killed, even if they were as rabid as a junkyard dog.

If what Bo had said was right and Lyn was out to start a war, he would have to be stopped at all costs. If that meant killing the wolf, then so be it. Rik knew if he were the one to do the deed, his life would forever be at risk for retaliation. The wolves wouldn't allow the killing of their own to go unpunished, especially if it was carried out by a were-cat. No one close to him could ever hope to be safe.

Char stirred and rolled over, making a soft, sexy purr as she did so. His gut clenched. He could never ask her to join him with the threat of Lyn and possible retribution hanging over his head. He'd sworn to Trey he would protect her, and once the wolf was apprehended and he was sure she was safe, he'd leave, no matter how much pain it caused him.

Let it be soon. The longer I stay with her, the more firm a grip she'll have on my heart.

"Rik?" Char's sleepy, sexy voice sounded.

He approached the bed and set his cell phone on the table. He'd turned it off, as he wasn't sure he wanted to hear any more news after the last call.

"Yeah, babe?"

"What are you doing?"

He stretched out beside her and gathered her in his arms. He buried his nose in her fragrant hair and inhaled deeply.

"I was watching you." He cuddled close to kiss the curve of her shoulder. "You look beautiful in the moonlight."

She gave a sleepy chuckle. "You need glasses. I'm chubby." She sighed. "I can never seem to lose the twenty pounds I put on in college."

"All women say that, even the ones with the stick figures." He suckled her earlobe and was rewarded with a shiver. "Meat is for men while sticks are for dogs." He licked the tender skin beneath her ear.

She wrapped her arms around his shoulders and tilted her head to allow better access. "I like that," she purred.

"I borrowed that line from a friend." He skimmed his hands up her back, enjoying the pressure of her ripe breasts against his chest. "I'll pass your pleasure along."

"Uh-huh." She scraped her nails over his nipples and his breath hissed between his teeth. "You're hard for me. I can feel you against my stomach."

He palmed her breast and teased her nipple with his thumb. "I just look at you and I want you again."

She smiled. "What a lovely thing to say."

"That's me, a regular poet."

He bent his head and nipped at her breast before taking her nipple into his mouth. She moaned and clutched his head as he teased and tasted her, rolling her pert nipple against the roof of his mouth then releasing it to torment the other.

She moved onto her back and he kissed his way down her body, nipping at her belly button and kissing the lush curve of her lower stomach.

The soft curls covering her fragrant mound were damp with desire and he inhaled her scent. Arousal shot through his system and the need to mate with her increased. The night was dwindling and the moon hung heavy in the sky. It was far past time for the cat to play.

"Open for me." His voice was hoarse. "I want to see you."

She slid her hands between her thighs, and parted her labia. He growled deep in his throat at the sight of her rosy, dampened flesh. He buried his face between her legs and seduced her with his tongue.

She moaned and her thighs tensed at the first swipe of his tongue over her clit. He closed his eyes and lost himself in the essence of this amazing woman. She clutched at his head as he worshipped her needy flesh with his tongue.

He lavished attention upon the hardened nub, dragging his tongue over her again and again until she was sobbing and thrusting against his mouth. It had been so long since he'd wanted to pleasure a woman as he did this one. While he'd always made sure his sexual partners reached release, he wanted more from Char. More touching, tasting, fucking, sucking — all of it.

He covered her with his mouth and stroked his roughened tongue over her clit. Holding the position he PPurrRReeddD…

Char came with a wild scream. Her back arched and her hips left the bed in a wild move that threatened to unseat him. Gripping her hips, he followed the movement and continued his sensual assault until she begged him to stop.

Desire burned hot and heavy in his bloodstream and he felt he would explode if he didn't take her now. He rose to his knees.

It was time to unleash the beast.

* * * * *

Her heart was still pounding as Rik urged her onto her knees. He knelt close behind her; his big body cuddled close and his cock pressed into her buttocks. He put his arms around her and palmed her breasts. Still shaking from her powerful release, she tipped her head back to rest on his shoulder.

"Are you always this insatiable?" She covered his hands with hers.

"No." He nipped at her throat. "Only with you." He slid a hand down to cup her mound then slipped his fingers inside.

She moaned and rubbed herself against his fingers, amazed at her own stamina. She'd never considered herself a sexual Olympian before, but now she was convinced she was headed for the gold medal.

Silently, he urged her to part her legs and he entered her from behind. She swayed, stunned by the stark eroticism of the moment. The room was dark and she couldn't see her lover, only feel him behind her, filling her, stretching her until she could take no more. The sensations were so powerful she moaned and strained against his grip as he began to gently thrust.

She tumbled forward onto her elbows and they both groaned as he sank even deeper into her. Sex in this position, with this man, gave her a pleasure richer than anything she'd ever imagined.

Rik began to thrust in earnest, his big body covering hers. The bedsprings squeaked in accompaniment to their muted groans and sighs. She arched her back, taking him just a few centimeters deeper than before while she strained to meet his thrusts. She was a woman consumed with the need for total possession. His possession.

His fingers dug into her hips and she knew she'd probably be bruised in the morning, but she didn't care. She wanted only this man's complete and utter domination of her body and soul.

He bent over her; his teeth grazed her shoulder as he reached between her thighs and stroked her clit. The sensation was earthy, powerful, and she teetered on the verge of release. He bit her shoulder and it was that slight flash pain that he soothed with his tongue that pushed her over the edge.

She came with a scream and a few seconds later, Rik joined her. Together they sank on the bed in a limp, sweaty heap with their hearts pounding in near unison.

He covered her like a human blanket and Char found she quite enjoyed the experience. She snuggled into the pillows and closed her eyes, relishing the feel of his warm skin against hers.

As far as lovers went, in her opinion, she'd found the best there was in New Orleans. Rik had definitely spoiled her for any other man.

* * * * *

Char came awake slowly with the sound of heavy purring in her ear. She batted her tangled hair from her eyes only to realize it was Rik making the odd sound in his throat. She grinned. He sort-of snored — how cute was that?

Sunlight poured in through the blinds, alerting her to the fact that it was much later than when she usually got up. She glanced at the clock.

Eleven-seventeen.

Yup, much later, but she'd had good reason to sleep in a bit.

Her lover was curled against her; his big arm tossed over her stomach and his face buried in the pillows. The bandage on his arm had come loose and one end stuck up. She pulled it the rest of the way off and tossed it on the bedside table. Her eyes widened when she saw the scratches. They looked amazingly good. In fact, they looked as if they were several days old. She frowned. Maybe they hadn't been as bad as she'd originally thought?

"What are you doing?" Rik's sleepy voice sounded from the pillows. His arm tightened and he snuggled closer.

"Checking your wounds. They look excellent."

"I heal fast." He pulled her into the curve of his big body and nibbled her neck.

"And you recover pretty quickly, too," she teased. His burgeoning erection prodded her in the hip.

"Well, it *is* morning." His teeth grazed her throat. She moved her hair out of the way and he nipped her earlobe. "And you know what that means…"

She rolled onto her side and snuggled her back against his chest to enjoy the caress of his tongue. "That I do."

He slid his arm around her neck, then secured her against his chest before he moved his hand between her thighs. She parted her legs and he entered her from behind. She sighed. They fit so well together it was frightening. His big arms encircled her, anchoring her in place, making her feel safe, cherished, as he began to thrust. Each movement was slow, easy, an unhurried dance of passion.

It was an incredible rush to be held so tightly she could barely move, only accept his inevitable possession. The tension built and he increased the pace. When she thought she could bear it no more, his fingers plunged between her thighs to stroke her clit and she reached release.

Just as she fell to the earth again she felt Rik tense and he growled out his release. They lay intimately entwined while their breathing slowed and their heartbeats gentled.

"That is the best way to wake up," he said.

She laughed. "You're such a guy."

He gave her a rough hug. "No, if I was a 'guy', as you put it, I'd say that having my cock in your mouth was the best way to wake up."

She shook her head and giggled. "Yeah, well, maybe next time."

He released her abruptly and rolled away, leaving her wishing she'd never said such a thing. Regardless of how she felt, this was still a one-night stand, albeit a leisurely one.

"I'm starving." He rose and presented her with an eye-widening view of his perfect buttocks and the strongly muscled line of his back.

She cleared her throat and thanked the gods the blinds were partially open so she could see him clearly. A vision such as Rik's naked body was one that should never be wasted.

"I can make some breakfast. How do you feel about eggs and sausage?" she asked.

He turned and grinned, causing her heart to flop. "I say bring it on."

Char got to her feet and grabbed her robe. "If you want to take a shower, go ahead. Just help yourself to whatever you might need."

"Great, thanks."

Mourning the sudden distance she felt between them, she scurried into the kitchen. She'd never been in this position before. Let's face it; she just wasn't that kind of girl.

She opened the fridge and pulled out the eggs and sausage.

Well, now she could be considered one of those girls but under normal circumstances she wasn't. She was more likely to spend her evenings alone with a stack of romance novels and a bowl of carrot sticks than she was to go out and partake of the multitude of sinful pleasures New Orleans offered.

On the rare occasion she'd contemplated going out and finding a playmate, she'd come up with a hundred reasons to stay on the couch. Never, in her wildest dreams, had she imagined she'd end up with a man such as Rik.

Sheesh, the man was an animal.

She tossed the sausages into the skillet and began scrambling some eggs. He was a big guy so she'd better make at least six eggs. Her cheeks colored. He was definitely a *big* guy.

Now what? She'd feed him and he'd leave? Would he call her again? Should she just send him on his way with a smile and a casual "see ya" or beg him to take her phone number?

She scowled and poked the sausages with a fork. She hated this feeling of indecision. She'd been brought up to let the man make all the moves and right now that lesson seemed really dumb to her.

"Are the sausages misbehaving?"

Rik stood in the doorway dressed only in his jeans and a wide smile. His damp hair was tousled and he looked good enough to eat.

Her stomach rumbled.

"Why do you say that?" she asked.

"You're making evil faces at them." He walked toward the refrigerator.

She grinned. "Don't worry, I know what to do with my meat."

He laughed and pleasure flooded her system at the warm sound. "Yes, you do. Do you want this fruit salad set out on the table?"

"Please. There's milk and juice in there, too. Just grab whatever you want. Glasses are over the sink."

He pulled the carton of milk out then made a face when he saw the label. "It's skim, what's the point?"

She gave his flat stomach a pointed look. "Some of us have to watch our weight."

He set the carton on the table then stepped behind her. He placed his hands on her hips before he dropped a kiss on her neck. "You do not need to watch your weight."

She grinned and reached for a plate to put the meat on before it burned. "Yes, I do. The women in my family run to chubbiness the second we hit thirty. I swear, at the stroke of midnight on my birthday, I put on four pounds."

He took the plate from her and sat at the table. "Trust me, after last night you burned enough calories to have a milkshake with your breakfast." He gave her a pointed look.

Her cheeks warmed and she placed a pile of scrambled eggs in front of him. "You too. Eat up."

She made some toast and listened to him grunt and groan over how fabulous the food was. She took a small portion of eggs and a sausage then sat down.

"It's just toast," she laughed as he snagged two pieces off the plate. "Don't you ever cook?"

"Not if I can help it. I'm a firm believer in take-out and it helps the local economy." He glanced at her plate. "Is that all you're having?"

"Well, I usually have cereal and fruit so this is a splurge for me."

He picked up an orange slice from the bowl of mixed fruit. "Like this?" He held it out to her, his eyes daring her to take it. "Would you like a bite?"

She leaned forward and took the proffered fruit from his fingertips. Heat ignited low in her belly when his fingers brushed her lower lip. She chewed and swallowed the sweet fruit.

"Well, not exactly like that." She reached for the bowl and pulled out a chunk of pineapple and offered it to him.

He caught her wrist and took the fruit before licking her fingers clean. When he was done, her skin burned where he'd touched her.

"I'm not sure, but some of this looks like it might be going bad." He fished out a plump strawberry. "We might need to check more of it to be sure." He bit the fruit in half then offered her the other half.

She mimicked him, taking his wrist and pulling him closer. She didn't miss how his gaze dropped to her mouth when she took the bite.

"I think you're right and I have something to help the situation. We wouldn't want to waste food." She rose and retrieved a container of whipped cream from the refrigerator. "This should cover up that slightly sour flavor."

She started to sit but he stopped her. Pushing back from the table he guided her to straddle his lap. His jeans felt decadent against her bare inner thighs.

"This is much better." His big hands landed on her hips.

"Mmm." She picked up a slice of peach and dipped it into the cream. "I think so, too."

Their gazes locked and he opened his mouth to take the morsel from her fingertips. As he chewed she picked up his plate and continued feeding him, taking bites for herself as well. When the plate was empty, Rik reached for the fruit.

"I think we need some more of this." He tipped the bowl ever so slightly and the cold juice splashed her chest and soaked her thin robe. She gasped as the icy liquid ran down her belly. Looking unrepentant, he put down the bowl and opened her robe fully.

"Sorry about that." His eyes gleamed. "Allow me to clean it up."

He tipped his head and began lapping at the sweet juice and her skin. Char leaned against the table and moaned as he suckled her sticky nipples. By the time he'd licked every inch of her chest, she was wet and ready for him. Rather than reach for her, he picked up the fruit.

"These peaches are really good." He pulled out a fat slice. "Would you like another one?" The juice ran down his fingers and dripped onto her breasts.

"I don't think one can ever have enough...fruit."

She took the sweet morsel from his fingers, taking time to clean his sticky fingertips. Rik licked his lips and she felt a near-delirious rush of power in the face of his obvious arousal.

"I'd say I have to agree with you." His voice was strained.

He slid the robe from her shoulders then grabbed her hips and stood, forcing Char to hang onto his shoulders or end up on the floor. He sat her on the edge of the table before he picked up the bowl of fruit, what little was left, and poured it over her torso.

Her lungs constricted as the cold juice ran down her stomach and between her thighs.

"The perfect dessert," he hissed.

He sat, gripped her hips and tilted her backward to feast on her flesh. Dimly, she heard some of the crockery hit the floor, but in the face of the magic he was perpetrating on her body, she didn't care if all her plates were destroyed.

His heated mouth suckled her breasts before he licked a determined path down her stomach. He spread her thighs and lapped at her drenched core. She braced her hands behind her, only to realize she'd stuck her hand into her plate of now-cold scrambled eggs. Shoving them, she heard the plate hit the floor and shatter as he began sucking her clit. The erotic sight of his tawny head between her thighs was almost as arousing as his touch.

She was close to release when Rik rose and unbuttoned his jeans to release his erection. She didn't have time to appreciate the magnificent sight as he spread her thighs and drove himself into her with a thrust that caused her breath to leave in a rush. He began to thrust, and beneath her, she felt the table shift and it gave an ominous creak.

"Rik, I don't think this table will survive much more," she panted.

He muttered something uncomplimentary about the stability of her table then picked her up. She'd expected him to head for the bedroom, but instead he lowered them both to the floor.

The tile was cool and sticky from the juice that had run off the table, but she didn't care in the slightest. They rolled across the floor, a tangle of sticky flesh and rampant need as they stroked and sucked any part of the other's body that they could reach. The taste of fruit juice and warm skin was a treat not to be denied.

Char ended up beneath him under the table. She arched her back and laced her legs around his waist as he entered her with a roar. She lost track of time and place as he took her again and again, forcing her into such an exquisite release she could barely breathe afterward.

After Rik found his own satisfaction they lay in a boneless heap on the floor. She hugged him tight, only to find a chunk of strawberry smashed on his shoulder.

She giggled and held up the massacred fruit so he could see it.

"So, how do you feel about lunch?"

Chapter Five

Rik stood with his hands on his hips as he surveyed the damage they'd created. Drying fruit juice coated the table and floor along with smashed pieces of fruit, shattered plates and melting dollops of whipped cream.

He couldn't wipe the smile off his face.

Char was in the shower singing an old disco hit about survival and it was wildly off-key. He could imagine her lush curves slick with soap and water, her rosy nipples hardened from the stroke of the washcloth. He could make quick work of this mess, then join in her in —

Before he could move, a knock sounded on her apartment door. He frowned and his hand automatically went to his knife only to realize it wasn't there. He cursed when also he realized he didn't have his boots on.

Knowing that Lyn would be coming for him, though it was doubtful he'd just knock on the front door, Rik ducked into the bedroom. He found the knife and tucked it into the back of his pants.

The knock sounded again, louder and definitely more impatient this time. Rik approached the door and was surprised when it opened and a large man stepped into the entry.

Human, no doubt.

Big, no question.

"Who the fuck are you?" The stranger's pale gaze moved over Rik, sizing him up.

"Who's asking?" Rik crossed his arms over his chest and widened his stance.

The other man's fists clenched then released. "You'd better start talking, *friend*."

Rik offered him a sharp smile that had cowed many humans over the years. "I'm not your friend and you'll do well to remember that."

The man shrugged. "Works for me."

Cheeky bastard.

"Who sent you?" Rik asked.

The man looked confused. "What the fuck are you talking about? No one sent me." He leaned to the side and tried to look down the hall past Rik. "Where is she?"

Rik moved to the side and blocked his view. "Not gonna happen, friend. Why don't you just turn around and leave before I knock some of those pretty teeth from your mouth? No matter what he's paying you, it isn't enough for new dental work."

The man only looked irritated and he cracked his knuckles. "You might try, but it won't happen." He leaned the other way and got a clear view into the kitchen. His eyes widened then narrowed when he saw the mess, and he started toward Rik.

Rik braced himself. While his attacker appeared to be human and it wouldn't take much for a were-cat to kill him, he'd just as soon avoid that. Women had a tendency to get a little touchy when people were slain in their home.

"You bastard," the stranger snarled and swung.

Rik barely managed to avoid the blow as he feinted to the left. The other man overextended and Rik moved to shove him against the wall. To his surprise, the stranger slipped from his grasp and shoved backwards, and Rik felt himself falling.

Tricky bastard.

Feeling a grudging sense of admiration, Rik gained his feet and caught the look of surprise on the other man's face. Cats were fast and nimble; it was a definite edge in a fight.

The stranger slammed into him and caught him around the waist, propelling him backward into the kitchen. His bare feet slid on the smashed remains of breakfast and together they fell onto the table. The flimsy piece of furniture disintegrated under four hundred pounds of enraged male muscle.

Rik landed on the bottom, and with a deft twist he overpowered the human and flipped the other man beneath him. Drawing his knife he grabbed the man's thick dark hair and wrenched his head back before he pressed the knife against the base of his throat.

"I'll ask you one more time, who sent you?" Rik ground out.

Behind him he heard the thud of bare feet approaching.

Char.

"Oh my God, what happened?" She skidded to a halt near them. "Why are you holding a knife to my brother's throat?"

Rik looked down at the man and noted the resemblance. They had the same reddish-brown hair, and the shape of his eyes was similar to Char's. He looked up at her.

"The cop?" he asked.

She bit her lip and nodded.

"Great...just great." Rik slid the knife into the back of his pants and stood. "Sorry about that." He held his hand out to the man on the floor.

Char's brother gave him a disgusted look and ignored the offered hand. No wonder the man had been tough to bring down; he probably had several years of street experience to back him up. Being a cop in New Orleans wasn't for wimps.

"Who is this freak?" The man brushed at the smashed fruit staining his shirt.

"Steph, this is Rik. A friend," Char said.

Steph propped his hands on his hips and glared at his sister. "Get some clothes on," he snapped. "You're practically naked."

Rik grinned when he noticed Char's robe was stuck to her damp body, and through the cotton, he could see her erect nipples. If it were his sister standing there dripping wet, he'd probably be surly, too.

She rolled her eyes. "I'm a grownup and you've just busted your way into my home. If you don't like the way I dress, then don't come here again."

"I didn't bust into anything. I have a key, remember?" He waved a hand at his sister and looked away. "So get dressed and I'll speak with your *friend* while we're waiting."

Char glanced at Rik then back to her brother. "Fine. But if I hear anyone throwing a punch or breaking any more of my furniture, I'll smack both of your heads together. You," she pointed at Rik, "leave your knife in your pants, and as for you," she scowled at her brother, "make yourself useful, Steph, and help Rik clean this mess up." With that she turned and stalked off, her butt clearly defined through the robe.

Rik licked his lips. She had the perfect backside. Plump and sweetly rounded—

"Stop staring at my sister like that."

Rik glanced at Steph. "I'll stop when your sister objects, not you."

He grunted and grabbed one end of the splintered table while Steph took the other. Together they carried the remains out to the dumpster behind the apartment. As they were walking back, the other man spoke first.

"You were expecting trouble?" Steph asked.

"It's always a possibility." Rik started picking up the cutlery and the few plates that had survived their sexual Armageddon.

"Does it involve my sister?" Steph fished the broom and mop out of the closet.

"It could," Rik said. "We had a little trouble at The Chamber last night and some threats were made."

"So you're saying I need to keep an eye on her?" Steph began sweeping the mess into a pile in the center of the floor.

"If I'm not around, yes, that would be a good idea."

"I hope you're not going to be around much longer," Steph grunted.

Rik couldn't help but grin. "If she were my sister, I'd probably feel the same way."

The other man propped his arm on the broom. "Where did you learn to fight like that?" He dumped the trash into the can.

"Military," Rik lied. It was his usual response to the question. The Shadow Hunters were a military, of sorts. "So you'll keep an eye on your sister?" He filled up the mop bucket with hot water and detergent.

"You don't even have to ask." He put the broom away and Rik started to mop the floor. "How long is this threat viable?"

"Hopefully only twenty-four hours at the most. I have some friends in the neutralization business."

"I should kill you for getting her mixed up in something dangerous." Steph leaned against the counter with his arms crossed over his chest.

"You don't have to. I've kicked myself enough for letting her get tangled up in it as it is," Rik said. "I don't take my relationship with Char lightly and I won't compromise her safety for my own."

A grudging look of admiration came into Steph's eyes. "My sister is a gentle soul and she doesn't need to get tangled up in something that could cost her her life."

"It's too late, she's already neck-deep, but I'm doing my damnedest to get her out of it."

"Does she realize she's in danger?"

"No."

"Let's keep it that way for now."

* * * * *

Satisfied that Char was in good hands, Rik left before she came back downstairs. Cowardly, yes, but he needed some time to gather his thoughts and get cleaned up. He turned on his cell phone to see several voicemail messages waiting for him.

The first was from Trey, cursing him because his cell phone was turned off and demanding Rik call at once. The second was from Marcus, asking him to call as soon as possible, but it was the final one was the one that set him on edge.

It was from Alexandre Saint-Juste, the head of the Council of Elders, requesting Rik call him after dark that evening.

Glancing at the clock in his car, he saw he had several hours before he could make that call and he opted to contact Marcus instead. Marcus would be much more fun to deal with than Trey.

The other man picked up on the first ring.

"Where y'at?" Marcus asked.

"Headed home to clean up and change my clothes."

The other man chuckled. "Was she worth the fight?"

"It's not like that."

There was silence on the other end. "So that's how it is."

Rik ignored him. "What else is going on?"

"Let's see, I bought a new handgun and it might come in handy, as Lyn is calling for your blood."

"That's no surprise," Rik said.

"No, but I found out there's a warrant out for his arrest in New York City. It seems he killed his human girlfriend, Serena. They found her body several days ago."

Rik felt a momentary pang for the young woman. She might have been in cahoots with Lyn to deceive Rik but she didn't deserve to die for her bad judgment.

"So the cops are looking for him?" Rik asked. "Good."

"And some Shadow Hunters. Trey reported back to Saint-Juste last night and it seems he wasn't happy with the latest turn of events."

"Imagine that," Rik muttered.

Marcus ignored him. "Rumor has it that you're being called before the Council for your actions."

"Oh yeah, this is shaping up to be a great day," Rik said.

Marcus chuckled. "With luck, the Hunters will have the wolf before nightfall, and the Council will probably do no more than slap you on the wrist."

"After they gnaw on my ass you mean?" Rik turned into his driveway. "It could be worse, I suppose."

"Yeah, Lyn could outfox the Hunters, grab your girl and start the war he hungers for."

"That isn't going to happen." Rik threw the car into park. "After I've changed clothes I'm going after him myself."

There was a moment of silence. "Going back in the Hunter biz, are you?"

"Just one more for the road, my friend."

Chapter Six

Char lay curled in her bed, watching the moonlight drift across her room. She wasn't sure why her brother had insisted upon staying the night. The last time he'd stayed here was when his apartment had been painted two years ago. Now she remembered why she'd resisted him staying here; even with the door shut, she could hear him snoring in the living room.

She rolled over and stuffed her pillow under her cheek. The burning question for her was why Rik had left without saying goodbye. Steph had assured her he'd done nothing, and Rik had left only a hastily scrawled note that stated he'd be in touch. One little note was no reassurance that he actually would contact her.

She sighed. She wished she could be the love 'em and leave 'em type but she wasn't wired like that. She was sentimental and she teared up over romantic movies, so it should be no surprise that she'd fallen head over heels for Rik. It gnawed at her that he'd left without speaking to her. Maybe she'd made it too easy for him or maybe he wasn't interested in anything other than wild sex on the kitchen floor.

She forced her eyes closed. No, he liked her, she was sure of it. They'd laughed and made love on her kitchen floor, the table and her bedroom. Surely he'd contact her sooner or later. No one could have made love with such zeal while feeling nothing for her.

She couldn't have dozed for long when the warm, familiar feel of Rik wrapping himself around her woke her.

"Rik." Her voice was thick with sleep.

"Yeah, babe, it's me."

"Where did you go?" she whispered.

"I had to deal with some business." He kissed her shoulder. "Sorry I had to run out like that, but it was important."

Relief blossomed in her chest and she laced her hands with his. "It's okay this one time, but don't try that again. A girl has her reputation to worry about."

He chuckled and she shushed him.

"Steph is out there." She pointed at the door.

"Mmm, I knew that. It sounds like he's sawing you a new kitchen table."

Char burst into giggles when Steph gave a particularly noisy snore. "He's always snored like that. He claims it's why he hasn't gotten married."

"Hmm." He covered her breast with one hand. "That and the fact he has the face of a carp?"

"Not hardly. Steph is very handsome, the women love him." Her voice grew faint as he stroked her nipple between his fingertips. She arched into his touch and he tweaked her other nipple.

"You sleep naked," he whispered.

"Not normally."

She parted her legs and he slid his cock between them. What was it about this man? He only had to touch her and all reason fled. She'd become a woman possessed by him. She tightened her thighs around his cock and he ran his tongue down her neck. He stroked her breasts until her nipples were hard, aching peaks. She pressed her hips backward into his and the movements dragged his cock back and forth against her swollen labia.

He gave a loud purr and the sound set her nerves on alert. She was very aware that her brother was only feet away, and the last thing she wanted was Steph busting in on them. She bit her lip when he slid his hand over her belly to part her dampened flesh.

He stroked her clit and her breathing grew strained. She felt the rush of liquid desire between her thighs. He continued the slow rocking motion, stimulating them both while not actually entering her. The tension mounted with each stroke until he rolled her over and urged her onto her hands and knees.

She parted her thighs wide, welcoming him. Instead of entering her, she felt him move away just before the soft slide of his tongue licked her damp flesh. She moaned and fell forward, pressing her face into the pillows to stifle her cries. His rough tongue teased her clit and sucked hard.

Using the pillows to stifle her cries, she felt Rik continue his sensual assault. His tongue teased her aroused flesh and he swiftly brought her to a mind-blowing climax.

Rik moved over her and she felt his thighs parting hers. His big hands landed on her hips and the broad tip of his cock nudged at her vagina.

Slowly, he entered her, filling her until she was fully impaled. He moved over her, covering her, his broad chest resting against her back. Propping his upper body on his elbows, he kissed her shoulder.

"Good?" he whispered.

"Mmm, perfect."

He started to move, slowly at first. Her hips arched to meet him halfway. He growled deep in his throat and his thrusts increased. She lost herself in the pool of sensuality that was making love with Rik. How many more times she came she didn't know. When she felt his release, a single refrain echoed in her mind.

He'd come back.

* * * * *

Rik lay in the darkness with his eyes closed. He never should have returned, but he couldn't resist her. He'd spent the day crisscrossing town on any number of wild goose chases while in constant contact with the Hunters who were also looking for Lyn. So far the wily bastard had eluded all of them.

Tired and frustrated, all he could think of was seeing Char, touching her face, kissing her lips and hearing her laugh. He was scheduled to meet with the Council, a crazed werewolf was on the loose in New Orleans, and he was hanging out in her bed, in her arms.

He definitely wasn't thinking straight.

He needed to get up and make a plan but he couldn't quite bring himself to move. He was warm, comfortable and Char's lush backside cradled his cock. What more could a were-cat ask for?

The soft beep of his phone jolted him into movement. He snatched the phone from his pants and looked at the display. Someone had sent him a text message: *Lyn located. Meet us at Gautier's and let's rumble.*

Rik checked the text message sender. It was Marcus. He rolled from the bed and reached for his clothing. He was only about fifteen minutes from the Gautier warehouse, as long as he ignored the traffic signals.

He laced up his leather pants and shoved his feet into his boots. Grabbing his jacket, he headed for the window.

Hopefully, within the hour they'd subdue Lyn and Char would be safe.

Rik slipped out the window as silently as he entered, and by the time he reached his car, was in full Hunter mode.

* * * * *

Char wasn't sure what woke her. She gave a noisy yawn and her eyes flicked open. The silence of the apartment was oppressive and very unusual. Even on the quietest nights she heard some street noise from Bourbon Street only a few blocks away—

Unease washed over her and she sat up. Steph wasn't snoring and the other half of her bed was cold. She glanced at the clock. It was a little after three a.m. Where was Rik? She slipped out of bed and picked up her robe from the floor. Maybe he went into the kitchen for a snack.

She frowned when she noticed the open bedroom door. She'd closed it when she'd gone to bed in a vague attempt to drown out Steph's snores. Not that it had helped much, as she was sure the neighbors could've heard him.

She stepped into the living room. The couch was empty and the blanket and pillow were tossed on the floor. She rolled her eyes and picked them up. Men! Why were they always pigs? She dropped them on the couch before heading toward the kitchen.

She turned the light on and her heart stopped when she saw Steph laying face down on the floor, a pool of blood spreading near his head.

"Oh my God," she reached for him. "Steph?" A movement in the shadows caught her attention.

Near the back door was a large, hulking figure in black leather with his back to her. For a split second she thought it was Rik, until he turned around. The overhead light caught on the stainless steel Asp baton he held in his hand. The stranger twirled it as if he were a cheerleader. When he smiled, long, wicked canine teeth emerged from between his lips.

"Hello, beautiful."

* * * * *

Rik knew the Gautier warehouse complex like the back of his hand. It was a series of dilapidated docks and warehouses that had been abandoned in the early nineteen fifties. Its secluded location made it a popular spot for all sorts of preternatural mischief. There was no better place for a pack of mangy werewolves to hang out.

He slipped in the side door of the warehouse, and almost immediately his senses detected the presence of several other preternaturals, most of them wolves and a few cats.

Taking cover in the labyrinth of wooden packing crates, he made his way to the center of the warehouse. The lights were on overhead and the silence was broken only by the slither of metal against metal and the beat of his own heart.

Rik peered through a gap in the boxes and he had a clear view of the center of the warehouse. Lyn stood near an iron railing overlooking a water-filled pit. Years ago, the pit had been used for bootlegging and before that, slavery. It opened directly onto the waterway and small, fast boats could slip under the pier to be loaded with liquor or slaves. When the building had been closed, the pit was sealed and now the water was black and stagnant.

"We wondered when you'd deign to join us," Lyn called out.

Rik stepped into the open. A few feet away from Lyn was Marcus, clearly unconscious and bleeding from a head wound. Next to him was Dirk, another Shadow Hunter Rik had worked with on several occasions. He sat on the floor bound with chains and gagged with a blue bandana.

Near him, perched on a wooden crate, was the wolf from the alley. His eyes glinted in an unfriendly manner and he had a smirky grin on his sharp-angled face. There were several other wolves behind him near the railing and their expressions varied from smug to leery.

Bo stood near the back of the group and he looked distinctly unhappy. It would appear that Lyn didn't have a united front to back him up after all.

"You're having a party and I wasn't invited?" Rik walked toward Lyn.

"Of course you were invited, you received my message, did you not?" He held up Marcus' phone. "I sent the message as your friend," he nudged Marcus in the side with a toe, "was indisposed."

"So you won't mind that I invited a few friends as well?" Rik asked.

Lyn's smile grew. "Of course not. The more the merrier."

"I thought you would say that. Why don't we settle this between ourselves, Fido?" Rik had reached Dirk's side. "We don't need to involve the others." He reached down and grabbed the other man's arm and hauled him to his feet.

"You'll need this." Bo stepped forward to toss a silver key at Rik.

"I see you've chosen your side then, *brother*," Lyn spat.

"I've chosen the side of peace, *brother*." Bo crossed his brawny arms over his chest. "I won't make war with you."

Lyn shrugged. "So be it."

"You and I, wolf. Let's settle this for once and for all." Rik removed the chains and gag from Dirk.

"Skin to skin?" The wolf gave a toothy grin and murmurs broke out in the pack. "Or animal to animal?"

"Just you and I, Fido. Man to man, leave the animals in their cages." Rik removed his leather jacket and draped it over the rail. He'd destroyed enough clothing in the last twenty-four hours, and he didn't want to add to the count.

Lyn removed his jacket and Rik approached, leaving Dirk to deal with Marcus. As they began to circle, the other wolves moved closer, each vying for a better viewing position. Only Bo held back with a look of resignation on his face. He turned and headed for the door. One down, six more to go.

Out of the corner of his eye, Rik noted the arrival of another wolf and with him, a woman with rumpled, reddish-brown curls. His heart stopped.

It was Char.

Chapter Seven

Her scream died when she saw Rik go down. The other man landed on him and they rolled across the floor in a tangle of long limbs. When they came to a stop, Rik was on top. He hit Lyn on the chin several times with his fist then rose. He grabbed the other man, and in a grotesquely graceful move that belied physics and human strength, he sent Lyn flying into a wall of crates.

The old wood collapsed and Rik leapt on Lyn. The men continued grappling amidst splintered crates and she winced at the sound of flesh striking flesh.

They're going to kill each other.

Several more men came in at a lope and a tall, dark-haired man waved them off. "Let Rik handle it himself," he said. "That's the way he wants it."

Char shook off the hand of the man who'd forced her to come here. With her gaze glued on the two combatants, she crept toward the railing and was going to lean upon it for support when she saw the black, stagnant water below. Her heart almost stopped.

She was deathly afraid of the water. Even as a child her parents had despaired of ever getting her into water that would go over her head. Even then she'd known it would spell her doom.

A crash brought her attention to the fight and both men were now on their feet. In a lightning-fast move she'd only seen in the movies, Lyn kicked Rik hard in the chest. Rik flew backward and skidded across the floor. Barely missing a beat, he gained his feet in one easy roll. Lyn ran at him and Rik slammed the heel of his hand into Lyn's face and snapped his nose, sending a gush of blood over both men.

"I broke your fucking nose, Fido." Rik had a bloodthirsty grin on his face. "Then again, you never were a pretty boy."

The other man's tongue licked at the torrent while Char's stomach roiled. "Delicious. I feed on my pain." Lyn's voice was low, guttural. "Just as I will feed on yours."

"Why? Did you run out of Alpo?"

A vicious snarl broke from Lyn and he threw himself at Rik. Their bodies slammed backward into the railing. The rusted metal bent as if in slow motion, and a scream caught in Char's throat as the rail gave way beneath their combined weight and both men fell over the edge in a tangle of limbs and anger.

Forcing her fear to the side, Char stepped toward the rail and her palms grew sweaty. Rik had landed on a small section of a cracked cement slab about seven or eight feet beneath where she was standing. Lyn hadn't been so lucky. The other man hung off the side of the slab and now dangled over the murky black water, his boots skimming the surface.

"Look at that, Fido. You're about to take a bath."

In a show of strength that was mind-boggling, Lyn vaulted himself onto the slab and threw himself at Rik. He landed a kick to Rik's ribs that knocked him off balance. Rik ducked the second punch then went in low and hard, catching Lyn around the waist. Both men plowed backward into a steel support and Lyn's head rang hard against it.

Rik trapped the other man against the pole with his body. He braced his arm against Lyn's Adam's apple and forced his head back.

"You're going to die, jackal," Rik snarled. "Your kind deserves to die a long, slow and painful death and I'm just the man to deliver the goods."

"With your woman watching? You'd forsake your sacred Hunter Covenant and reveal to her the animal you are?" Lyn panted.

"If it means I save innocent lives, then yes," Rik hissed.

"Pussy."

Lyn clawed at Rik's face and Char had to press her fist to her mouth to halt her scream when she saw the bloody furrows left behind. Rik jerked away, his grip loosening, and Lyn slid down the pole to freedom.

Taking a running leap, Lyn flew through the air and caught one of the rusted chains that were suspended from a winch in the ceiling. He soared through the air like Tarzan to land on the cement slab on the opposite side of the pit.

Terrified, Char's teeth dug into her knuckles as Rik performed the same move. When Rik landed, the other man pulled a knife from his boot and took a swipe at her lover's exposed belly. At the last minute he sidestepped, barely evading the wicked blade.

"So much for man to man," Rik mocked.

"It's overrated," Lyn growled, his speech somewhat garbled now.

Char's eyes widened when she caught sight of his enlarged canines. Did his teeth suddenly get longer?

"I'm going to slit your belly open, Ulrik the Fair, and my pack will feast on your guts."

"You'll try and you'll lose," Rik said. "Your kind couldn't kill one of mine, as we don't go down as easily as a human."

They circled and taunted each other, leaving Char so nervous she felt she would leap out of her skin with the tension.

"We'll see about that, pussycat," Lyn snarled.

Before her very eyes Lyn began to change. His teeth and nose elongated and she blinked several times just to make sure she was seeing right. His hair shortened and seemed to move down his back in a dark wave. Ears appeared on his head and they resembled those of a German Shepherd. His hands were transformed into claws and he flexed them; his nails clicked together. His eyes glowed red and with a howl of rage, of loathing, Lyn charged at Rik.

My God, what were these people?

Shaking now, Char's breath caught as Rik tipped his head back and gave a scream like that of a cougar. A wild, ear-shattering sound that sent shivers down her spine.

Her lover leapt into the air, and with a sharp flick of his leg, kicked the knife from the other man's hand. With a second kick, right into Lyn's dog-shaped face, the other man's feet flew out from beneath him and he landed heavily on his back.

Rik stood over him, his chest heaving with exertion. "You're done, Fido." He grabbed Lyn by the throat and hauled him to his feet.

The other man grinned; his face had reverted to its human form with the exception of his elongated canine teeth. Blood ran from his nose and had splashed onto his chest. "That's what you think, pussy."

The man who'd abducted her from her apartment had stood silently beside her, but now he grabbed her arm and hauled her toward the section of broken railing.

"No!" Char resisted, trying to push away from the pit but the man seemed to be unfazed by her struggles. She looked up into his dark eyes and he gave her a cold, toothy smile.

"Ulrik," he called out. "Release him or lose your woman."

Char's body went numb as he hauled her to the edge. A soft keening sound welled up in her throat as she teetered between safety and sure death. Her nails dug into her tormentor's hand but he didn't flinch.

"Char!"

Her gaze shifted to Rik. He stood on the edge of the pit and his eyes were strangely golden. His hair looked longer and his teeth...his teeth...

Oh my God...not him too...

Lyn lunged for Rik's unprotected back.

"Look out!" she screamed.

The floor tilted and her captor released his grip. She managed to catch a piece of the broken railing and her nails clawed at rusted metal. The faded paint flaked off to embed itself under her nails.

It wasn't enough.

She screamed as her grip loosened and she fell into space. She flailed her arms and legs in the air and it felt as if she were falling in slow motion. Down, down, down she plummeted into the stagnant black water. She'd barely managed to take a deep breath before the darkness closed over her head. She struggled in the inky water and her sense of time and space was obscured.

Foul water invaded her mouth and filled her nose. She clawed at the darkness, all the while bemoaning the fact she'd never conquered her fear and learned to swim. Her all-consuming terror of the water had caused her to go into hysterics when her parents had signed her up for swim classes as a child and they'd pulled her after the first day.

A sense of inevitability settled over her. She would die here alone in the darkness and her family would probably never find her. Her body would be sucked out into the bayou and become croc kibble.

That horrifying thought sent a jolt of panic through her. She kicked her shoes off and clawed the water, trying to reach the surface and fresh air. Her abused lungs ached and spots danced before her eyes. Images of her parents, brothers, and Rik flashed against her eyelids.

Whatever he was, whoever he was, he'd cared for her. She knew that as sure as she knew her own name. Too bad she would be dead before he would ever know how she felt about him. Oh, why hadn't she told him?

Dizziness assailed her and shadows shifted. A deeper, thicker darkness descended over her. The water didn't seem as cold or alien as when she'd fallen into it. In fact, it was almost...welcoming.

As she lost consciousness, she imagined a hand reaching out of the darkness.

Chapter Eight

She hurt all over. Every inch of her body felt used and abused, and she wanted nothing more than to let herself slide back into sleep. At least there she didn't experience any pain.

"Charlene," a firm female voice spoke in her ear.

Char forced her eyes open and the blinding overhead lights caused her to whimper. Pain lanced through her skull and her throat felt raw.

"I'm sorry. Let me turn the lights down."

The voice carried the soft twang of the south. Almost immediately, Char began to feel better just hearing that melodic voice.

Taking a deep breath, Char slowly opened her eyes. The light had been turned down, leaving the room dim, and she sighed with relief. She blinked several times, trying to clear her fuzzy vision.

"Would you like to sit up a little bit?" the soft voice asked.

"Please." Her voice was horribly raspy.

"You have to be feeling like hell." The voice came closer and a mechanical whir sounded. Char felt the head of the bed rise a few inches until she was in a partially reclined position. "I have some soda for you. Are you thirsty?"

Images of the dark water rushing up to meet her caused her to shudder. "I shouldn't be." Her attempt at humor fell flat.

The other woman chuckled. "You swallowed quite a bit of that nasty water but we pumped your stomach just in case."

Char blinked several more times and slowly her murky vision cleared. She lay in a hospital-style bed complete with metal rails, except the sheet was pale pink. Her gaze moved around the room. If she really was in a hospital, it was unlike any she'd ever seen.

The walls were painted a soft, butter yellow and there were paintings on each wall. Several feet from the foot of the bed was a comfortable grouping of overstuffed chairs arranged near a small fireplace. In the center was a coffee table that sported a towering arrangement of flowers.

"Where am I?" Char asked.

"The Clinic. The cats brought you in a few hours ago."

Char's gaze moved toward the young woman standing near the bed. She was petite, with short hair that stood straight up in different colored spikes. Her lower lip was pierced and her eye shadow was a shocking blue. She wore a neat white lab coat over a worn Ramones concert T-shirt.

She gave Char a wide, welcoming smile. "My name is Sasha." She reached for a glass of clear, sparkling soda and she held it so Char could take a drink.

The cold liquid felt like heaven on her abused throat and she took several deep swallows, then indicated she didn't want any more. The woman put the glass on the bedside table.

"What kind of clinic is this?" Char whispered.

The woman's smile widened. "This is a clinic for the Shadow Dwellers."

"What are the Shadow Dwellers?"

Sasha's smile slipped. "You don't know?"

"I'm feeling like Alice in Wonderland and I've just fallen into the rabbit hole." Char let her head fall back against the soft pillows. The linens smelled of fresh lemons.

"The Shadow Dwellers are those who live on the fringe of the mortal world. The vampires, were-cats, wolves, the creatures most humans don't believe exist." She waved her hand to indicate the sumptuous room. "This is where the Shadow Dwellers come when they need medical attention."

Vampires?

"What kind of medical procedure would a vampire need?"

"A blood transfusion?" Sasha grinned and Char couldn't help but smile.

"Are you a w-w-were-cat?"

Sasha shook her spiky head. "Oh no, I'm a vampire."

Char sunk farther into her comfy bed. "Oh." Her voice was faint. "That was my second guess."

"Charlene, are you new to our world?" Sasha asked in a gentle voice.

"I don't know what I am right now," Char admitted.

Sasha patted her on the hand. "If you don't mind me saying, our world isn't much different than the world of the mortals. We love, live, and have productive lives."

"Just with more teeth."

The other woman laughed and nodded. "For some of us that's true. Most of us aren't anyone to be feared. We don't live under the beds of children to grab them when they stick their feet out from under the covers. Many of us are more humane than most humans."

"And what is Rik? Is he a cat?"

"We call them were-cats. They are very similar to a werewolf from your American movies. Their kind are cat shapeshifters and they're known for being very sensual creatures."

That explained a lot. Weary, Char allowed her eyes to slip closed.

"It's a lot to take in."

"It is. Just take it slow and trust that all will work out in the end." Sasha stroked Char's arm. "Rest. I'm sure Rik will be back any minute."

Just what the hell had she stumbled into? Vampires? Did they really exist or was Sasha some deluded freak and she'd landed smack dab in the middle of some sort of cult?

Lyn's wolfish face came to mind and she shuddered. No, what she'd seen was real. He had changed shape before her very eyes. She shook her head then regretted the movement as a soft wave of pain washed over her.

The soft murmur of voices warned her that someone was approaching. Rik materialized in the doorway and his golden gaze centered on her. He was dressed in loose, dark blue scrubs and he looked disgustingly hale and hearty. Three scratches on his right cheek marred the perfection of his face, but she was pleased to see they'd been cleaned and attended to. When he saw she was awake, he smiled and her stomach clenched.

She was definitely in trouble.

"How are you feeling?" He kissed her on the forehead and she inhaled his familiar, beloved scent.

"Shaky," she said. "My brother—"

"Is pissed but he'll live." He took her hand. "Just hang tight and everything will become clearer—"

The soft sound of someone clearing his throat brought her attention to the door. A tall, dark-haired man clad in an immaculate Armani suit was watching her from the entrance. His skin was pale and his eyes were a mesmerizing green. Behind him came a second man that Char recognized from the alley and the warehouse.

"Char, this is Alexandre Saint-Juste, the head of the Council of Elders," Rik spoke. "The Council is akin to the American Congress."

The tall man smiled. "Only more efficient." His cool gaze moved over Char and she fought the urge to squirm. "I trust you are feeling much better?"

Char forced a weak smile. "Much, thank you for asking."

"And this is Bo, Lyn's brother." Rik indicated the second man.

"A werewolf." Char's voice was flat.

Something flickered in the man's eyes and he nodded.

Alexandre looked at his watch. "If we may speak freely, Rik?"

Rik took her hand. "Of course."

"We need to discuss the recent events involving you, Weylyn and this young woman. I understand that the wolf is dead."

"He is." Rik spoke and Char shuddered. As long as she lived, she would never forget the look of pure animal rage on Lyn's face as she fell into the water.

"Just how did he die?"

Rik squeezed her hand. "I killed him, Alexandre."

The vampire frowned. "You were told to avoid confrontation, and killing someone is definitely a confrontation. What do you have to say for yourself?"

"I killed him in order to save the life of the woman I love," Rik said.

Char froze at his words. He loved her? Did she hear him right?

"That's not a very—" Alexandre started.

"Your honor," Bo stepped forward, "if I may add something to your line of questioning."

Alexandre nodded. "Go ahead."

"My brother had plans to set Rik up from day one. He paid his human lover, an unmarked lover I might add, to seduce Rik into bedding her."

"For what purpose?"

"He wanted a reason to start a war, sir."

Alexandre frowned and his electric gaze moved from Rik to Bo then back again. "What brought this on?"

"Mikhail recruited him to start a war between the cats and wolves in the hopes that it would divide the Council and leave you vulnerable to attack.

"Several weeks after Rik returned home, Lyn put his plan into action. He murdered Serena in New York and came here demanding an apology from Rik. I found out about her death only after our meeting with Rik turned sour."

"What happened during that meeting, Rik?" Alexandre asked.

"He wanted me to grovel at his feet and he pulled an innocent young woman into it." Rik raised their linked hands, ensuring Alexandre saw them. "He threatened her life and I was forced to defend her."

"This is most distressing news." Alexandre's gaze flickered over her, and to Char it felt like she was being caressed by a low voltage line. "While I am glad that your human was unharmed, I think it illustrates the danger of forging a relationship between humans and one of our kind."

Her heart caught in her throat and her gaze locked on Rik. She didn't know what power Alexandre held but if he forbade their relationship, she was prepared to throw herself at his feet and beg for mercy.

"I am aware of that," Rik said. "I was a Shadow Hunter for several hundred years and I am very familiar with the dangers involved in crossing that line."

He raised her hand and brushed his mouth over the back of her knuckles. The depth of emotion in his eyes took her breath away.

"But there are times we can't help who we fall in love with," he continued. "Love is like a train with no brakes, running downhill at full speed and you're helpless to stop it. When the odds are against you and you already know you're sunk, all you can do is hang on and hope for the best possible outcome."

Her eyes stung and she swallowed hard. "That's the nicest thing anyone has ever said to me, I think."

Rik grinned. "I should hope so."

"Given that Lyn was acting on Mikhail's behalf, I think the Council will be in agreement when we say that you did nothing wrong in your dealings with the werewolf, Rik," Alexandre said. He turned toward the wolf.

"Bo, I would like to speak more with you about this."

"If you insist." Bo's tone was stiff.

"I can't insist; your clan does not recognize the Council," Alexandre said.

Bo gave a slow nod. "I think I would like to sit down and discuss a few things with you."

"Excellent. Who knows? We may salvage something good from this unfortunate situation." Alexandre headed for the door. "I have to get going; the sun rises soon. Charlene, I hope you feel better soon. Rik, I'll be in touch."

The tall vampire left with the wolf on his heels and Char couldn't bring herself to tear her gaze from her lover's. Her eyes stung and she whispered, "Now what?"

"That's an excellent question." Rik lowered the bedside rail and sat on the edge of the bed. She scooted over until he slid his arm around her and she laid her head on his shoulder. "We need to sit down and have a long discussion."

"A very long one," she agreed. "Can we get something to eat first? I'm starving."

He chuckled. "I don't know...the last time we had a meal together we almost killed each other."

Her cheeks heated at the reminder of their erotic breakfast. Her grip on his waist tightened. "I think we can contain ourselves for a few hours."

"I certainly hope so. I was in the cafeteria a few minutes ago and I saw some New York cheesecake and the cherry topping did remind me of you."

About the author:

J.C. Wilder left the world of big business to carry on conversations with the people who live in her mind, fictional characters that is. In her past she has worked as a software tester, traveled with an alternative rock band and currently volunteers for her local police department as a photographer. She lives in Central Ohio with 6,000 books and an impressive collection of dust bunnies.

The award-winning author also writes as Dominique Adair.

J.C. Wilder welcomes mail from readers. You can write to her c/o Ellora's Cave Publishing at 1056 Home Ave. Akron, Oh 44310-3502.

Also by J.C. Wilder:

In Moonlight anthology
Ellora's Cavemen: Tales from the Temple II anthology
Tactical Pleasure
Tactical Manuever

Writing as Dominique Adair:

Blood Law
Last Kiss
Party Favors anthology
Tied With a Bow anthology
R.S.V.P. Anthology
Single White Submissive Anthology
Southern Submissive: Holly

Twofold Desires

Ashleigh Raine

Non-Dedication

This story is not in any way dedicated to our best friend Carrie. Nope. Not at all dedicated to her. No way. No how. We wouldn't dedicate this to her. Nuh-uh. Not Carrie. Not the lovable, charismatic, vibrant, wonderful, loud, fan-damn-tastic, electric, hyper, bodacious, awesome, spectacular, intrepid, ballsy, funky-spunky, musical, lyrical, outer-spacial woman we know and love.

So Carrie, now that this story has NOT been dedicated to you, whatcha gonna do about it?

Chapter One

Can't close early.

Want to close early.

For the two hundredth time in the last five minutes, Jill Evans looked at her wristwatch. Had the hands even moved? She glanced up at the wall clock and sighed. Foiled again. Closing time wasn't for another long, drawn out, painfully frustrating fifteen minutes. Ugh. She fought the temptation to flip the sign on the door to closed. Who was going to shop for flowers at 7:45 at night a few days before Halloween?

No, she couldn't do it. What if a young girl wanted to buy a flower for her first love? Or what if a gentleman needed a corsage for his lovely lady? Or better yet, what if a single handsome stranger wanted a solitary red rose to bring to the party tonight?

Oh crap!

Tossing her pliers back onto the workbench, Jill whipped around the counter to her computer. She'd never printed up her ticket for tonight's *Singles Haunt* at *Silver Twilight*. She typed in her webmail address. While waiting for the site to load through her incredibly slow connection, she skipped over to the sink and attempted to clean some of the orange and black flower dye from under her fingernails.

Three days until Halloween and everyone seemed to be getting in the spirit. Just today, Jill had sprayed a batch of gladiolus black and orange and carved a few pumpkins. But tonight's bash was the highlight of her holiday. She'd always hoped that one day a man would walk through the door of *Jill's Bloomers* and sweep her off her feet. Yet in the five years since she'd opened, the only sweeping going on involved her broom.

The men who came in weren't looking for a woman, they were looking for flowers for the woman they already had. Although that was great for business, it wasn't great for her love life, or even her go-out-on-a-date-once-every-blue-moon life.

So it was time to take the bull by the horns. Time to go out and get noticed, to live a little dangerously and maybe go a little wild.

And hopefully find someone to go a little wild with her in the process.

The party tonight incorporated all of her newest resolutions. Less than a year ago, *Silver Twilight* had been a strip club. Now it was under new management, offering live music and dancing every night. It was *the* place in Talisman Bay to go for fun.

She cast a glance over her shoulder as she scrubbed. It looked like her e-ticket had arrived. Shutting off the water, she grabbed a towel and did the happy dance back to her computer, letting out a giddy giggle.

Before clicking on the *Silver Twilight* confirmation and e-ticket, she skimmed her incoming messages and noticed one of her old college friends had sent her a Halloween funny. Her grin widened. Charlene always sent the best zingers. Jill had learned to never drink while reading Charlene's emails, to avoid spewing soda all over the monitor. After clicking the appropriate button to print her e-ticket, Jill opened the joke email.

She didn't even get to read the first line before her printer jammed.

"No, no, no. Darn it." At least her stupid printer decided to eat something of hers rather than a receipt for a client. But she needed the printout in order to get in. That darn printer would not ruin her plans to finally have some fun!

Jill yanked on the jammed sheet of paper, extracting it as though opening a Chinese fan, fold by fold. "All right, you silly old thing. Are you going to play nice now?" Offering up a prayer to the god of crappy computers, she returned to the e-ticket email, clicked print again and watched. "Thank heavens." Her printer appeared to be cooperating.

"Okay. Now then, what good joke did Charlene send me?" She opened the email.

"Top Ten Things to Avoid on Halloween"

Never —

Interrupting yet again, the printer started to eat the page, making a horrendous squeaking sound. "But you were being so good!"

Oh well. There wasn't enough time to deal with it anymore. She grabbed a knife from her worktable, shut off the printer from hell and slashed the page free. Luckily, the e-ticket and confirmation number were on the top half.

She tucked the ticket into her purse and for the third time, clicked to open Charlene's email.

Her computer froze.

Jill stuck her tongue out at her computer as she powered down. Okay, obviously she wasn't supposed to read that email tonight. Too bad. It would've been fun to see how many of those so-called rules she could have broken.

She glanced at the wall clock. Only five minutes remaining. She swallowed her grin, reminding herself to stay professional.

Screw it! Closing five minutes early was hardly cause for anyone to be upset. Hurrying about, she pulled the display buckets from the front sidewalk and began tucking all the necessary delicate blooms into the refrigerators.

The bell on the door jingled merrily behind her. Fudge! She hadn't locked it yet.

Turning to the latecomer, she offered up her best retail smile. Hopefully, the fun at *Silver Twilight* wouldn't run out before she got there.

* * * * *

By the time Jill had escaped work, showered, dressed up, discovered her nylons had holes instead of feet, rushed to the corner store, put on her new pair while driving, and finally arrived at *Silver Twilight*, the party was in full swing. People were talking, mingling, drinking...having fun. The music was loud, and servers weaved through the crowd handling drink orders. It was the definition of organized chaos.

Devils, pirates and warriors shared the dance floor with vixens, French maids and a few dominatrices. Most everyone was dressed in dark shades, the most common colors vamp red and soulless black.

Her sparkly white fairy costume with petite silver gossamer wings made her stick out like a sore thumb.

No, she chastised herself, not like a sore thumb. She was unique and original. And so out of place she suddenly wondered what the heck she was doing there.

Butterflies fluttered wildly in her stomach. As much as she'd been anticipating tonight, looking around at the room full of costumed people trying to make a love connection, she realized she had no idea what to do next. Should she just jump in and start dancing? Maybe buy a drink, then walk around hoping someone would talk to her? Paste a smile on her face, praying it made her look friendly and approachable rather than three sheets to the wind?

She shook her head and sighed. No wonder she was still single. She had no clue about this kind of stuff.

An overweight vampire, blood smeared on both of his chins, winked at her as he sauntered into the bathroom. She stifled her giggle. Okay, maybe she wouldn't be a complete failure with the men tonight. But should she wait around for another vampire? A pirate maybe? What about one of the knights in rusty armor?

Wait a minute. Why should she wait around for some clown, or cowboy, or whatever that thing in the corner was to come to her? Tonight she was a fairy. And as a fairy, there was no reason she couldn't flit around, grant wishes, flirt profusely and have a darn good time in the process.

Jill took a deep breath and thrust her way into the crowd. She expected to be bounced back out, rejected with a big red "vetoed" stamp on her forehead, but instead the swarm swallowed her up, welcoming her into their midst.

The rest of her worry evaporated as she noticed a familiar face on the dance floor. Jake, who co-owned *Rare and Unusual Imports*, was dancing and laughing, surrounded by a group of women all vying to be the one he took home that night. His eyes met hers and he grinned, gesturing for her to join them.

Not one to turn down an invitation to dance, she smiled and weaved her way toward him, already beginning to move to the music.

* * * * *

Arden snarled inwardly as he scanned the festive crowd. With the way the women were dressed, it was more like a flashers convention than a costume party. Everywhere he looked, breasts spilled out the top of too-tight spandex. Disgusting. Appreciating beautiful women was one thing, but watching them use their bodies to try to hook some poor fool for a night was almost painful. Was there not a decent woman in the whole place?

An all too familiar voice mentally interrupted his internal tirade. *You're growling again. No wonder you're still sitting by yourself.*

Arden cursed the telepathic, empathic and downright annoying connection. *Get out of my head, Leo.*

If you're not even going to try, then why are we here? Through the crowd, Leo shot Arden the usual scowl.

I thought there'd be potential here, not a roomful of women only interested in a quick lay in the back alley.

Oh ye of little faith. You see my following. There's tons of potential.

Arden scanned the group of women surrounding Leo, then turned his back on all of them. *Big deal. We're not here just to get laid.*

Leo's annoyance permeated Arden's consciousness. *Dammit. This was your idea in the first place. "We're running out of time," you said. "We can't give up yet," you said. "We can still find the one." All of that bullshit and now you're backing out?*

Arden downed the rest of his beer and gestured for the bartender to hand him another. *This wasn't what I had in mind.*

*You know what, Arden, if you're going to be a dick and give up, maybe you should just pick yourself out a vamp, maid, dominatrix or whatever and at least get laid one last—*Leo's spiel came to an abrupt halt.

Wondering what had caused the interruption, Arden glanced back toward Leo, but his gaze was drawn to someone else. A woman, dressed in sparkling white and silver, weaved through the crowd as Leo continued. *Or how about a fairy? Now, she definitely has potential.*

For the first time that night, hope stirred inside of Arden. The beautiful fairy glowed as she moved, unknowingly portraying a bright innocence that made her outshine every other woman in the room. Shoulder-length brown hair framed a heart-shaped face. Wide brown eyes seemed to watch everything at once, unabashedly soaking in the world around her. She was pure and sweet and exactly what he was looking for.

A moment of guilt slashed through him. Did she deserve to be pulled into their cursed existence?

Did they have a choice?

Leo interrupted his troubled thoughts. *If you're not interested...*

I am, Arden fairly growled.

Good, Leo replied smugly. *Because it looks like our fairy queen is thirsty.*

Chapter Two

Jill spied an empty barstool and her aching feet turned longingly in that direction. After putting in a full day of standing at work, then dancing nonstop for forty-five minutes, she was ready for the sit, drink and chat-with-whoever-was-nearby part of tonight's festivities.

Breaking from the dance floor, she made her way along a row of small tables, aiming for the short set of stairs leading to the bar. Jill passed table after table of flirting couples, heads pressed close to hear each other over the pounding music. She even saw the double-chinned vampire from earlier, cuddled up with a latex-clad goddess of equally dynamic proportions. She grinned. Love—or at least lust—was in the air tonight.

At the last table next to the stairs, what could only be described as a gaggle of women surrounded someone Jill could not yet see. A few even leaned over the railing from above, smiling and flirting with whoever was seated below. They all laughed in unison and one of them moved, giving Jill an opportunity to see what all the fuss was about.

Wow.

Double wow.

No wonder so many women were hanging around his table. The man had one of those classically beautiful faces, as though a sculptor had taken his time, meticulously carving out every rich detail of expression, the sharp arch of each golden eyebrow, the proud, aristocratic nose, down to the sinful expanse of his mouth. White blond hair disappeared over his shoulders and down his back. Long, dark blond eyelashes framed almond-shaped amber eyes that sparkled with mirth, as though he knew a secret that all the women were desperate to learn.

The closer she got to him, the closer she wanted to get to him.

He sat crookedly, one arm resting on the table, the other casually lying along the back of his chair. Although clad in dark colors, mostly grays and browns, unlike the rest of the crowd, he would never blend in. He was a royal leader holding court, mesmerizing the women with his mere presence.

Too bad Jill wasn't one to compete. With a bevy of eager babes at his disposal, the man was probably a player anyway.

She turned away from the blond god and, resting her hand on the railing, began to climb the few steps to the bar. For a split second, a warm masculine hand covered hers, fingertips clasping possessively around her wrist before retreating.

Who had touched her? Jill looked down, expecting to see a red flush where her skin tingled. There was only one man close enough to lay his hand on her. She turned her gaze toward him as he straightened in his chair. Her breath caught as his amber eyes locked with hers. Awareness flooded from where her hand and wrist still tingled, to every cell of her body. His eyes danced, those full lips curling up into a knowing smile. She returned his smile, her heart thumping wildly against her rib cage.

No wonder he had a harem ready to serve him. His smile alone could charm the cheap spandex off any woman in the room.

Too bad she wasn't just any woman. Wanting to avoid temptation, she tried to break from the blond man's stare, afraid if she didn't, she'd launch herself over the railing and into his lap. Instead, she rammed full force into someone at the top of the stairs.

"Whoa, there. I got you." Strong arms wrapped around her waist, pulling her flush against a warm, male body, keeping her from careening backward down the stairs.

Trying to regain her mental balance as well as her physical, she grabbed onto his arms and got a handful of rock-hard muscle.

She squeezed her hands, getting a firmer grasp of his biceps. This man could easily bench-press a truck. He was probably one of *Silver Twilight's* bouncers, sent to kick her out for excessive levels of drooling.

Prepared to state her case, claiming dehydration and possible chemical reactions from the glitter makeup sprinkled lightly across her face, she lifted her head. Her stomach dropped to the tips of her tired toes as she looked at her rescuer's face.

Holy moly! Two hot men in a row. Where had these hunks been hiding all night? Although this man was an exact opposite of the blond god. He was dark. Rough-edged. Beautiful in a sexy, dangerous, probably-shouldn't-take-him-home-to-mom kind of way.

Wavy dark brown hair fell raggedly to his shoulders. Dark eyebrows slashed deliciously over black eyes deep as night. Strong cheekbones complimented his sturdy nose and late-night stubble covered his jaw. His mouth tilted up questioningly as he spoke. "You okay?"

She nodded, not quite able to get the words past her lips. His voice was deep, almost more of a growl. He should have scared her, the whole package of dark, rugged male. But she wasn't frightened. Instead, her body reacted to his nearness, heating from the inside out. Between this man, and her brush with the hot blond god earlier, her internal temperature had skyrocketed.

One of his arms slipped from around her waist, brushing her flyaway hair back into place.

Realizing that if she didn't say something soon he'd probably think her an imbecile, she grasped for the comfort of the line she'd been using all night. "Need a wish granted?" she asked, forcing her voice to come out light and flirty.

His mouth widened in a crooked grin but before he could answer, someone bumped into him from behind. His arm circled tighter around her waist, pulling her even closer against the warmth of his body. Now within licking distance of his neck, she indulged her curiosity and inhaled, taking in his scent. He smelled like the outdoors, like the wind on a hot summer day.

Warm lips pressed against her ear, his breath caressing her neck. She suppressed a needy shiver as he spoke. "You grant wishes? Have a drink with me?"

Jill wondered if screaming yes and dancing a jig would be an inappropriate response. She turned her head toward him to answer. His lips were so close, she wanted to trace them with her tongue, to see if he tasted like sunshine, too.

Instead, she licked her own dry lips, and said, "Wish granted."

Keeping an arm around her, he guided them through the crowd to a small table set up as an afterthought in the far corner next to the bar. He gestured for a server, while settling her into a chair.

She finally got a chance to study the man whose body was most definitely worth falling down stairs for. Heavy black boots, black jeans and a gray shirt with a weathered black leather jacket completing the look. Guessing by the way he wore everything so comfortably, it was more normal attire than a costume.

He took a seat across from her, then, resting his forearms on the table, leaned forward, closing the distance between them. "So, just how many wishes are you willing to grant me?"

She matched him, leaning forward and speaking conspiratorially. "Depends on what they are."

"My first wish is to know your name."

Sticking with the comfort of her fairy persona she said, "Tonight I'm a fairy, escaped from my world for a few hours of mischief and mayhem. But when my wings disappear tomorrow, I'll be plain ol' Jill Evans again."

"Certainly not plain, Jill." He shook his head, his gaze sweeping over her before returning to her face. "And tonight I am a great warrior from a strange world, seeking freedom I have long been denied. Tomorrow I'll simply be Arden Griffin, graphic designer extraordinaire. Are you in need of a battle won? A website built? Or maybe my warrior can rescue your fairy and we can escape our worlds together?"

"And then what?" Even though she knew this was only a game, she found herself caught up in the fairy tale he was spinning.

"And then we live happily ever after, or so they say…" The tips of his fingers lightly brushed over hers, and her heart rate accelerated, feeling like it would beat its way right out of her chest. Then he winked and gave her a lighthearted grin. "But who really believes that stuff anyway?"

The moment was interrupted by the appearance of a server. Jill smiled up at the woman and placed her order, then waited for Arden to do the same. She took that moment to catch her breath and regain control of her senses. This man was overwhelming in every meaning of the word. Tall, broad-shouldered, dark and intense, yet with a sense of humor and a way with the fantastical that seemed to contradict his outward appearance. So how much was real and how much was a part of the fantasy character he was portraying for the night?

When the server left, Arden's gaze returned to Jill. "So, my fairy queen, Jill. What do you do when you're not granting wishes?"

"I own *Jill's Bloomers*," she replied. "It's a flower shop."

His eyes lit up. "On the corner of Hayden and Third," he said as though continuing her sentence. "Your window displays always grab my attention. I think it's your use of colors and shapes in composition. They beckon to the designer in me. But then I always think to myself, 'I don't need any flowers' and I keep on going. Boy, am I an idiot, huh? Look at what I've been missing all this time." His gaze washed over her face, centering on her eyes.

"You've been missing out on the best flower arrangements in town," she teased, unable to think of anything else to say. It wasn't like she heard this kind of stuff everyday. At least not about herself. Her shop, yes. But the way he was looking at her led her to believe that flowers were the last thing on his mind.

"Well, I'll have to change that in the future." Arden was about to say something more when their drinks arrived, brought by an incredibly well-built and handsome bald man. The two men exchanged handshakes and grins. "Diesel, I'm surprised you're getting your hands dirty."

"Hey, now. I don't just run the place," Diesel said, making his point by grabbing a towel from his back pocket and wiping off the table.

"No, you're a workaholic just like me." Arden shook his head, a self-deprecating smirk on his face.

"Add me to that list." Jill laughed. "It sounds like we all need to get out more."

"*Silver Twilight's* my mistress and she's not very forgiving if I take a night off." Diesel glanced around the club, the pride evident in his demeanor. "And I haven't found anyone willing to play second fiddle." He held his hand out to Jill. "I'm Diesel."

Arden shifted forward. "Shit, I'm sorry. Jill, this is Diesel, he owns this place. And Diesel, this is Jill, she owns *Jill's Bloomers*."

Her hand was swallowed up in Diesel's. "It's great to meet you," she said.

"The pleasure's all mine." Diesel let go of Jill's hand and when she lowered it back to the table, Arden moved his hand close to hers.

"So, Diesel, what brings you over here?" Arden asked.

"Actually, I just wanted to thank you again for the website. This whole party never would've happened without your redesign and addition of all the online contact stuff that you claim to have thrown in for free."

"All in a day's work, man. I'm glad it's working for you, though. This gig's a hit." Arden smiled and purposefully returned his gaze to Jill.

"And that's my cue to leave," Diesel grinned. "You both have fun. Drinks are on the house." He headed back to the bar and the crowd waiting there.

Arden watched Diesel walk away and breathed a sigh of relief. He genuinely liked the man, but he didn't want to share Jill with Diesel for even a minute.

The clock was ticking and he wanted to make every moment count, wanted to take his time with her, court her, prove himself to her, because after eighteen years of looking, he knew she was the one. But taking his time wouldn't be possible. There were only three nights left.

Shit. Why couldn't he have met her before? What he needed from her was too much to expect anyone to give in such a short period of time. Maybe he should just walk away now, give up, let her go to find another man—hell, maybe even Diesel—who could give her a future without sacrifice.

But that thought left emptiness in his gut, and made anger burn across his flesh. Maybe this was his true curse. After so many years of looking, to finally find the one who could make his world right again, only to lose her forever because time had run out.

Jill took a drink from her beer, then cocked her head to the side and gave him a concerned smile. "You okay? You got quiet. Don't tell me I'm boring you already."

"No, actually quite the opposite."

"Uh-oh. Is that good or bad?"

"It's good. Very good." He was about to reach for her hand, ask her to dance, something to get his mind off the big picture and focused on just Jill Evans, but she beat him to the punch.

Jill downed the rest of her beer and pushed her chair back. "Do you dance? Or...or...do you want to?" She gave him a glowing smile, but he noticed the nervousness in her eyes.

"You read my mind." This time he did take her hand as he swept her onto the dance floor. The first slow song of the night was playing, encouraging interested couples to get a little closer. A man crooned a ballad of love lost as Arden pulled Jill into his embrace. She settled against him as though they'd danced this way a thousand times before, one hand curled over his shoulder, the other still clasped in his.

His free hand rested on the small of her back, holding her as tight as he dared. She relaxed against him, her face turned into his neck rather than away, her breath a sweet sigh whispering across his skin. A sign of trust he was so afraid to shatter. Her soft hair brushed against his cheek, and he inhaled, breathing in the scent of wild strawberries.

You look enraptured, Leo said. *Is she what we expected?*

Even more so, Arden replied. *She's the one.*

Right. Sure. We've been down this road before, and it always ends with the woman running away from the "crazy freaks of nature".

Don't give me shit. I just know, okay? Arden spotted Leo exiting *Silver Twilight*, a tall blonde on his arm. *And the blonde?*

Another option. If the fairy queen isn't what you claim —

She is.

I hope you're right.

There was no need to respond. They both knew what would happen if she wasn't.

Too soon, the last strains of the ballad morphed into a raw techno beat. Couples around them broke apart, adjusting their movements to match the music. The primal pounding of the bass urged him to throw her over his shoulder, to take her away from the masses. All his muscles flexed and tightened as he fought against his animal instincts. The mild annoyance he'd felt toward Diesel's earlier intrusion had heightened a hundredfold. If he didn't get her alone soon, he knew his control would snap. Although being alone with her would be another trial in and of itself.

Jill lifted her head and graced him with a beautiful smile. "The song's over," she said wistfully.

"And I'm not ready to let you go," he admitted.

A group pushed past them and someone chortled, "Geez, you guys. Get a room."

A blush swiftly covered Jill's face and traveled down her neck beneath her costume. She tried to pull away from him, but instead he kept an arm around her and drew her off the dance floor toward the exit.

"Let's get out of here." It came out as a growl and he cursed the need that had him near crazy, then added in a calmer voice, "Please."

She stopped in her tracks and tipped her head up, meeting his gaze. Her cheeks still glowed pink. "Where?"

Although she seemed willing, he heard the uncertainty in her voice. Shit. He was scaring her already. "Anywhere," he said softly, hoping to reassure her. "I just… Let's just get away from the crowds and the noise so we can talk. There's an all-night diner I go to sometimes. Can I take you there? Buy you dinner? Coffee? Or where do you want to go? It's up to you."

Jill was quiet for a few moments, long enough for him to convince himself that the asshole with the "get a room" comment had ruined things between them and that she was trying to come up with a good excuse to get as far away from him as possible. Then her lips tilted up in a flirty smile. "You're right. It's time for us to make our escape." She started walking again. "So my warrior, where should we fly away to?"

Her acceptance brought immediate relief. Together they walked out of the club toward the parking lot. "You like to fly?" he asked with a grin as he motioned to his custom motorcycle, parked in front. Now free of *Silver Twilight's* sensory overload, he felt more at ease. The night air was crisp, but not too cool. Perfect night for a ride, but he wasn't sure he should suggest it. Jill looked a little too sweet and innocent. Like asking her if she wanted to go for a ride would give her the wrong idea.

"Wow. This is yours?" Her eyes wide with appreciation, she began circling his bike. Then giving him a pleading look, she asked, "Can I touch it?"

Oh God, she was going to kill him. Those words coming out of that angelic mouth. And the desire in her eyes. Okay, maybe the desire wasn't yet for him, but it was a start. He nodded his approval and she knelt down next to his bike, caressing the green flames on the tank.

"Yeah. My little toy." He knelt next to her. "You've got wings to fly, but have you ever been on one of these?"

"Not one like this. One of my brothers was a bike mechanic back home. He used to take me riding, but I've never thrown a leg over a custom like this. Wow!"

Her hands continued to slide all over his Steed Quarterhorse SE. It was obvious that she knew what she was looking at and he didn't even care that she was getting fingerprints all over the paint. When he'd first gotten the bike, he'd caressed it, too. This motorcycle was no average showroom model. He'd had it custom-made. In fact, there wasn't much on it that hadn't been turned or smoothed by hand. She smiled over at him. "Let me guess. With a bike like this, you don't even own a car, do you?"

"Nope." He shifted his stance, his erection growing larger as he watched every stroke of her graceful hands on the motorcycle.

"Does this thing really have the hidden LED gauges? My brother only told me about them. I've never seen them. Sheesh! It's been ages since I've even been near a motorcycle. And never a machine like this."

"Y-you know about hidden gauges?" Arden put the key in the ignition and turned it, allowing all the gauges in the rearview mirrors and on the tank to light up.

"You have to take me for a ride," she blurted out.

"Well, shit, you're good...granting my wish before I could even speak it. But you're going to freeze in that sweet costume of yours."

"Oh yeah. Ummm..." She glanced around the parking lot, her eyes twinkling mischievously. She backed away from him, lifting her hands up reassuringly. "Don't go anywhere, okay? I'll be right back. I'm going to grab some jeans from my car."

Within the time it took him to fantasize about helping her out of her skirt, reminding himself that he shouldn't be thinking that way, and pulling a spare helmet from his saddlebag, she was already back. And he'd never seen a woman look so good. She'd thrown an oversized purple sweater over her white leotard top, and a pair of jeans replaced the skirt, hugging her thighs and tapering down... Dammit, she'd caught him looking. Her grin widened and she wiggled excitedly, her hips doing a quick side to side. He couldn't help it, he laughed. She was something else. Something special. And now he wanted her even more.

He forced his attention down to the helmets in his hand, hoping he'd regain control of himself. When he returned his gaze to her, he realized she was missing one thing. He set the helmets down on the seats, took off his leather jacket and held it out to her. "I wouldn't want you to get too cold. You know how it can get."

Tentatively, she reached out to take his coat. "But what about you? Won't you get cold?"

Like that would be possible with her body close to his. "I insist. Besides, this shirt is thicker than it looks." He plucked the sleeve of his lightweight cotton top, hoping she'd believe his lie.

She slid his jacket on over her sweater. It was so large it could probably wrap around her twice. For some reason that turned him on even more, and he had to force himself to get on the bike and out of there or he would end up throwing her against the bike and consuming her like she was consuming him.

He handed her the emerald green helmet, then put on his dark green one, snapping the clasp into place. "Let me know if you need help adjusting the strap," he offered but she'd already settled it on her head. "You sure you're ready for this?"

"Oh heck yeah! I'm always game for a good ride." She bit her lower lip, her face pinking in a way he was already becoming addicted to. "I-I mean...yeah...I've always wanted to go for a ride on a custom chopper, so let's go."

He grinned and shook his head knowingly. "There's a good diner just up the street. We can get coffee or something. Sound good?"

"Sounds great."

Arden mounted his bike and she climbed on behind him, her body rocking against his as she situated herself. Her hands settled on his shoulders, then smoothed down to his biceps. Maybe she didn't know where to put her hands? He had several inappropriate suggestions, but stuck with something more suitable so she wouldn't think him a pervert. "Sorry, there's no bar on the back to hold on to, and the tank is—"

"That's okay. I prefer to hold on to the rider." Answering his unspoken request, she wrapped her arms around him, resting her hands flat against his abdomen. With her breasts pressed against his back, her thighs surrounding his, and her hands inches from his cock, it was all he could do to start the bike and get it upright. If he hadn't spent over half his life riding, he probably wouldn't have made it out of the parking lot without wiping out.

Throughout the short ride, the wind whipping past cooled his fevered body. But all it took was one shift of Jill's hand, bringing it flush against his cock—a move he was sure she didn't realize she'd made—and his blood was boiling again. His raging erection banged against the tank. He was stuck. Either he could keep banging his cock into the tank, or slide backward, nestling deeper into Jill's body. Which would probably just make his erection grow impossibly larger and he'd still manage to dent the damn tank and bruise his dick.

He slowed down as the diner came into view, wondering how he'd be able to hide the very prominent bulge in his pants when he got off the bike.

"Arden?" Her voice came from behind his right ear as he coasted to a stop on the street in front of the diner. "Don't stop. Please. I just want to keep going. If that's okay with you…"

She had no idea. "I'm always game for a ride, too. Is there somewhere in particular you'd like to go?"

"No. Anywhere's fine. On this bike…with you…the diner just wasn't far enough of a ride."

He checked his gas gauge. Still full. Arden wondered what she'd say if he told her he never wanted to stop.

*

Chapter Three

Jill couldn't remember the last time she'd felt so free. The Pacific shone dark and beautiful on her left, and she had her arms around a man who'd quickly become irresistible. She had no idea what the rest of the night would bring, and she didn't want to know. She just wanted to let go and live.

As he slowed down to make a turn, Jill gathered her courage and gave word to her desires. "Arden, go faster."

"What?" he called over his shoulder.

"I said, faster, Arden."

"Are you sure?"

"Yes! I want to fly with you."

"Your wish is my command. Now hold on tight." He twisted the throttle and let the chopper fly.

Mile after mile whipped past them, exchanging the lights of Talisman Bay for endless coastline. Everything was perfect. The sky was clear, the brilliant stars adding to the magic of the night. This was nothing at all like riding with her brother.

Jill's heart kept pace with the whirring of the engine. She'd never felt this alive — or turned on. The faster he went, the more she wanted him. Was she becoming an adrenaline junkie, or just an Arden junkie? Her entire body vibrated, and she couldn't blame it solely on the ride. It was mostly the rider who made her skin tingle, her body burn, and her insides clench with unfulfilled yearning. The constant vibration between her legs only accelerated the sexual desire that had begun the moment she'd fallen into Arden's arms at *Silver Twilight*.

When they passed a small hotel, she bit her lip to keep from begging him to stop. How would that look? Don't stop at the café for dinner, but please stop at this hotel for dessert? Because as much as she wanted to have sex with Arden, she didn't want him to think she was a one-night stand kind of woman.

Keeping one arm tight around his waist, she let the other hand wander, stroking up to his chest. The muscles beneath her exploring palm tightened and she shivered at the sign of barely restrained power. The smell of earth and sunshine surrounded her, in the leather jacket she wore, and coming directly from Arden himself. It was heady and addictive and she couldn't inhale deep enough to satisfy her craving for all things Arden.

He slowed down, pulling to the side of the road. Twisting to face her, he said, "Are you afraid of heights?"

"No. Why?"

"There's a really pretty spot off the beaten path that I want to show you."

"Hey, I'm just along for the ride," she teased. "You can take me anywhere."

"Don't tempt me, Jill." He grinned, his teeth shining white in the darkness. He turned back around, but before pulling onto the road, he ran his hand down her leg from thigh to knee. But this wasn't a casual caress; this was a promise of things to come. His fingertips claimed and possessed, his hand circling, kneading, burning through her jeans and making her flesh beg for more of his touch.

Wherever he was taking her, she hoped he got there fast.

A few minutes later, Arden left the main road, slowly weaving along a dirt path. When it became too narrow to continue, Arden drew the bike to a halt, turning off the engine. She expected the sudden silence to surprise her, but the roar of the engine was replaced by the roar of the ocean somewhere in the distance. Not to mention the roar of blood pulsing anxiously through her veins.

He took off his helmet, hanging it from one of the handlebars before brushing a hand through his hair. She matched his movements, removing hers as well, but unless her arm grew an extra six inches she wouldn't be able to hang her helmet. Still she tried, wrapping herself around him like she was playing a game of Twister.

"Here. Let me," he said, taking the helmet from her outstretched hand. Before she could thank him he mumbled, "Aw, hell," and crushed his lips over hers.

Arden did taste like sunshine. The heat blistered her lips, soaking into her body. But it wasn't enough. Wrapping her arms around him, she slammed their bodies together, opening her mouth, begging for more.

The helmet thumped to the dirt as Arden brought his hand to her cheek, his tongue sweeping recklessly into her mouth. The kiss became a battle as they both fought for more of each other. Tongues tangling, teeth nipping, groans ripping from their very souls. An arm swept beneath her, and in one swift movement, she was lifted off the bike, spun around and lowered, her legs straddling Arden. She didn't know how he kept his balance and the bike from falling. It was all she could do to breathe.

She shrugged off his jacket, no longer needing it to stay warm. Both of his hands trailed underneath her sweater, massaging the middle of her back. She wrapped her legs around his waist, bringing her crotch flush against his erection. He groaned and his hands lowered, cupping her ass, grinding their sexes together. The hot friction made her gasp and squirm, desperately seeking relief. At what point would the denim separating them burst into flame?

Arden stood up, taking her with him. Much to her dismay, the kiss had to end or they'd fall over in a heap of hot flesh and metal. Untangling their legs from the bike and each other, Arden lowered Jill to the ground, then leaned the bike over onto its kickstand. He paused, catching his breath. "Although you probably won't believe this, I didn't bring you here just to ravish you."

Trying to hide how her knees were still shaking, she bent over and picked the leather jacket off the ground, brushing off some leaves and dirt before hanging it on the bike. "Really? Well that's disappointing. You're pretty good at ravishing."

He chuckled. "Well, we'll get back to that in a minute. First, there's something I want to show you." Taking her hand, they began walking between trees and bushes, the air growing misty with sea breeze.

They broke through the trees and Jill froze in wonder. The earth fell away less than a dozen feet from where she stood. Beyond that, the great Pacific Ocean filled her vision in all its vast glory. It blurred outward and upward, melding with the star-filled sky. Jill crept closer to the edge of the embankment, Arden's arm wrapped protectively around her waist. There, secluded from the road by trees and high above the crashing waves, the cliff top afforded a view for miles.

"It's magnificent," she murmured, almost afraid to speak and break the magic of the night.

"I stumbled across this place a few years ago, right after moving to Talisman Bay. It's become my favorite secret escape spot. Come here." He tugged on her hand, taking her closer to the edge, pointing off in the distance. "See those lights over there? That's the Talisman Bay pier. You should see it at Christmas time."

"I bet it's beautiful."

"From here, all the twinkle lights look like fireworks with the spray distorting them. We'll have to come back here in a couple months so I can show you."

"I'd like that." She smiled up at him, her breath catching when she met his eyes. No one had ever looked at her like that before. Desire...need...yet it was more than that, something deeper. Like she alone could make his world right—or like she was the only person in his world. But that was crazy. Not yet. Not after only a couple hours together.

"T-thank you," she whispered. "For tonight. For everything. It's been amazing."

"It's not over yet." Both his hands cradled her neck, his thumbs framing her face, running up and down, caressing her cheeks.

"Thank God," she whispered as he leaned in and kissed her. He brushed his lips over hers, back and forth, softly, taking his time. His mouth teased along her jaw, his teeth lightly scraping down her neck. Then he moved back to her mouth and started all over again.

This was more than a seduction. It was a slow, sweet worshipping, making her feel cherished and adored. Yet beneath his tenderness, there was a sense of urgency in the way he kissed her, the way he held her. Like the moment would shatter if he pressed her too close. It was such a contradiction from their frantic entanglement on the motorcycle. Why was he holding back now?

When his lips returned to hers, she opened her mouth, rejoicing when he accepted her invitation and swept his tongue inside.

Arden had mastered the art of kissing. He kissed with his whole body, his mouth like a live wire that filled her from head to toe with electric energy. Unlike the duel of earlier, this time his tongue slowly thrust and retreated, mimicking two bodies in the throes of lovemaking. Her fingers dug into his shoulders and she arched into him. She wanted to melt and explode, to find a way to relieve the pressure building inside.

He growled, sliding his hands from her neck to hips, arousing the flesh beneath her clothing. Not breaking the kiss, he lifted her into his arms, taking her down to a small patch of grass beneath a lone tree. His hair brushed against her neck and she wanted to purr, wanted to feel those wayward strands tease all along her body. The thought alone had her letting out a strangled moan. She couldn't remember ever being this hot before, to the point she was ready to rip a man's clothes off and take advantage of him.

He pulled away, his breath ragged, arms trembling as he held himself just above her body. "Jill...damn, you're killing me."

"Sorry," she whispered, lifting up and kissing his jaw.

"No," he rasped. "I mean, you deserve better than this."

"I wouldn't be here if I didn't want to be."

His eyes darkened and he kissed her again, fully lowering his body over hers. She loved the feeling of his weight pressing into her, his heat burning through their clothes. His erection throbbed against her thigh and she shifted her leg, rubbing his cock through the denim.

A low growl of pained desire came from deep inside Arden. He broke from the kiss, his eyes pinpoints of flame in the darkness. Desire. Fear. Regret. Hope. Her heart ached at the mix of emotions visible there. He didn't outwardly portray vulnerability, but she knew it was there, just beneath the surface. Unsure of what to say, she tried to show that she felt a connection to him, too. She stroked his jaw, his face, tracing along his temples. With a harsh groan he buried his face into her neck and began to love her further.

While his mouth traced along the neckline of her sweater, his hands skimmed down her sides, coming to rest on the slopes of her breasts. He cradled and caressed, his fingertips lightly brushing over her erect nipples. She cried out as a shaft of desire shot from her nipples to deep inside her body. Liquid heat filled her, making her feel like she was being boiled alive.

There was still too much clothing separating them. Jill sat up and pulled the sweater over her head. Arden nodded his approval then lowered his head to her breast. Through the thin fabric of her leotard, his warm mouth suckled, his teeth tugging on the nub of flesh. His other hand slid down her abdomen, stopping when his fingers hit the zipper of her jeans. She whimpered, pushing up against his hands and mouth and body. "Arden..." she moaned, tossing her head back and forth.

There was a rustle in the bushes to her right. Visions of rapists, murderers, and other creepy things from the late night news filled her mind. Could it be the wind? No, the wind had died down. And Arden hadn't noticed anything—was she imagining it? She blinked, trying to focus in the dark.

Glowing lion eyes blinked back at her. Before she could draw breath to scream, a lion jumped back into the brush.

"Oh my God!" Jill scrambled out from underneath Arden, yanking on his arm, trying to pull him with her.

"Jill? What's wrong?"

She pointed a shaking hand in the direction the lion had disappeared. But had it even existed in the first place? It had been so quick...

He lifted her to standing, his arms surrounding her protectively. Arden's concerned face filled her vision. "Jill? What did you see? What's wrong? Was someone there?"

Trying to come to grips with what she'd just seen—or thought she'd seen—Jill looked back into the bushes. Nothing was there. "A lion...I swear I just saw a lion. It was watching us..." She shook her head. "I must be seeing things..."

"We should go just in case," he said.

"Yeah." Jill swallowed hard, her eyes still trained on the last location of the lion her mind had most probably fabricated. "I'm sorry."

"It's okay, Jill." Grabbing her discarded sweater, Arden tore her away from the cliff and all the fiery passion they'd shared there. She threw one last glance behind her. No lion. Just the undisturbed beauty of coastline.

Arriving back at *Silver Twilight*, Arden parked next to her car. "You going to be okay?" he asked as they dismounted.

"Yes. I'm okay now. More ticked off at myself than anything. A lion? I mean, what was I thinking?" She sighed. "I'm sorry it ended that way—"

"Shhh…" He pressed a finger to her lips. "Can I see you tomorrow night? To avoid lions, we'll take it inside this time. My house? Dinner?"

"You cook?"

"And clean." He winked.

"Then I'll definitely be there." She smiled, relieved that he wasn't taking tonight as a blow off. "I get off work at five. I'm all yours after that."

He pulled his wallet from his back pocket, then handed her a business card. She traced her finger over the embossed lettering. "Griffin Designs—Arden Griffin—Owner" and a phone number beneath it.

"Call me in the morning and I'll give you directions to my place." As though sealing the deal, he placed a hand on her cheek and kissed her so sweetly, her knees weakened. His other hand trailed down, resting on her hip. "I'll see you then."

Chapter Four

Jill's stomach fluttered excitedly as she drove toward Arden's place. Today had felt insufferably long and even though she'd been remarkably busy, the day had dragged by. Especially after she'd spoken with Arden. All she'd wanted to do was close up shop and spend the day remembering the way he had kissed her. The way he used his whole body when he kissed, the strength, heat and power of him melding with her. Every part of her had felt that touch, even though he hadn't touched the parts of her that burned the hottest.

Jill blushed at the memory. She wasn't the type to have sex on the first date, but she'd been more than willing last night. Right there on the cliff overlooking the deep dark ocean. If she hadn't been spooked by the lion, or what she'd thought was a lion, she would've happily gone for it.

"Lions and tigers and bears, oh my," she sang in a high-pitched voice. The stupid thing was that she still couldn't completely convince herself that she hadn't seen a lion. Although she knew it was near impossible that a wildcat would be prowling around the outskirts of Talisman Bay, in that brief moment it had seemed absolutely real.

She turned onto Arden's street and parked in front of his house. No lion was going to screw things up tonight. Grinning, she grabbed the bottle of wine she'd brought as her portion of tonight's dinner and practically skipped up to the house, following the flagstone walkway that led to the front door.

Before knocking she took half a second to assess herself, smoothing the wrinkles out of her pale pink sundress. Did she look too *Little House on the Prairie*? Darn it, she might as well have put on a bonnet and gone barefoot. She should have attempted a more casual, please-have-sex-with-me outfit. Although she was wearing tiny lace panties and a white lacy bra—not exactly über-vixen but it was the closest she got. But like he was going to see them underneath her Amish attire! Maybe if she loosened the laces over her breasts, exposed a little skin...

"Arden was right. He lucked out when you bumped into him last night."

Jill jumped and whipped around to face the man behind the voice, her heart practically beating out of her chest. But the surprise was far from over. "You? But..."

That same knowing smile she remembered from last night covered his face. In fact, he looked much the same, his long blond hair cascading down his back, amber eyes alight with mischief, his arms full of groceries.

Wait a second. Groceries? Just what was he doing here?

He looked pointedly at her arm, his smile widening. "You can lower the wine bottle. I'm just bringing home some stuff to make a salad. I'm not going to hurt you."

Jill looked over at her arm, realizing that she was hefting the bottle like a weapon. Smirking, she lowered the bottle. "Well, that's what you get for sneaking up on me."

He laughed, a rich golden sound that made her insides feel like putty. He shifted the bag of groceries into one arm, held out his hand and winked. "Sorry. We weren't properly introduced last night. I'm Leo."

The man's—Leo's—charm was just as apparent and appealing as it had been last night at *Silver Twilight*. It was like he immediately drew you inside of him, making you feel like you belonged, even when you were caught off guard by his overwhelming presence.

She mentally kicked herself in the rump, then, promising herself she'd ask about Arden in a second, she took Leo's offered hand. "I'm Jill." Her gaze wandered from his eyes to his dark green T-shirt, leather jacket and finally to his faded blue jeans.

For those few moments, Jill couldn't remember why she was there or who she was there to see. She shook it off, returning her gaze to Leo's face. Perhaps the blond god was more dangerous than appearances suggested.

"Jill, it's a pleasure."

Leo's hand was warm and firm, swallowing her smaller one. The same tingling sensation she'd felt last night when he touched her wrist assaulted her senses. What the...

The door behind her opened and a familiar deep voice said, "Hey, beautiful." Feeling like she'd been rescued from drowning, she turned toward Arden with a smile just in time for his lips to land soundly over hers.

Oh my...

Strong arms—Arden's arms—surrounded her and she melted against him, tipping her head back to give him better access. His tongue parted her lips and slipped inside. Her whole body reacted to his kiss, the intense longing and desire that had been floating around inside her all day flooding to the surface.

He pulled away and she blinked up at him, his dark eyes staring back down into hers. His hand cupped the base of her neck and he smiled. "I see you met my brother Leo."

She blinked again. "Brother?" No wonder she found Leo as irresistible as Arden. It must run in the genes—or jeans since they both knew how to fill out a pair. She chastised herself for noticing their matching asses—um...assets—then shot her gaze to Leo, who was watching their exchange with interest.

"Brother," Leo repeated. He squeezed her hand—she was still holding his hand?—then let it fall. "The brother who is wishing he hadn't let you go last night. Leave it to Arden to rub it in by bringing you home for dinner. Not that it bothers me. Tonight it's my turn to win you over." With a vibrant twinkle in his eyes and that telling phrase, he entered the house.

Jill knew her eyes were probably as wide as saucers. She expected Arden to say something, stake his claim, or even make fun of his brother. Instead he turned her in his arms so she was facing him, then kissed her again before leaning his forehead against hers. "I'm so glad you came tonight, Jill. I haven't stopped thinking about you all day."

"Feeling's mutual," she said breathlessly, her rapidly pounding heart somehow managing to stay inside her chest.

"Good...now do you mind that Leo's here? He'll be on his best behavior—which probably means you'll be flirted with nonstop." He grinned. "Not that I blame him for it, of course. But just say the word and I'll kick his ass to the curb."

"That won't be necessary," Jill said with a laugh. "I'm sure I can handle the both of you."

Jill waited to be struck down for that lie. What the heck was she thinking? It was one of those moments she wished she could freeze in time, dissect, and figure out exactly what to do next. Two hot men. Two brothers. And she'd be in the same house, spending the evening with both of them. Well, maybe Leo would bow out early. But it was his house, too. How could she expect him to bow out? It was too much to think about. Should she be worried? Nervous? Scared even?

Yeah, right. Try excited and enthusiastic. Truthfully, she had a feeling that Leo flirted with every woman who crossed his path, but the double attention was more than she was used to. Why shouldn't she enjoy it? As long as Arden didn't mind, why should she?

"You sure?" Arden asked.

"I'm sure." She nodded for emphasis. "It'll be fun."

"Well, good," Arden replied with a wicked grin, then took her by the hand and into the house.

Immediately she was hit with the aroma of garlic, herbs and tomato sauce.

"I hope you like spaghetti," Leo called from somewhere in the back of the house.

"Of course! Only heathens don't like spaghetti," she joked as Arden led her toward the kitchen and dining room area, taking the bottle of wine out of her hand. There was something more than just the scent of marinara sauce wafting around her. Like magic sparks were floating in the air, something about being in that house with those two men felt incredibly...well...stimulating.

Arden pulled out a sleek cushioned metal chair at the glass dinner table. "Please, have a seat. Dinner will be ready shortly."

"And it'll be good," Leo added. "Promise."

Jill wasn't sure who to reply to so she smiled instead. "Thank you." She watched as Arden joined his brother in the well-equipped kitchen. Swiftly, he grabbed wineglasses from a rack above the counter and proceeded to uncork the wine.

"You got that okay?" Arden motioned to Leo, who had a spoon in each hand, stirring the contents of two different pots on the stove.

"Easy as pie. Salad?"

"Definitely."

Arden brought Jill a glass of wine, setting it down gently on the glossy black placemat in front of her. He swirled his own liquid-filled glass. "Nice coloring, wouldn't you say?"

"Everything about her is delightful." Leo looked up from his stirring and winked. "Oh, you weren't talking about Jill, were you?"

She couldn't help but chuckle. What was it about these two guys? Why did she feel so at ease and really in the mood to enjoy everything they had to offer?

Everything? her inner slut taunted. She gulped, barely avoiding choking on her wine. Her libido could easily go into overdrive around these two. She had to remember that "everything" only included dinner and conversation. The rest was for Arden alone.

"Well, of course everything about her is wonderful, but shouldn't you pay more attention to what you're cooking?" Arden swallowed some wine before heading back into the kitchen.

"Only if you do. I'm nearly done and yet there's nary a scrap of lettuce chopped or carrot peeled. Just how do you intend on serving the first course before the main?" Leo tossed a tomato to Arden, which he caught in one hand.

He set his glass down and rolled his eyes. "Back to work." In moments, Arden had the salad ingredients sprawled over the countertop. Chopping, shredding, dicing, slicing, the man was an expert with a knife, taking care with the tomatoes, sloshing just enough dressing, shaking just the right amount of herbs into his masterpiece.

Swishing the contents of one of the pots, Leo produced a spaghetti noodle and walked over to Jill. "Tell me. How do you like your pasta? Is this al dente enough for you?" He leaned his fork close to her lips and she retrieved the noodle with a little slurp.

"I wish I was on the other end of that noodle." Leo grinned. "Good?"

"Yes." Jill laughed. "Perfect, actually. But would you be on the other end of the noodle or have me whipping you with it?"

"Hey now. There'll be no noodle-whipping without me involved." Arden chuckled as he lobbed a radish at Leo who adeptly caught it while returning to the kitchen.

"I'll whip the both of you. I'm an equal opportunity noodle-whipper."

The two of them stopped and gave her identical looks of interest. She laughed and took another swig of wine. Her shoulders were finally starting to unknot from the day spent leaning over her worktable. She hoped they'd completely quit aching within another few sips. Tonight held tons more potential than her average humdrum evening and she didn't want tight muscles interfering with any of the fun to be had.

Leo moved the spaghetti pot to a back burner, then glanced toward Arden and watched him expertly toss the salad. "Not bad, brother."

"You've never expected anything less, have you?"

"True. Very true, Arden. But the real test will be on the palate, won't it?" Leo looked at Jill and playfully raised an eyebrow. "Don't mind him. He's just showing off."

Arden slid his brother a look of amusement. "Let's see how that sauce of yours turns out, huh? Then we'll see who's showing off." He plucked a cherry tomato out of the salad bowl and walked over to Jill. The tomato glistened with oil from the salad dressing and with a sensual grin, Arden traced it along her sealed lips. "It's all in the presentation," he said huskily. "Then when the time is right, you can fully indulge."

Entranced, her mouth opened beneath the tomato. The burst of flavor startled her, but it tasted even better when Arden placed his mouth over hers. His tongue flicked out, stealing the oil from her lips. She shivered under the onslaught of taste and touch and knew she'd never eat a tomato again without thinking of this moment.

Arden had only just backed away when Leo stepped in his place, this time with a spoonful of sauce, his other hand ready to catch any stray drips. "The secret's in the sauce." He stared at her lips as she reached for the spoonful of what smelled like herbed tomato heaven.

"Tangy enough, I hope?" he asked.

She nodded, but then a drip escaped the corner of her mouth.

Leo wiped it away as though it never happened, but his eyes told another story. Their eyes met as they shared the intimate tingle of his skin grazing hers.

Jill looked away and licked her lips, tasting salad dressing and sauce, Leo and Arden. She wanted to close her eyes and moan, to get lost in the feast of the senses. Her body physically ached, her nipples tight, her inner thighs awash with yearning heat. This desire for both of them wasn't healthy, and she needed to calm her raging hormones and not let herself ruin the relationship she wanted with Arden. He may have said he was okay with his brother flirting with her, but she couldn't imagine he'd be okay with the thoughts running rampant through her head.

She spoke carefully, trying to keep her voice light and flirty so they wouldn't suspect her inner turmoil. "This is incredible. But you both should probably stop feeding me or I won't be hungry when dinner is ready."

"Don't lose interest yet," Arden said, refilling her wineglass as Leo retreated back to the stove. "If you like his concoctions so far, dessert's going to be heaven."

If she survived until dessert. At this point, it wouldn't surprise her if she spontaneously combusted halfway through dinner.

Arden returned to the kitchen and the men gathered plates and silverware, moving as though they were choreographed. When Arden dropped a fork, Leo's hand was right underneath it to capture the stray flatware as though it was second nature. They moved fluidly, almost in unison, Arden finding a spare hand to grab his wine as he followed Leo to the table.

The presentation of the fully loaded salad and hearty spaghetti marinara had Jill's mouth watering. Or was that because of the company? She wasn't sure, but their light dinner conversation kept her laughing and smiling, while each bite was a taste of heaven. The thought of dessert had her wondering how it could top such a dinner. Okay, maybe just hand her a can of whipped cream and let her coat the nearest male specimen. Either way, the dish would be delicious.

And she really should stop thinking like that. She was there for Arden. One man was enough for her, no matter how much she was enjoying the attentions of two.

"So, Jill, I already know you've got one motorcycling brother. Any other brothers or sisters?" Arden asked before taking another sip of wine.

"There are eight of us, actually. I've got four brothers and three sisters."

"Must be nice. All I've got is Tweedledum over here." Leo gestured at Arden with his fork before taking the last bite of his salad.

Arden tossed him a sideways glance as he wrangled up another forkful of spaghetti.

The way these two acted around each other was a fond reminder of home. Jill grinned at the brotherly...umm...affection. "Don't get me wrong, I love my family, but there's a reason I moved across the country. When you're part of a group like that, you never get to do anything on your own." She paused, struggling to put her feelings into words. "Sometimes that's a blessing. But I needed to prove to myself that I could succeed with no outside, well-meaning family help. That's why I moved here after college and opened *Jill's Bloomers*."

Arden nodded as he cleaned the last bite of spaghetti off his plate. "Well, I for one am glad you got here."

"And I'm sure I don't really need to second that, do I?" Leo charmed her with a grin while reaching for the nearly empty bottle of wine.

Jill caught a glimpse of the bottom edges of a tattoo peeking from beneath one shirtsleeve. He retracted his arm, hiding the four catlike legs. "You have a tattoo? What is it?"

After setting the bottle back down, Leo lifted his sleeve to reveal a lion proudly ready to pounce.

"Leo, the lion." Arden smirked, then lifted his sleeve to reveal an eagle in much the same vein, soaring while searching for its prey.

"And Arden, the eagle," Leo finished.

"Wow, they're beautiful. So lifelike." She leaned forward, tracing her finger over the lion on Leo's arm. "Did Arden tell you I saw a lion...well, thought I saw a lion last night?"

"Maybe you were just thinking of me while you were with my brother." Leo wiggled two perfectly arched golden eyebrows.

"Don't get your hopes up, Leo." Jill laughed. "Besides, I didn't know you had a lion tattoo until just now."

Leo's gaze remained intent on hers. "Maybe you recognized—"

"So Jill," Arden interrupted. "Do you have any tattoos?"

"Um, that would be a big no. Needle phobia." She rolled her eyes. "But yours are so beautiful it makes me wish I wasn't a scaredy-cat." She traced her fingers along the eagle's wings, spread wide in flight. "Let me guess, you designed them yourself, right?"

"Actually, we both did," Leo answered. "We co-own Griffin Designs."

"Wait a second. A lion and an eagle. The two animals together make up the mythological creature gryphon. So am I right? Is that how you two got your first names? Your parents had too much fun when they named you." Jill sat back in her seat, proud of her deductive skills.

Arden and Leo were quiet for longer than Jill expected, yet she had a feeling they were somehow communicating. She could feel tension rising between them. But why? What had she done? "What? Am I wrong? Did I screw up my mythology?"

"No. You're right." Arden grinned, but it looked forced. "You just surprised us. No one's made the connection before."

"At least not until we told them," Leo leaned over the table, taking Jill's hand. "But you're more understanding, more open-minded than everyone else."

More understanding? Confused, Jill looked to Arden for some type of clarification.

Arden shot his brother an irate glare before taking Jill's other hand and helping her to her feet. "Let's go into the living room while Leo perfects dessert."

Leo stood up, his body tight and angry. He grabbed the spaghetti platter, and strode into the kitchen. But Jill couldn't let him clear the table all by himself, didn't want the night to go downhill because of a dispute between the brothers she'd somehow unknowingly caused. "Where I come from, we all help." She began stacking up the salad bowls.

"But you're our guest, Jill," Arden argued half-heartedly, but he followed her lead, stacking up the plates. They both filed into the kitchen, depositing tableware in the sink and dishwasher.

"Jill? What are you doing?" Leo took the last few bowls out of her hands. "Arden, don't let her—"

"She insisted and I can't look her in the eye and say no." Arden threw out the used napkins.

"I don't blame you," Leo agreed. "I just didn't want the guest to see the dessert before it's perfect."

"Look, you two. If I'm the guest, I can do whatever I want, right?" She smiled at both of the unsuspecting brothers. They appeared startled, or unsure of themselves. She couldn't quite put her finger on it. But at least the tension between them seemed to have dissipated. "You look like you've never seen a person help before."

Arden regained himself first. "That's probably because we haven't." He leaned down and touched his lips to hers. "Thank you." His smile warmed her from the inside out, making her heart soar.

A cork popped from a wine bottle and she turned to see Leo pouring pink liquid into three glasses. "Okay, if our dear guest still wants to be helpful, she can take one glass and bring it into the living room. But if she grabs a second, Arden and I might have to tackle her." Leo winked as he handed the glass to Jill.

"Oh, all right. It's killin' me, though." She playfully reached for a second glass, only to have Arden snatch it out of her grasp.

He laughed and looked toward Leo. "Then again, maybe I should've let her take it, huh?"

Jill swatted at Arden as she headed into the living room. "So, what's this amazing dessert you two have planned?"

"An old favorite of mine. You'll see." Arden waited for Jill to sit down on the couch before sitting next to her, his thigh pressed against hers. He took her hand. "Are you having fun tonight? We aren't scaring you away, right?"

"I'm having the time of my life."

"Good," he said as he leaned in closer. "Because I'm hoping to convince you to make this a nightly event."

"Mmm...yes, please," she breathed against his lips. In seconds the kiss had deepened, Arden's body coming to rest over hers. Jill welcomed the urgency, wrapping her fingers in his hair, grinding her lips, her body, all of her against him.

"Ready?" Leo called out, footfalls entering the room.

Arden lifted himself off of Jill and gave Leo an annoyed smirk.

"Well, it looks like you two were skipping to another kind of dessert," Leo said shamelessly.

Jill thought about being embarrassed, then changed her mind as she noticed what Leo was carrying. A silver tray full of big luscious strawberries, each dipped in chocolate. Some dark, some milk, some white and some in a combination of all three. "Oh wow, wow, wow, wow, wow..."

Leo knelt in front of her, holding the tray like an offering. "My lady."

It was almost impossible to select only one. But a dark chocolate one had started to melt, making it look even more delicious and sinful. Unable to resist temptation, she lifted the strawberry to Arden's lips.

He took hold of her wrist, and proceeded to eat the luscious treat from her hand. When he'd finished the fruit, he suckled each of her fingers into his mouth, then moved to her palm, licking in ever widening circles. Jill watched, awestruck, wondering if her panties were flame retardant.

"Delicious, dear brother." Arden grinned.

"No need to brag," Leo said. "I have no doubt Jill's flavor surpassed that of the berries."

Feeling a blush coming on again, Jill pulled a small white chocolate strawberry from the tray and put it in her mouth, savoring the smoothness of the chocolate and the sweetness of the berry. "Yes, Leo, the berries are absolutely delicious." She picked up her wineglass and held it high in tribute before taking a sip. "Everything here is phenomenal."

"Just you, Jill." Arden sipped his wine.

She looked from brother to brother and chuckled in spite of herself. "Wow. If my mom ever found out I was alone in a house with two men, she'd run to church and beg for her daughter's sins to be forgiven."

Arden and Leo looked at each other for a moment and Jill couldn't keep the words from coming out of her mouth. "Wait. Do you guys do this all the time?"

Leo answered first. "Well, we've both dated the same woman—"

"I just thought you might enjoy meeting my brother," Arden interrupted, as though trying to change the subject. "And his culinary skills are the easiest thing about him to swallow."

"Wait a second. You guys dated the same woman? At the same time?"

"Yes," Leo replied simply.

Arden gave her an embarrassed grin. "We have the same taste in women. So, yeah, it has happened a few times."

"And it doesn't bother you? You two don't get jealous of each other?"

"If the woman is happy and enjoying herself, then why should it bother us?" Leo shrugged.

Jill looked between the two of them, torn between shock and absolute fascination. They watched her expectantly, as though waiting for her to say or do something. "Well...um...that's definitely...um...different."

The sound of a cell phone ringing somewhere deep in the house interrupted the awkward moment. Arden set down his glass and stood up. "Sorry. That's got to be a client. I promise I'll be right back." He headed down the hallway.

Jill's gaze followed Arden until he disappeared, leaving her alone with Leo. Small talk…small talk…what could she say? "So, uh, are you guys on call all the time?" She rolled her neck, trying to loosen her muscles and avoid looking Leo in the eyes.

"It often seems that way. People get inspired at the craziest moments and forget that it's better to email." Leo finished his ice wine.

"Yeah, they get excited and just can't wait to tell someone. I've had people leave me messages on my shop answering machine at all hours of the night. Some people forget that you might have a life away from work." Jill rubbed her shoulder. The wine was definitely helping, but there was still one stubborn muscle that wouldn't relent.

"Life away from work. What a dream that would be." Leo set his glass on a side table and walked behind Jill. She wasn't sure where he was going until she felt a warm hand slide under where her own hand had been. "If you don't mind, I can help you a little bit."

Both of his hands pushed and soothed her neck and shoulders to the point where all she could do was nod and breathily reply, "Yes. I mean, no, I don't mind."

Maybe he had a second job as a masseuse. Jill was so lost in the ecstasy brought about by his deft fingers that she couldn't gather the words to inquire about his incredible skill. She was putty in his hands. Truly. And then her mind starting thinking sinfully again, causing wetness to pool between her thighs. She wanted Arden to come back so they could continue what they'd started last night. She wanted Leo's hands to move from her neck and stroke every inch of her body. Closing her eyes, she lost herself in a fantasy that no good girl from West Virginia would ever think about having.

She smelled sunshine seconds before Arden's mouth covered hers. Fantasy became reality as his tongue demanded then claimed, and she willingly opened for him. He lowered onto the couch, knees pinning her thighs, hands framing her face while he dove deeper and deeper into her mouth. And still Leo's hands continued to work their magic, her muscles liquid beneath his palms.

A mix of contradictory emotions filled her, relaxed and comfortable, needy and desperate. It was so confusing, she didn't know how to react, relying on instinct alone to guide her. And instinct told her she wanted to be possessed by these men or her arousal would rage out of control.

Moaning her acquiescence, she tangled her fingers into Arden's hair, holding him to her. His lips sought her neck, and his tender bites burned the skin that Leo had so recently soothed. Leo's hands moved to the middle of her back, rubbing beneath the clasp of her bra. At some point the top buttons on the back of her dress had been undone, and now it gaped in the front, offering Arden a view of her white lacy bra. His hands followed his eyes, cradling her breasts.

But it wasn't only Arden's fingers caressing there. Leo's hand skimmed over the lace-covered flesh, while Arden slipped her other breast from the fabric shell. Two matching growls of approval filled the air before Arden took her rigid nipple into his mouth.

Jill cried out as Arden suckled her flesh. The tiny nub was a power center of nerve endings, igniting an explosive fire in her clit, between her legs, down her spine...everywhere. From behind her, Leo kissed the back of her neck, one hand kneading the base of her spine. His other hand cupped and massaged, tugging on the nipple opposite Arden. With both breasts being stroked, she felt like lightning bolts were striking all over her body. Each touch caused her body to shudder, her toes to curl, her fingers to wrap tighter in Arden's hair.

"Beautiful," Arden said, barely above a whisper.

So many hands, mouths, sensations, her body was on overload. She gasped, lost, not knowing what to do, how to react.

The dress hung off her body, the buttons along the back now completely undone. But still, the sudden release of her bra surprised her, as both breasts spilled completely from their constraints. Two sets of hands undressed her, smoothly sliding her dress and bra down her arms, leaving her naked from the waist up.

Then Leo's hands were gone, and for a moment it was just her and Arden, his dark hair brushing against her nipples as he kissed her stomach.

Like tiny butterflies, need rippled across her skin. Everything became brilliantly clear. It was Arden she wanted. He was the reason she'd come here tonight. He was the only reason. She couldn't make it more than that.

Leo knelt next to her, fingertips tenderly brushing across her cheek then down along her collarbone. "It's too much," she whispered.

All motion stopped as both men looked at her for confirmation. She couldn't tear her gaze from Arden, his eyes full of all the emotions she remembered from last night. Jill laced her fingers with Arden's, then forced herself to meet Leo's gaze. Embarrassed at her wanton behavior, she grabbed her dress, lifting it to cover her breasts. "I-I'm sorry."

Leo nodded, a slight smile forming on his lips. "Enjoy my brother as I know he'll enjoy you." He kissed her forehead before standing up and moving away from the couch.

Jill watched Leo walk down the hall, surprised when a flicker of guilt and sorrow made her tremble. Why did she feel like she'd just made the wrong decision?

Blinking back tears, she struggled with the conflicting emotions that hadn't disappeared with Leo's exit. How could she care so deeply about both brothers already?

Arden lifted their linked hands above her head and pressed his lips to hers, bringing her attention back to the two of them. She saw and felt nothing but his earthy sunshine. Her senses reeled again and she let the dress drop to her waist, surrendering herself to Arden.

The dress fell to the carpet as he lifted her to her feet. Wearing nothing but sandals and a tiny scrap of white fabric, Jill felt strangely empowered. The liquid heat of Arden's gaze as he took her in from head to toe made her legs tremble, but she forced herself to remain upright as she returned his stare.

Arden pulled his shirt over his head while Jill kicked off her sandals and shimmied out of the tiny piece of lace passing as underwear. She kept an eye on Arden, admiring as each bit of flesh was revealed. Bronze skin sprinkled with dark brown curls, powerful muscles, every bit of him firm and tight. When he lowered his jeans, she sucked in a deep breath. God how she loved a man in black briefs. It was better than presents at Christmas time — and oh how she wanted to unwrap him.

As though reading her mind, he raised an eyebrow and gestured for her to approach. She'd thought she would take her time, smoothing her hands down his body, tracing each muscle, tasting him all over, but the moment she pressed her nipples against his bare flesh, they both went into a frenzy. She didn't know if Arden lifted her or if she'd climbed him, but her legs were now around his waist, her back arching as he rasped his teeth over her nipples.

They weren't speaking with words now, only desires. Too much wanting, too much need — Jill knew their first time would be as fast and furious as the feelings ripping through her. She needed that violent outlet — slow sex would probably drive her insane.

Jill slid his briefs down enough to free his cock. She couldn't see it, only feel its heat wedged between their bodies, throbbing against her clit. It was enough to make her cry out and squirm against him.

Arden groaned, his hands clamping down on her ass to keep her from moving. But that just shoved him tighter against her clit. Already over the edge, she sobbed as an orgasm shot through her body.

Unable to stop herself, she rocked against him as the tremors burst through her.

"Oh, fuck, Jill," Arden cursed through gritted teeth. "You're gonna make me come."

They dropped to the couch, Jill still trembling. She needed him inside her so she could come again and again and again. This was crazy. It had never been like this before. She'd never climaxed so quickly—and never without having to help herself get there after the guy was finished.

Arden slid his briefs off completely then knelt over her. Sweat dripped down his chest, his arms trembling. "This time is gonna be fast. I'm sorry." And in one easy thrust he was sheathed inside her.

It felt fantastic. Beyond fantastic. Out of this world. His cock slammed in and out, faster and faster, his breath coming in rapid pants against her neck. "I want you. I can't get enough, Jill. I just want more. More."

His words drove her unbelievably higher and she stifled a scream. He buried his face into her neck, teeth scraping as he thrust even faster. Tilting her head to the side, she found herself staring into Leo's eyes.

He stood in the hallway, gaze locked on their writhing bodies. She wanted to be shocked, offended, upset, but his eyes…in his eyes she saw every bare emotion she'd seen in Arden. Need, desire, and lust twisted inexplicably with fading hope. She knew that all she had to do was hold out her hand and Leo would come back and somehow, everything would be all right.

Arden trembled beneath her hands, his whole body arching as he made one final thrust. His seed shot hard and hot inside her, each liquid pulse taking her higher and higher, making her fly. With Leo filling her vision, Jill began to come, her pussy rippling, keeping Arden deep inside.

Jill shattered, her eyes slamming shut, her cries mingling with Arden's moans. She threw out her arm, reaching for Leo.

But when she opened her eyes, he was gone.

Chapter Five

Leo pushed open the door of *Jill's Bloomers*, silencing the welcome bells with his palm before they could chime.

Behind the counter, Jill was hard at work, her fingers wrestling with wire and green tape, a floral masterpiece in progress. She hummed along with the radio, her hips swinging from side to side. With her back to him, he was able to watch unnoticed as she continued to dance, occasionally singing along with the music.

So she was in a good mood after her late night with Arden. No surprises there. The two of them had fucked until the early hours of the morning.

Leo had watched then without her knowing, too. Well, she'd noticed once, her eyes focusing on him only while Arden rutted away inside of her. But Leo'd made sure to be out of view when her eyes opened post-climax.

Call him a detached bastard, but adding emotion into the mix right now would only fuck things up. Arden was already so wrapped up in Jill, Leo had no choice but to be the balance. The charming seducer, the guilt-free pleasure, the clinical half who could show Jill that it wasn't a competition, but a cooperative venture.

And if he gave up now, there wasn't a chance in hell of survival.

He gave the bells on the door a gentle swing, ready to announce his arrival.

Without turning, Jill called out, "I'll be right with you." She held up the stem wire she'd attached an artsy twig to, nodded and laid it down next to a pile of purple chrysanthemums, then spun around, a welcoming smile wide on her face.

"Leo…" Her smile wavered, and she averted her gaze, a blush covering her face. "Um…so…so what brings you here?"

"I'm not exactly sure what I need. No, check that. I know what I need. Flowers." He gestured around the store, giving her an open smile. "And your advice on everything about them."

Wiping her hands on her apron, she lifted her gaze back to his face. "Everything?" Her lips curled upward teasingly, the blush fading to a rosy glow on each cheek. "You might want to be a bit more specific or we could be here for a while."

"I don't have any plans." He chuckled when she smirked. "Okay, okay. Well, I want to impress a lady. Show my honest sincerity with the right flowers and an apology."

"An apology? What did you do?" Jill stepped from behind the counter, but as though realizing she no longer had a barrier between them, she drew to a halt several feet away from him.

He smiled, trying to find the best angle of approach. "Hmmm… Let's just say I may have gone too far, too fast."

"All right then." Her eyes narrowed. Had she figured out the real reason behind his visit, or was she being the good salesperson and trying to decide which flowers would do the trick?

In any case, he knew he couldn't screw this up. "I know you probably get this question all the time from guys like me, but what kind of flowers would you want someone to get for you?"

She crossed her arms over her chest. "That depends who's giving them."

"Really?"

"Well, yeah. Any guy who buys me flowers knows going in that I own a flower shop. How can he get me something that I haven't seen before? I don't get flowers. I get chocolates." She laughed. "But we're not talking about me, are we?" She unabashedly looked him straight in the eye.

Damn, she was quite a challenge, keeping him on his toes. "But would that mean you'd want the most beautiful blossom in the store or…"

"A pot of dirt? A wilted lilac?" she quipped.

"You're not helping," he sang.

"And make your job easier? Now why would I do that?" She cocked an eyebrow, her eyes sparkling mischievously.

"Because that's *your* job." He lifted his eyebrow and matched her stance.

"Okay, okay." She laughed. "Does this...*mystery* lady...like you?"

"Well, that remains to be seen."

She nodded. "Okay...does she think whatever you did was so awful?"

"I hope not." In spite of himself, he moved closer, nearly towering over her. He stepped back. Crowding her now would be a big mistake.

In a surprising turn, she regained the space he'd put between them and placed one finger dead center of his chest. "Then I think you should pick out the flower or flowers that most remind you of her. Women like that kind of stuff, you know."

"Wow. Tall order." Leo swallowed and his mind raced for a winning response. "I think I'm going to have to buy the whole store because in each flower, I can find something that reminds me of her."

Jill made a muffled snort, and started to pull away. "You're so full of..."

He pinned her retreating hand between both of his. "Okay, you want the truth? There isn't a flower here that touches on what I feel for this woman. I'm completely in awe. She's got me mesmerized by the look in her eyes when she laughs, the way she turns pink from head to toe when she's embarrassed. I'm absolutely addicted." He brought her hand to his lips and kissed it before continuing in a whisper, "She's so damn special and if I don't get a chance to make things right, I'll lose my mind."

"I think you just did," she whispered, her fingers curling around his hand.

"So am I forgiven for overstaying my welcome last night?"

The door behind him jingled and he swallowed a curse as Jill jumped away from him. So damn close! He turned to see a woman with pink and purple spiked hair striding into the shop, her eyes widening as she looked between the two of them.

"Carrie!" Jill exclaimed. "Umm...done with the early deliveries already?"

"Sure am, boss lady," the multicolored Carrie replied. "I'm ready for the afternoon run. That is if I'm not interrupting any--"

"Nope. Everything's ready," Jill said overly cheery, dashing behind the counter, handing Carrie a stack of papers.

While Jill was occupied, Leo glanced around the shop, compelled to locate the perfect flower. A single peach daisy—the only one of its kind he could see—called out to him. He plucked it from its display vase and stepped up to the register where Jill and Carrie were going through orders.

Carrie looked up at his approach. "Well, I'll just be in the back room...taking my time...getting the flowers...doing my job...not bothering you..." Grinning, she disappeared through a swinging door.

Jill turned back to Leo and paused when she saw the flower in his hand. He pulled out his wallet, and as she wrapped up the flower and rang him up he said casually, "You know, I think this might be the one. At first glance, you're struck by its simple beauty. Then the more you hold it, you realize that it's exactly what you're looking for."

She handed the flower to him with a gentle smile. "I hope it is, too."

He took the flower. "Seeing as how I somewhat overstayed my welcome last night...and I'm sorry about that." He handed the flower right back to her. "I'm hoping it won't keep you from coming over tonight."

In an unconscious gesture, she lifted the flower to her face and inhaled. Her eyes met his calculatingly over the peach bloom. "Okay, I'll be there. But I'm bringing dinner this time."

"Ouch!" He grabbed at his heart. "You didn't like our cooking?"

She laughed, her carefree attitude returning. "You know I loved it. But tonight it's my turn."

"If you insist."

"I do."

"Then I'll be waiting anxiously." Caught up in the moment, he leaned down to kiss her, but just before their lips met he changed his mind, not wanting to scare her away. When she didn't retreat, the urge to kiss her grew stronger, but he held back, knowing the anticipation would make tonight more memorable. "Thank you."

"You're welcome." She breathed the words against his mouth before pulling away. "I'll see you tonight."

He nodded and headed out of the store, a grin creeping over his face. Hot damn, that had been a bigger thrill than he'd expected. There was more to Jill than appearances implied. Shutting him down, making him really work to win her over…the chase was always better when they put up a fight. The blood raced through his veins at the challenge that awaited him tonight.

Leo glanced up at the eagle flying overhead. *One step closer…*

* * * * *

The moment Leo walked out the front door, Carrie erupted from the backroom. Not that this was unusual for her. Carrie was a walking entertainment center — approaching everything in life with a through-the-roof level of energy and enthusiasm. She hiked herself onto the counter next to where Jill stood. "Hello! He was good. Smooth as buttah! And not that crappy diet stuff I've been eatin' lately. I mean, I was gonna get up on him, all flowers and apology hottie, if you didn't—and you know I don't do dick." Turning her head sideways and using her hand, she mimed a blowjob. "So I take it Mr. Blond and Beautiful is the reason you've been bouncing around here the last couple days?"

Jill nodded absentmindedly, watching as Leo paused outside her door and looked into the sky. He tipped his head, his white blond hair shining like spun gold in the sunlight. Then he was gone, disappearing around the corner.

"That's it. My boss has finally found a man who makes her cream. Fuck yeah! You get him, girl. Make him show you a real good time. I'll just go home to my vibrator...alone...and jealous." Carrie hopped off the counter and swept Jill into the air, smashing her in a bear hug. "I'll be out doing deliveries, but if you decide you want to leave early to do the horizontal mambo, I'll cover for ya." Carrie danced into the backroom, preparing to load the delivery van.

Jill took a shaky breath, inhaling the light scent of the Gerbera daisy. There could be no misconstruing what she'd just agreed to. She wasn't only dating Arden anymore—she was dating both brothers.

Obviously she'd lost her mind sometime in the last ten minutes. Why would she agree to a situation so far beyond the boundaries of a normal relationship?

Five hours later as she walked up to their house, Jill still didn't have an answer to that question. But being around Arden and Leo made her happy. Since they'd never once tried to force her into something she didn't want, she felt safe to explore this twofold relationship.

Arms full of three large sodas and Chinese food, Jill leaned over precariously and rang the doorbell. The door swung open, Leo coming to her rescue.

"Whoa! Jill, you under there somewhere? Let me get that for you." He chuckled as he gathered the bags from her.

"Hey, when I say I'm bringing food, I bring food. No one goes hungry under my watch." She closed the door and followed Leo into the kitchen. He looked incredible tonight, wearing a long-sleeve button-down maroon shirt that emphasized his beautiful blond hair and blue jeans that had a comfortable worn appeal to them. He was barefoot, and for some bizarre reason Jill found that incredibly endearing—maybe Leo would finally stop putting on airs trying to impress her.

He set the bags down and dug through them. "Which army are we feeding? Or did you bring a ton of food so you never have to leave?"

Jill grinned sheepishly. "Okay, the truth is when I ordered the family-size meal, I had no idea it would feed a family of twenty."

"Dammit. I was hoping you were staying indefinitely." Leo pouted.

Laughing, she glanced around the room. "Where's Arden?"

"M.I.A." At her quick look, he shrugged. "It's coming down to the wire on an important project."

"Oh." Which would explain why Arden hadn't been the one to make the date with her tonight. It felt strange though, like she was cheating on him. Did he even know she was here?

"Hey, there." Leo swiped his thumb across her lip, and she realized she'd been nervously biting it. "He has to come home sometime."

His thumb continued to smooth over her lip, back and forth, back and forth. It was hypnotic, the glide of flesh over flesh. She swallowed hard, trying to regain some control over the situation. It didn't work. The heat from his gaze, his touch, blazed a path of reckless need through her body, making her breasts tingle. How could she fight these traitorous desires? She didn't need to look down to know that her nipples were straining to break through her turtleneck. Geesh! She hadn't even been in the house for two minutes and she was already horny.

Forcing an unaffected smile, she said, "I hope he'll be hungry."

Leo's amber eyes darkened. "I'm sure that won't be a problem." He withdrew his hand, and his behavior returned to that of the gracious host. "I thought we could eat outside, if that's okay with you."

"Sounds fantastic." Jill grabbed the sodas while Leo picked up the bag of food and they exited to the backyard.

A table was already set up, a bottle of wine chilling in an ice bucket, a dozen candles under glass hurricane shades lighting up the darkness. There were three place settings. Relief skittered down her spine. Obviously, Leo expected Arden to be home any minute.

They dug into their food, the earlier awkwardness disappearing. Leo was the charmer she knew he could be, but she still couldn't help but miss Arden. Last night had been so memorable—the unbelievable dinner combined with the brothers' flirting and antics—tonight seemed almost solemn in comparison. It made her appreciate how well the brothers worked together.

"This food is delicious. Good choice, Jill." Leo raised his soda in a mock toast. "Too bad my brother's missing it."

"Yeah, it is too bad, isn't it? Tons of food and this incredible wine. Is he working with a client on a website?"

"Honestly, I'm not sure on all the details. This one's his pet. Usually, I reel people in and get them started and then Arden irons out the details and we start doing whatever's necessary. This time, I'm on the outside anxiously looking in. It's a big project and I don't want to sabotage all the work he's put into it."

"Does he work late a lot?"

"We both do."

"On the same projects?"

"Sometimes. We tend to switch jobs from creative to technical all the time." Leo poured himself another glass of wine. "But I usually do the ads and he does the web stuff."

"That's good. Maybe I could hire him to redo my website. It's pretty boring. He could probably add some real life to it."

"I'm sure he could." Leo took a long drink of his wine. "I'd be happy to help, too." He grinned. "Maybe we could trade. You teach me more about flowers, I'll help you with your website."

"I don't know," she teased. "Sounds like I'm getting a raw deal. You don't seem like someone who could easily be taught. Arden, however —"

"Ouch! You wound me!" He shook his head, a self-deprecating smirk on his face.

"Sorry." She bit her lip to keep from laughing out loud and raised her wineglass. "To friends and flowers."

Leo clinked his glass against hers and they both took a drink.

When the phone inside the house rang, Jill was stunned to see that an hour had passed since they'd started eating. She could've spent all night talking to Leo. He'd captivated her, made her laugh and even surprised her. There was more to him than a pretty face, broad shoulders and a tight ass. A lot more…and she was infatuated with the whole package.

Leo pushed out of his chair. "Maybe that's my brother." He strode into the house, returning seconds later with the phone, holding it out to her. "Arden, wanting to beg your forgiveness, I'm sure." When she took the phone, Leo began clearing the table.

"Hey, beautiful," Arden said. "Turns out I'm missing a really good time, huh?"

"Hey yourself." Jill smiled. "'Bout time we heard from you. I thought maybe I'd scared you away."

"Never," he stated emphatically. "Never. I mean that. You have no idea how badly I want to be there with you right now. This damn…" He paused and Jill could envision him running his hand through his hair. "Is Leo being good to you?"

Jill met Leo's eyes and smiled. "Perfect host."

"He'll take care of you. I promise. You can trust him...with everything."

Jill shivered involuntarily. Interesting word choice. "So will I see you tonight?" she asked.

"Tell me you'll be there waiting and I'll be there as soon as I can."

"I'll be here," she whispered and Leo nodded his approval.

"Good," Arden replied, sounding relieved. "Until then, have fun with my brother."

"Yeah...okay. See you soon." Awareness rippled over her flesh as they said their goodbyes.

"Everything okay?" Leo covered her hand with his as he took the phone.

She studied him in the soft glow of the candlelight. Something in his demeanor had changed in the last hour. His expression was open and honest...and a little bit resigned. Like he'd finally let down his guard and was willing to let her see the real Leo. Without his charmer façade, he bewitched her mind, body and soul.

"Yeah. Everything's great." She smiled up at him. "Ready to go inside?"

He grinned, offering his arm. "Sounds like a plan."

She threaded her arm through his. Clutching his forearm, she stood up, walking with him into the house.

Chapter Six

Now Leo knew what it was like to be a death row prisoner starting his walk to the execution chamber. Helpless. Hopeless. Resigned to his fate.

Even though he'd hoped for a stay of execution, time was drawing to a close, and he had yet to win Jill over.

He'd thought it would be easy to charm her like he'd charmed all the others. Hell, none of those women had come through in the end either—so who was to say it hadn't been his fault all along? He'd always found women willing to offer their bodies. Now he and Arden had found one who would offer her heart—but only to one of them. Second place had never felt so fucking horrible.

You better be good to her. Arden's voice forced its way into Leo's head.

Like he needed this now. *I can't work if you're going to fuck with me. You're forgetting I need this as much as you do.* He shoved all doubt to the back of his mind. He couldn't lose. To Jill he said, "We've got a little time to kill before Arden gets here. Care to watch a movie in the meantime? There's a home theater upstairs."

"Sure. But are you an action adventure guy, or are you comfortable enough in your masculinity to watch a chick flick without getting embarrassed?" She headed toward the stairway.

Leo grinned as they climbed the stairs to the black box room. "I refuse to answer your question on the basis that it could incriminate me later." Jill laughed out loud and Leo continued, pointing at the DVD collection. "But I'll let you choose the movie anyway."

"You're in trouble now," Jill teased as she began going through the DVDs.

Arden was restless, it was too obvious. Leo felt the tension, adding to his own. *I'm coming home,* Arden declared.

No, you're not. If you don't get your emotions in check, we could lose her. Let's not do that.

Leo, this is not some kind of game. Don't you dare hurt her. If you're just going to fuck her and —

Give me a little credit. If you want this to work, you won't barge in here. You won't screw this up.

"Wow! Your collection's not half bad. I've heard great things about *The Color of Rain.* That okay with you?" Jill asked.

Dammit Leo. If you can't treat her with respect, then we need to end this charade now and let her go.

Arden, hear me well. I'm not gonna discuss this. I only needed you to call her because it looked like she was still uneasy about us. Now let me do what I need to do and stay out of it. Leo hid his rage and nodded at Jill. "Yeah, *The Color of Rain* sounds great. I haven't watched it yet so it'll be new for both of us."

Jill stood up and playfully tossed the DVD case at him. "I'm going to get comfortable while you do the manly job of starting up the player." She brushed past him and bounced over to the curved theater-style couch.

Arden refused to let go. *I'd rather you sent her home than let her get hurt.*

You've made that pretty damn clear. Now listen to me. I will not hurt her, Arden. Let me work. Leo terminated their telepathic connection. He couldn't deal with two conversations at once. Especially not where Jill was concerned. He needed to focus on her completely. Hell, he wanted to focus on her completely and skip the movie, but that would make his intentions too obvious.

She was quiet as he put in the DVD and set it to play. Too quiet. He turned to see what she was doing and caught her watching him. Smiling, she patted the sofa next to her.

Jill had taken off her shoes and socks, curling her legs up underneath her. She looked completely comfortable, as if she were where she belonged. Like he could come home from work every day and see her sitting there in her faded blue jeans and light blue turtleneck, smiling at him, making him feel like a million bucks.

God, he was thinking like Arden now. When he sat down next to her, he placed a hand over hers. "I guess I'm practically the consolation prize, huh? Sorry about that." He kept his tone light, wishing he'd thought more clearly before opening his big dumb mouth. Too many of Arden's words were echoing in his head. Too much pressure. Too much fucking pressure. Did Arden have any idea how much extra pressure he'd introduced? As if there wasn't already a ton.

"No, Leo, I—"

"It's okay, Jill. Really. Just like last night, I understand."

"But last night, I wasn't sure."

"It's okay. You don't need to explain."

She continued slightly above a whisper. "Tonight, I'm sure."

The movie opened with a silhouette of lovers on a beach in the surf underneath a brilliant twilight sky. The credits ended and the lovers walked from the water, still caressing each other, into a house on the beach. The scene cut to them in a large shower, washing each other, loving each other with their hands and lips.

It took those few minutes for Leo to process what Jill had said. Thinking he must have misunderstood, he faced her, and was further surprised to see that she wasn't watching the movie. She was turned sideways, elbow resting on the back of the couch, an amused smile on her face, watching him. He tried to get his mouth working, but the only thing that came out was a lame, "I had no idea."

"I know." She let out a carefree laugh then reached out and began playing with his hair, her fingers twisting and tangling in the long strands. She looked like an angel—no make that a nymph—enjoying the simple pleasure of stroking his hair. His cock, already stirring because of the love play on the screen, surged to life.

And that's when he noticed all the subtle nuances he'd somehow been blind to before now. Her eyes were stormy, mouth parted, breath coming in soft pants. Even in the darkened room her nipples were visible, rigid beneath the tight cotton.

He'd never felt so absorbed with a woman before, and still the only place they touched was her hand in his hair. He wanted to hold onto the moment, study it, try to understand what made this—her—different, but on a soft sigh of need, she closed the distance between them and pressed her lips to his.

It was the sweetest damn kiss he'd ever received. Full soft lips tenderly brushing his. There was no demand, no rush to get past the necessary first step of the kiss and on to the fucking. She breathed hope into him, the final chance he'd thought most likely lost. It was like she was awakening him from a nightmare, pulling him from a dark place into her sweetness and light. He wrapped his arms around her, holding her to him, not wanting to ever let go.

Sinking back into the couch, he kept her with him, wanting to feel her weight above him, covering him, their scents mingling before they mated. He slid a hand under her turtleneck, fingers running up and down her spine. She arched and purred, completely malleable beneath his worshipful exploration of her body. With his other hand he cradled her neck, holding her in place so he could delve deeper into her mouth.

When her lips parted and her tongue danced with his, he drank his first taste of pure joy and it made him want to laugh out loud. He knew he was thinking like a lunatic, but it didn't matter. Arden had been right. Jill was the one they'd waited their lifetime for.

Leo couldn't get enough of her flavor; it was a drug, a need so pure he couldn't deny himself. And she kept providing him with more things to get addicted to. Soft moans, ragged sighs, the press of her flesh against his. It could never be enough.

She maneuvered her hands between their bodies, and within a minute his shirt was unbuttoned and spread open, baring his chest. She tried to pull her mouth from his, and when he wouldn't relent, she lightly bit his lip. He grunted and let her go, and she laughed.

"Minx."

Laughing again, she lowered her mouth to his chest. All he could do was moan. So fucking sweet. Her hands, fingers and lips slowly traced over every muscle, every contour of flesh. His dick was so hard it would take hours for him to lose his erection. Hours he planned to spend buried deep inside her body. Anywhere, everywhere, wherever she would take him.

Maybe he'd let Arden join them. Maybe not. He wanted time to pleasure her alone. At least a little time, he knew they couldn't spare much, but he wanted to know when she moaned, that those sounds were his alone to enjoy.

"My turn, Jill."

She lifted her head from his chest, her lips swollen, eyes smoky with desire. When his hands grasped the bottom of her turtleneck, she nodded in agreement and lifted her arms. He tugged the tight fabric over her head, then stared in awe at what was revealed. Beautiful opalescent skin, luscious curves…a true feminine beauty. As he stared, her skin grew pink, but as though denying her embarrassment she reached behind her and undid her bra, sliding it down her arms and tossing it to the floor.

Bared from the waist up, she was truly glorious. Her breasts were slightly larger than he usually liked, but on her, he couldn't imagine wanting anything different. He instinctually reached out to possess one of them. She inhaled sharply as he thumbed her tight bud. Her dusky rose areola darkened to deep plum at her nipple, her generous breast spilling over his palm. He wanted to take all night to learn, taste, discover all of her soft curves. He'd seen her nude the night before, but now that she wanted him in return, he found it difficult to restrain himself, to make the night last rather than burn up in a fiery flash.

They both turned toward the forgotten movie as the moans of the onscreen lovers became more than they could ignore. The woman was on her knees in front of the man, taking his dick deep into her mouth. Leo's cock jumped as he imagined Jill taking him that way. He cursed. "I had no idea this was a porno marketed as an art film."

"I did," Jill whispered.

Surprised, Leo looked back at Jill. Her eyes were still focused on the screen, her breath coming faster and faster. Damn, she had picked this one on purpose. He would use it to his advantage.

Shrugging off his shirt, he moved behind her and murmured into her ear. "Stand up."

Her feet fell to the floor and she stood up, facing away from him. He moved to the edge of the couch, and from behind unbuttoned her jeans, lowering the zipper, sliding his hands between denim and hot flesh. When the curve of her ass was revealed, he leaned in, kissing the base of her spine. She shivered, legs trembling. As he pushed her jeans to the floor, he knelt behind her trailing kisses along the backs of her legs, taking special care in the sensitive spot behind her knees. She laughed and moaned, swaying to steady herself. Finally the jeans were removed and she stepped out of them. She started to turn, but he stopped her by placing his hands on her thighs. "Stay right there."

God, now he knew why some men became submissives. Kneeling behind this woman, staring up at her naked flesh, he knew he'd do whatever she commanded. He slid his hands from the outside of her thighs inward, one hand tracing her folds, landing over her clit. She let out a quiet moan and shifted her legs, inviting him to further claim her. Oh dear God, did Jill have any idea what she was doing to him?

Her gaze strayed over to the movie. The woman lay spread-eagle on a bed, the man's head buried between her legs.

"Like what you see, sweet Jill?" Leo kissed the back of her thigh as he caressed her swollen bud with his finger.

Her only answer was a moan.

"Lean forward, sweetheart, and brace yourself on the couch. Just like that. Good girl. Now spread your legs. God, you're so damn beautiful."

She did what he asked, her gaze flitting from him to the screen and back again. Bending over with legs splayed, she gave him access to her beautiful pink pussy, wetness coating her swollen lips.

With tender care he placed his hands above her knees, running upward, then back over her ass. Damn, she was gorgeous. He moved closer, inhaling deeply of her arousal. Pure, sweet honey. He had to have a taste.

Slowly, he outlined her lips with his tongue, then explored between them, the entrance to her cunt. Absolutely divine. He'd never tasted such lustful candy.

Swirling his tongue, drawing her juices into his mouth, he dove deeper. She gasped and fell to her elbows, her legs threatening to bend. He grasped her knees, supporting her weight and holding her to him. She was like a drug. The more he tasted her, the more she consumed him, the more he wanted to give her everything he had. A strange euphoria washed over him as she writhed and mewled under his exploration of her canal. He'd never found himself so wanting to please a woman that he felt his control waning. He could vaguely hear the onscreen lovers, the woman's moans had turned to screams.

Or wait. Was that Jill?

"Leo!" His name fluttered from deep within her throat as her pussy began spasming around his tongue, drenching it in delicious drops of her wetness.

How he wished his cock was tight inside her sheath as it contracted. He continued to drown in her flavor as the waves of orgasm hit her, renewing the frenzy in her cunt.

Dammit. He needed her. He needed her now.

As he began moving his body up her legs, she took her weight back onto her feet and elbows. In the blink of an eye, he managed to yank down his jeans and free himself from his briefs. He slid his cock along her inner thigh slick with sweat and juices, burning in her heat, desperate to lose himself in her liquid velvet. As soon as his shaft reached her drenched folds, he moaned. She responded by rocking her ass against his hips and tilting downward. He buried himself to the hilt, her luscious pussy rippling and tightening around him. They both cried out at the sudden overwhelming pleasure.

She was his now — theirs now. God willing, they'd convince her to stay with them when everything about them changed.

Chapter Seven

Jill curled her fingers into the soft leather of the couch. It was the only thing she could grasp onto as the world spun beautifully around her. Everything felt so good, the pleasure near violent in its intensity. Part of her felt disconnected from her body, floating on pure ecstasy while the rest of her reveled in every thrust of Leo's shaft deep into her pussy, his sharp groans when he seated himself completely inside, and the sound his testicles made as they rhythmically slapped against her.

She had only a few seconds to comprehend the pounding of footsteps running up the stairs. Throwing her gaze toward the doorway, she saw Arden round the corner into the room, completely naked. And very aroused. His cock towered straight out from the dark curls covering his groin. But there was also an air of wild desperation about him. The minimal light coming from the movie didn't allow her to see his eyes. Was he angry? Hurt?

Leo must have sensed her worry because he slowed his thrusts until he was barely moving within her, letting go of her hip with one hand and soothing down her spine. She shivered as Arden stalked toward them. Had she made the wrong decision?

Arden knelt next to her, his strong hands brushing sweat soaked strands of hair off her face. He ran kisses over her forehead, eyes, cheeks, murmuring, "Sweet beautiful Jill. God how I want you." He stopped kissing her, looking deep into her eyes. "Will you take us both tonight? Let us take care of you?"

"Yes," she gasped, nodding her head in case he didn't understand. "Yes."

Relief and lust shone in Arden's dark eyes as he leaned in and kissed her, his tongue claiming her mouth with the same possessiveness that Leo laid claim to her pussy. She was pinned, unable to move forward or back, left only to accept and enjoy every blast of pleasure their touches evoked.

Arden's hands cupped her breasts, his thumbs lightly stroking her erect nipples. It was like adding flame to the fire already burning so hot inside her. She whimpered into his mouth, her body trembling. All of her muscles quivered. She wouldn't be able to hold herself up much longer.

Leo groaned, his fingers digging into her hips. "Fuck Jill, you feel too damn good. Dammit, I can't—" With a ragged moan, Leo spurted hot seed into her channel.

Pulling her mouth from Arden's, she cried out at the liquid invasion. The stream of Leo's come shooting hard against her womb created a ripple effect throughout her body, tearing another orgasm from her soul.

Unable to hold herself up any longer, she crumpled onto the couch, her head landing on Arden's chest. Leo slumped over her, their bodies still attached.

"I just need to pass out for a couple minutes," she mumbled between deep gulps of air. She closed her eyes, listening to the rapid beat of Arden's heart.

Jill didn't think she'd slept, at least not for more than a few minutes. Somewhere in the back of her consciousness she heard Leo get up and the sound of a door sliding open. Arden shifted her into his arms and stood up, carrying her with him. She snuggled against his chest, loving his familiar scent.

Cool air washed over her, awakening her completely from her orgasm-induced daze. She opened her eyes as Arden stepped outside onto a balcony.

"Um, Arden. Naked. Outside. People..." Feeling even more nude than she had moments ago in the house, she tried to cover all her pertinent parts.

"It's okay. No one can see us. Well, not unless they're really trying," Leo answered.

Jill turned her head in the direction of Leo's voice, finding him sprawled comfortably in a spa. Steam rose from the hot water, misting in the air around them. The spa was surrounded on three sides by wood paneling, sheltering it from the wind and any neighbors with voyeuristic tendencies. Although somehow she had a feeling the brothers didn't have the paneling to protect their virtue. Being naked outside didn't seem to bother them in the slightest.

"Give me the word and we'll go back inside," Arden said. "I just thought—"

"No, it's fine. Really. It just surprised me." She smiled up at him. "And by the way, I feel ridiculous holding a conversation with you while you're carrying me and standing naked on the balcony for all the world to see."

"It doesn't bother me." Arden winked. "Besides, I like carrying you, especially when you're like this...all sleepy-eyed and sated."

She stuck out her tongue at him and he laughed. "Okay, fine, he-man. I'll admit it. I was kinda out of it post...um...coitus." She felt the heat of a blush staining her cheeks. Sheesh! After what she'd just done, how could she still feel embarrassed? "But I'm all back to normal now and fully capable of walking."

"Damn Leo, you must have been lacking if she's already back to normal." Arden smirked as he climbed the steps to the spa.

"Well, shit, I guess we'll have to try harder then." Leo stood up and for a second Jill was entranced by the water sluicing down his very nice body. Like the first time she'd seen him, he mesmerized her with his overwhelming and commanding presence. Leo continued, "Wouldn't want her walking away from us before morning."

"Ha ha, very funny," Jill intoned. "You can put me down now, Arden."

"Okay." With an impious grin, Arden pretended to toss her into the spa, making her shriek. Instead, he handed her off to Leo who lowered her onto his lap under the water. He was already erect, his cock nudging her thigh. The stamina of these men.

"Oh…" she sighed as the hot water coaxed her into submission. "I was going to be mad at you two for teasing me, but now I don't even have the energy to care."

"You don't need energy," Arden said. "We'll take care of you."

Between lowered eyelids she watched Arden begin to climb into the spa. His erection looked almost painful. She shook her head and slid off Leo's lap. "Stop right there."

Arden looked at her questioningly as he stood half-in, half-out of the water. He was truly a work of art, chiseled muscles, dark curls sprinkled over his chest, down his stomach, trailing to the masterpiece below. With the steam rising around him he looked like something out of a dream. But it wasn't a dream—tonight, both of these men were hers.

A drop of pre-ejaculate glistened at the tip of Arden's cock. The thought of taking him orally made her pussy clench longingly and a shiver race down her spine. It surprised her how sexually open she was with these men. It was a side of herself she'd never known existed.

"I want to take care of you now," she said, kneeling on a small shelf in front of Arden.

He looked down at her, those gorgeous dark eyes of his so full of lustful adoration she could barely breathe. He didn't say a word, just sat down on the edge, his feet dangling in the water, spreading his legs so she could settle between them.

Keeping her balance by grasping the powerful muscles of Arden's thighs, she wrapped her mouth around the head of his cock. Her tongue circled the tip, tasting his essence. Expecting to find it bitter, she was surprised that the salty taste didn't bother her and in fact, she enjoyed it. She suckled him deeper into her mouth, wanting to taste all of him at once. His low rumble of approval urged her on, as did his hand weaving through her hair, encouraging her to continue. She felt the tension in his body, the tremble of muscles tight and desperate for release as he fought the urge to thrust into her.

She loved his texture, smooth velvet over hard steel. Using her tongue, she traced along the engorged veins of his shaft until she'd reached the base. Wanting to explore even further, she curled her fingers through his coarse, dark hair, then followed it lower to his sac, rolling the flesh over her palm. His breath hissed out between clenched teeth as she took his cock deep into her mouth again, while her hands caressed his balls. Arden's musky smell—that enticing mix of male, desire, sex, power—surrounded her, and she felt the evidence of her arousal building inside like a dam waiting to burst.

Desperation growing, her ass thrashed in and out of the water as she worked Arden harder, her body searching for a way to ease her ache. Fingers gripped her hips, stilling her frantic motions. Leo smoothed his hands over her rear, spreading her cheeks. She didn't have any time to comprehend what was happening before something warm and wet soothed her tiny hole. Oh dear God, Leo was licking her *there*. And it felt good. So unbelievably good. How could something so immoral feel so fantastic? She couldn't hold back her moan of absolute pleasure. It vibrated up Arden's length, and he reacted instantly.

Groaning, Arden stopped holding back, beginning to plunge in and out of her mouth with short, quick jabs. Leo continued to circle her anus with his tongue. Jill didn't know what would happen next; her skin felt too tight for her body, her ears buzzing, body trembling. Not an orgasm, at least not like she was used to. This didn't end; it kept building, growing stronger and stronger.

Arden's whole body grew rigid and he shouted, his seed shooting into her mouth. It came so fast she almost choked, but she carefully swallowed, continuing to manipulate his flesh until he finished. Arden stroked her hair, finally lifting her face from his shaft. He dropped from the edge of the spa and into the water, gifting her with a tender kiss. "Thank you," he murmured against her lips.

Jill couldn't answer, strung tight on the edge of something unexplainable. Replacing his tongue with his finger, Leo began a gentle massage, one finger pressing into her hole. Involuntarily she tightened up, offering resistance against the foreign invasion. He calmed her, making soothing noises while layering kisses along her spine. He kept up the light stimulation against her anus, while Arden joined his brother, his hand beginning a similar massage around her clit. It felt so good, those matching touches, she could barely breathe. If Leo and Arden weren't holding her, she probably would have sunk beneath the water.

She almost did fall when Leo's finger slipped past the barrier and entered her tight hole. Whimpering, she rocked back and forth, wanting more, wanting less, needing an explanation for all the contradicting waves of pain and pleasure that felt too good to ignore. Leo pressed his finger deeper, then retreated, a cautious in and out. The more he moved, the better it felt as her body adjusted to the intrusion.

Arden reached out of the tub, handing a bottle to Leo. Warm oil trickled down her crack, and Leo rubbed the oil over and into her sensitive flesh. He retreated completely and for a moment she felt bereft and empty. Then something larger nudged against her opening. Even though she'd known this was coming, his girth scared her. How could she take him that way?

He must have covered his cock with the same oil, because he was slick against her anus. Slowly, cautiously, he pressed forward, gently invading her. She gasped as her muscles fought against his presence, while the rest of her welcomed it. Forcing herself to relax, Leo pushed deeper with small, digging thrusts. Her arms trembled, body shuddering as he seated himself all the way in.

Once there he didn't move, giving her time to adjust. It burned and ached, being stretched so tight. She shifted, trying to acclimate herself. The longer he was there, the more intense her desire grew. Her skin was hot, sensitive, needy.

"Leo...Arden...please..." Jill didn't recognize the husky, ragged voice as her own, didn't even know what she was begging for, only knowing that if they didn't do something her body was going to explode or implode or burst into flames— whatever happened, with all the pressure building inside, she figured she was going to take out half of Talisman Bay with her.

Arden sank two fingers into her pussy and began thrusting in and out, Leo matching the motions. Desperately she reached out, her hand circling Arden's shaft. He was still semi-hard, even after his orgasm. "Now...Arden, I want you now. Both of you..."

He kissed her again, this time delving into her mouth. His hands cradled her cheeks, holding her still so he could sink deeper and deeper inside of her. While he kissed her, their sexes found each other beneath the water and she lowered herself onto his cock, her pussy stretching to accommodate him. The two brothers moved in unison, taking her, breaking her down. It was an assault on her heart, a discovery that she craved forever with these men. Tears ran down her cheeks as she kissed Arden back, wishing she could kiss Leo too, wishing there was some way she could explain to them that she somehow, inexplicably had fallen in love with them both.

Reaching up and behind her, she wrapped one arm around Leo, the other around Arden. She was a conduit; every movement made felt by all three of them.

Leo kissed her neck, nibbling and loving her skin. She broke from Arden's kiss, turning her head to kiss Leo. He worshiped her just as possessively, claiming her mouth with as much ardor as he claimed her ass. Arden's teeth scraped down her exposed neck, suckling the skin where it met her shoulders.

Everything became a blur of feeling, motion, friction. The orgasm surged from deep inside her, shimmering outward like a great blast of light, ricocheting through her and into Leo and Arden. As though merging into one, they came together, hot liquid pulsing fire. She was trembling, soaring, flying, bound to the men she loved.

* * * * *

They lay in euphoric silence, the only sound the gentle lap of water stirred up by their desperate lovemaking. Arden's heart returned to its normal steady rhythm, but the rest of him felt different...content...complete. He caressed Jill's shoulder, never wanting to be separated from her, but the water's flow created an easy disengagement. She sweetly sighed, lowering her head to his shoulder. One of her hands tangled with Leo's, keeping the three of them connected.

Leo's voice slammed into Arden's head, shattering the blissful afterglow. *Do you feel different? Is the change happening?*

Arden forced his thoughts away from how Jill made him feel and focused inward. Muscles rhythmically tightened and released, contracting of their own accord, making concentration difficult. It felt similar to the moments just before he shifted form. Had Jill broken the curse? He met Leo's intent gaze. *I feel different...better...more alive.*

We need to tell her, Leo warned, his eyes fierce. A muscle ticked in his jaw, and his teeth clenched. Whatever was happening to them, Leo was feeling it, too. *We're in too deep now. She needs to know.*

I know. Arden kissed the top of Jill's head. Her breathing had deepened, her warm exhales caressing his neck. She was asleep, or close to it, oblivious to the damning situation brewing around her. God, more than anything, he didn't want to disrupt what might be their last peaceful moments together.

But Leo broke the silence. "Jill, you're amazing. We knew you were the one."

She let out a muffled sigh, rubbing her face against Arden's neck.

Giving Leo a quelling look, Arden stroked down her spine, hoping his touches could gentle the blow their confession would impart. "I've never felt like this before." He paused to take a breath, to gather his thoughts, to find a way of easing into the heart of the matter. "*We've* never felt like this before."

"And that's exactly why we need to tell you something," Leo finished.

Lifting her head from Arden's shoulder, Jill blinked away grogginess. She stretched languorously and gave them a sheepish grin. "I'm sorry. I guess my lack of sleep over the past few nights is finally getting to me. What did you need to tell me?"

So sweet, so beautiful, so innocent. He didn't want what he loved about her to become fractured when the truth surfaced. "Something we should have told you before things went this far…"

"We've got a secret we've been keeping for eighteen years," Leo offered, softening his words by stroking her arm from shoulder to wrist.

Arden took a deep breath, shouldering the burden of revealing their first lie. "We're not brothers."

"You aren't brothers?" She scrutinized Leo, then Arden, her eyes growing wide. "Are you…are you lovers?"

"No. We're not lovers…we're not brothers. It's confusing." Leo gripped her hand and met her worried gaze. "We're cursed."

"C-cursed?" Jill repeated. Although she didn't move, Arden could see the subtle change in her demeanor, the beginning of an emotional retreat. His heart rate accelerated, a rocky cadence of fear thudding angrily through every vein.

Back off, he demanded. *We're scaring her.*

We're out of time, Leo argued. *Would you rather she has no warning if we change?* To Jill, he asked, "Do you believe in magic?"

"Magic?" She paused, teasing her bottom lip between her front teeth. "Like hocus-pocus, saw-a-lady-in-half magic?" Her gaze darted between the two of them, uneasiness weighing down her smile.

"I wish it was that simple." Arden took her hand, finding it unnaturally cold. Her body's reaction to fear, he guessed. Grasping her fingers between his palms, he gently massaged each digit. He needed more time to ease her into the truth, but the muscle contractions were growing in strength, a ticking time bomb waiting to explode. "When we were eighteen, we were rather open in our love interests."

"We dated multiple women," Leo revealed.

"But that's normal," Jill laughed, although confusion still tempered her expression. "What's not normal is two men dating the same woman at the same time. Like this...us..." Her voice trailed off. "But that's not what you're trying to tell me, is it?"

Arden's guilt hit him with hammer-like ferocity. They were making a mess of this. "Two of the women we dated were witches—powerful witches—and when they discovered our tendencies, they cursed us. Telling us if we wanted to be with multiple women, then we should be two."

Glancing from man to man, Jill shook her head. "What is that supposed to mean? You should be two? You are two!"

"We weren't then." Leo ran a hand over his damp hair. "We were born one man. Now we're two halves of that same man."

"A man you might be meeting in a moment or two here," Arden finished.

"What? There's three of you?" Jill's eyes widened. She jerked her hand from his grasp, crossing her arms protectively over her exposed breasts. "Ummm, I'd really rather not meet him like this."

"No. It's not like that." Arden paused, unsure of how to continue. "I don't want to scare you."

"Well, you are," she whispered. "You *are* scaring me. Nothing you're saying makes any sense."

Leo stepped between Arden and Jill. "We don't want to scare you, Jill, but we're running out of time and there's more we have to tell you. Even before we were cursed and split into two, there was a duality to our nature. We're shape-shifters."

"This isn't funny." Jill jolted to her feet and grabbed a towel from the shelf nearby. Climbing from the spa, she wrapped the fabric around herself tightly and rushed inside the house.

Arden chased after her, ignoring the towels. "No. Jill, please listen. The curse had a time limit. We were eighteen when we were split, so we had eighteen years as separate halves to find someone to make us whole again. And now our time is up."

"So what next?" Jill plucked her jeans from the floor and stepped into them, struggling to pull them up over her damp skin. "Please tell me there's a punch line coming."

"It's no joke," Leo replied from behind Arden. He crossed the room and stood naked in front of Jill. "Without your love, we're dead."

"So let me get this straight." Jill dragged her turtleneck down over her wet hair. "You two are cursed shape-shifters who have spent years screwing the same women in the hopes one of them would be gullible enough to fall in love with both of you, thereby solving all your problems. Did I miss anything?" Her words were laced with sarcasm, hurt and betrayal.

Frustration and fear surged through Arden. She didn't believe them. His muscles contracted to the point of pain and he swallowed a groan. Everything was spiraling out of control and he was helpless to stop it.

"I'm sorry I have to do this, Jill, but you need to understand." In a blur of flesh and fur, Leo shifted to his lion form.

Jill's shocked gasp echoed in the sudden quiet. Arden cursed his other, impulsive half and stepped in front of the animal, blocking Jill's view.

But it was too late. Jill stared past Arden. "Oh God. A lion...a lion. Leo's a lion." She backed away in fright, grasping her shoes and socks like a lifeline. "Leo the lion...Arden the eagle." She spoke the words softly as tears began to fall. Her liquid gaze accusatorily locked on Arden, like a dagger stabbing into his heart. "You're an eagle."

"Yes," he replied simply.

"I want to see it," she demanded, shivers racking her tiny frame.

"Jill—"

"Do it." Her voice was eerily calm…distant.

The normal pain of shifting was dull in comparison to the pain of facing the withdrawal of the woman he loved. Arms became wings, hair became feathers as the shift to eagle worked toward completion. Before the urge to fly free took over, he returned to human again, rippling from one form to another with practiced ease. He held an arm out to her, but she backed away, turning toward the stairs. His last hope died with her retreat.

One foot on the top step, she paused, her voice so quiet he had to strain to hear her. "You got what you wanted. I did love you both." She pounded down the stairs.

Leo returned to human form and started after Jill. Arden grabbed him, pulling him back. "We lost her." Arden felt a blow as the front door slammed shut. "Just let her go."

"No!" Leo roared, eyes flashing angrily as he tried to disengage Arden's grasp. Muscles rippled violently beneath flesh. "I love her."

"Nice of you to finally make the goddamn admission, but it's too late. No matter how much we love her, we can't make her stay."

Leo's fingers dug into Arden's hand, urging it to unshackle. "We can convince her. I won't let her leave us. I'd rather die than live without her."

"So you're going to force her to stay?" Arden shook his head. "You shouldn't have shifted."

Leo swiped at Arden and growled. "If you had just told her the truth the other night at dinner—"

"She would've run away then. Can you blame her?" Arden released him and turned toward the open sliding glass door. He could fly away, leave the racking, burning pain behind. His vision blurred as another round of rapid muscle contractions surged through him. He gritted his teeth, refusing to fall to his knees. Maybe the curse hadn't been broken and death waited just around the corner. He couldn't summon the energy to care.

"If you fly away, we are dead." Leo's words echoed both in Arden's mind and in the room around him.

Arden gripped his head as the world blurred again. "Yeah, well you said it yourself." He began his shift. "Without her…"

An explosion of pain knocked him off his feet as a million bursts of bright, furious light blasted from every cell of his body, ripping him apart.

Chapter Eight

A cold fist squeezed Jill's heart, draining all happiness from its depths. Fear kept her moving forward and into her car, when she would've rather sunk to her knees and let the tears run dry. But then everything she'd lost when her reality catapulted into fantasy would crash through her mind, furthering her torment.

What had happened back there? Jill had a death grip on the steering wheel as she drove away from their house. Jesus, she'd thought falling in love with two men was crazy—but this...this was straitjacket, need-to-be-heavily-medicated insanity. The men she loved were animals. Raw, powerful, beautiful...beasts.

Hot tears scalded her cheeks. She brushed them away with the back of her hand, but more fell in their place. Love had never hurt so badly.

Looking through the windshield, she realized in her daze she'd turned down a street that dead-ended overlooking the ocean. Her tires crunched over gravel as she slowed to a halt, parking near the cement embankment. She rolled down the window, and closed her eyes, letting the chill ocean breeze wash over her. Salty air mingled with tears washing down her face.

Leo the lion...Arden the eagle. The wordplay they'd exchanged last night over dinner when she'd noticed their tattoos held all-new meaning now. Plus the oddity of seeing a lion on the cliffs of Talisman Bay had been explained. Leo watching her with his brother...other half...whatever their relationship was.

How could they be the same man split into two? Heck, how could they be animals? Magic...curses...it was too much to take in. Jill's head pounded, the ache spreading from her heart throughout her body.

Leo had stood before her, naked and beautiful, water dotting his skin. Then he blurred, his shape losing focus. It wasn't a mist, and it wasn't like he'd melted. The air had stirred around him and one moment he was man, the next, lion. Water droplets clung to his fur, the same luscious gold as his hair. Even in lion form he was regal, mesmerizing...the same characteristics that had drawn her to his human half.

And Arden...his change had been almost too quick to comprehend. Man, eagle, man. A flash of dark feathers, wings, and then he was human again. Although his eyes had remained the same through the change. Human, emotional, full of love, fear and regret.

Leo, too, had watched her while the lion paced. Begging her to understand, to accept them in all their forms. Begging her to stay.

Without your love, we're dead.

God, what had she done? Would Leo and Arden cease to exist because she'd run away from them?

Starting the car, Jill slammed into reverse, desperate to get back to their house. She felt the clock ticking with every beat of her heart. Ice-cold fear made her teeth chatter and her fingers clench tighter on the steering wheel. How could she have feared them? They would never hurt her. She *knew* that, just like she knew they loved her, too. The moment the three of them came together in the spa, a deeper connection had been born, their love a tangible presence in the water around them. No one else could ever make her feel the way Leo and Arden did. Emotionally, physically, sexually...they completed her.

The three minutes it took to get back to their house felt like an eternity. She bolted from the car, scared at what she might find inside. The door was closed but unlocked.

"Arden! Leo!" she called as she threw the door open, already moving toward the stairs.

There was no response.

Darting up the stairs, she entered the home theater. The room was empty...dark. The movie had come to an end, reverting to the DVD menu screen. Behind the options, two lovers were locked in an embrace. The movie's theme music, sad, longing, beautiful, poured from the speakers.

Leo's clothes were scattered throughout the room, marking the path of their lovemaking. The sliding door was still open, cold air filling the room, numbing her heart, freezing the tears on her cheeks.

They were gone.

She felt as though she were moving in slow motion as she canvassed the rest of the house. Their bedrooms, office, the living room, kitchen, backyard, everything was as before, beds made, dishes left over from dinner stacked haphazardly in the sink. Yet the house was an empty shell all the same, lacking the life brought to it by its inhabitants.

A pile of clothes was stacked on the floor in the living room—Arden's clothes, which explained his nudity when he'd come upstairs earlier. His leather jacket was draped over the back of the couch. It was as though the two men had just disappeared, leaving everything behind undisturbed.

A sob froze in her throat. She was so cold...couldn't think...couldn't breathe. Picking up Arden's jacket, she fingered the butter soft leather, lifting it to her face and inhaling his sunshine. She smelled Arden and Leo, their combined scents a heavy musk on her skin. The evidence of their lovemaking lingered in every aching muscle, their fluids mingling with hers. She could still taste them on her lips. A small spark of hope flickered to life inside her numb heart.

They couldn't be dead. She loved them. Had never stopped loving them. If her love was the only key to keeping them alive, they would not die tonight.

Wrapping Arden's jacket around her, she ran to her car. In her haste to get in the house, she'd left the engine running.

Sliding behind the wheel, she murmured a prayer, hoping she was right and that they were still within reach.

Finding the coastal road she and Arden had ridden on two nights ago was easy, finding the cliff was not. Two hours passed as she made stop after stop, hoping she'd found the spot, feeling more disappointed each time she returned to her car alone.

Pushing the growing weariness and fear from her mind, she pulled over again at yet another familiar-looking location. Unfortunately, almost everything appeared familiar under the glow of the full moon.

Pocketing her keys, she closed the car door and headed down a dirt path, too narrow for her car. Her hands and face were scratched, her clothing muddied from an earlier fall. To avoid a repeat performance, she studied the ground as she walked.

Her heart tumbled erratically as she noticed a slight groove in the dirt, resembling a tire track. Frantically she surveyed the area. Yes! This was it.

Energy surged through her and she ran through bushes and trees, ignoring the pain of branches whipping against her body, snagging her hair and skin. Rejoicing, she broke through the trees and onto the cliff, the Pacific Ocean filling her vision.

There was no one here.

Spinning in a circle, she studied the bushes where she'd first seen Leo in lion form, glanced beneath the tree where she and Arden had lain, even looked to the sky, praying for a glimpse of wings.

Nothing…no one…she was alone.

The final spark of hope winked out. She'd lost.

Time passed as she stood there, grief numbing her to the bone. The roar of the ocean continued unhampered, a strange occurrence when everything else felt beyond repair. She crept to the edge, watching the waves crash against the rocks below. Nature in all its violent beauty.

Wind whipped the air as the night sky grew darker, clouds drawing over the moon like curtains at the end of a performance. She lifted her face, surveying for evidence of a storm.

Silvers of moonlight reflected off something in the distance. She narrowed her eyes, searching the night.

A shadow split from the darkness, leveling downward. Joy ricocheted through her as the black crown of an eagle's head became visible. Arden was alive!

His wings spanned the night as he flew toward her, black feathers melding downward into a lighter golden shade. But the gold didn't look like feathers, it looked like fur...

This wasn't Arden...this wasn't an eagle.

This was mythology come to life.

Fantasy converged with reality as the gryphon stretched out its claws, gracefully landing on the cliff in front of her.

The creature lifted its head, and in a blur of motion, the gryphon was gone. A nude man stood in its place.

Golden brown hair brushed his wide shoulders. He was lean, muscular, beautiful, a body built for flight. A tattoo of a gryphon in vibrant shades of black, brown and gray graced his upper arm. A sprinkling of bronze hair began at his chest and arrowed downward converging at the vee of his thighs. His cock was magnificent even at rest, lying in its bed of curls. Under her steady perusal, his shaft grew larger.

Physically, everything about him was familiar, yet different, a confusing combination that made her stomach twist in anxious longing.

His arm flexed as he reached out to her, making the tattoo of the gryphon appear as if it were jumping into flight. "Jill..."

The voice was familiar, part growl, part smooth seduction. She lifted her gaze, studying his face. Full lips, craggy jaw, strong cheekbones, the face of a leader, a lover, a friend. Finally, she met his golden gaze, and in his eyes she saw the souls of the men she loved.

A cry ripped from her throat and she threw herself into his arms.

She tried to touch him everywhere at once, her hands taking inventory, basking in his vitality. As though he was waiting for her full acceptance, he remained still, letting her explore the new man he'd become. His muscles flexed beneath her fingertips, straining to respond. Rubbing her face against his chest, she listened to the steady, reassuring beat of his heart. Leo and Arden had come back to her. They weren't dead, just in renewed flesh.

Sighing, she pulled his mouth down to hers. Their first kiss, a tender recognition evolving into frenzied reunion.

"My love. Mine. Forever," he murmured, his lips laying claim to her neck.

"Yes...forever..." She gasped as he tugged her fabric-covered nipple between his teeth. "I thought I'd lost you."

She shrugged off the jacket, needing to feel his flesh against hers. As she tugged her shirt up, he lowered her pants, pausing to kiss just below her belly button. "Jill, you never need to worry again." He kissed lower as she ran her hands through his soft locks of hair. "You've already seen the worst of my oddities." After laving her clitoris with tender wet kisses, he turned his head sideways and hugged her to him. "I love you."

"I love you, too." The words erupted from her throat as her body began to tingle. Giddy, alive, in love. The man holding her was more than twice the man she'd ever dreamed of.

He gazed up at her and with mischievous fire in his eyes breathed, "Show me."

"Mmmm..." Jill smiled and wiggled out of his grasp. Her darn shoes and socks were still on, preventing her from stepping out of her pants. Once down on the grass, she removed every last stitch of fabric. As he watched her disrobe, a droplet grew on the tip of his cock, glistening in the moonlight.

She had every intention of teasing him, learning his new shape, but as soon as her hand met his thigh, she couldn't hold back. All of her need, welling to the surface, pooling between her legs, all of her love shimmering along her skin. Touching him magnified every sensation. A thigh brushed his, her knee swept to his hip. Using her fingernails, she traced from his hip up to his shoulder letting her lips continue the path, laving his neck, tasting his stubble, losing herself in his sunshine.

Shifting her body weight, she ground her hips against his just to feel his heat, his hardness. Jill buried a hand in the locks tumbling to his shoulder and he grabbed her ass, his fingers kneading. Her juices coating his shaft, she raised and lowered her hips, rocking her clit against him.

As she continued stroking toward heaven, he brought his hands to her breasts, cupping them, toying with her nipples. Another moan escaped her lips as she spread her legs, straddling him, nudging his shaft until finally impaling herself on his throbbing length.

They both cried out. She was complete with him buried inside. Her cunt squeezed tightly as they rocked together, matching each other's motions. She sat up straight, riding him deeper and deeper against her womb. He seized her hips, grinding, combining sex and love as their bodies became one.

A dynamic frenzy built with each thrust, each rub, each stirring thrill. Their fervor equal in every action, their gazes locked. Jill needed this man more than she'd ever needed anyone. She needed his seed planted within her. Needed his sunshine, his magic, his everything.

Her orgasm erupted from somewhere deep inside, urging him to join her on the primal, beautiful bonding of two souls in love. She collapsed on his chest, their bodies still attached, writhing gently. His arms enclosed her tightly as she cuddled into him, lost in pleasure, lost in lust, lost in love.

And somewhere in the fog of completion, she discovered the one question that hadn't occurred to her sooner. "What should I call you?"

She felt his smile against her forehead. "Leonard. My name is Leonard."

* * * * *

Jill woke to the first rays of morning sun caressing her flesh. The dawn was cool and crisp, and she inhaled, filling her lungs with fresh sea breeze.

They'd never left the cliff last night. Leonard's tight embrace kept her warm, and she'd fallen into a deep, peaceful sleep.

Eyes still closed to avoid the sun's glare, she stretched, awakening muscles sore from yesterday's many activities. Behind her, Leonard shifted in sleep, his hand lifting to cup her breast. Something warm and soft caressed up her bare leg, brushing over her flesh. Fur teased the back of her knee and she giggled.

Wait a second? Fur?

Jill's eyes shot open.

A golden pelt shone brilliant in the sunlight, nearly blinding her. A lion slept peacefully in front of her, his tail curling around her legs. A lion...not a gryphon.

But how? Who?

Jill sat upright with a jolt, the male hand cradling her breast falling into her lap. She faced the man who until moments ago had been spooning her. Dark curls covered a sleepy-eyed gaze, morning stubble thick on Arden's beautiful, rugged face.

"Jill? What's wrong?" he asked, slowly coming awake.

The animal behind her stirred, its soft head nudging her back while he purred. She reached back, stroking the silky hide. The purring grew louder, and a sandpaper tongue laved over her shoulders and along the back of her neck.

Arden shot upright. "What the hell?" He looked down at his flesh, patting himself disbelievingly. He studied his tattoo, once again a soaring eagle. "How?"

"At least I'm not the only one flabbergasted." Giddiness filled her and she laughed. She'd never thought she'd see them again in their separate forms. This was strange, wonderful, too good to be true. Even if it were to only last a few moments, she wanted this time to remember Leo and Arden—Leonard—in the forms she'd fallen in love with him...them.

Beneath Jill's hand, she felt a shift...muscles trembling, fur becoming flesh and Leo's voice, "Well, this is a surprise." He lifted her hand, tangling their fingers together.

"Yeah, no kidding." Jill shook her head. "How do— What do—?"

Arden shifted quickly into eagle form and then back, his eyes registering astonishment and fascination. Then both Leo and Arden elevated off the ground, their humanity transforming into eagle and lion before morphing together, flowing into the shape of a gryphon. The beautiful creature spread its wings to their fullest and stretched its legs as it softly landed. Bowing to Jill, the gryphon brought its wings forward. Swinging back, they transfigured to form arms as its body became Leonard's.

As though he was just passing through, he lifted once more, his essence separating into fur and feathers. As lion and eagle, they landed and paced before lifting again and returning to Leonard.

Jill lost herself in the magic of the ever-changing menagerie. There was a sensuality to the shifts, watching two bodies become one, then two again, animal to human, the ripple of muscles underneath tight flesh, fur and feather. Desire flowed through her body and her toes curled into soft dirt. Their show of power and strength had a very interesting effect on her libido.

Leonard appeared again, shifting out of gryphon form. He smiled, kneeling in front of her. "I guess I got more than I bargained for. We'd always thought once we became one again, we'd be just that...one."

He shifted to Leo and Arden. "Sorry if we scare you. We—I am still getting used to this." They spoke in unison.

"I think all of us are trying to make some sense of this." Lounging backward onto her elbows, she grinned. "I don't care how many of you there are, or what you look like, or how high you fly, fast you run, whatever. You're mine."

Arden and Leo shifted through gryphon form back to Leonard. "I think, at this point, that's the only thing I'm sure of. I'm all yours." He studied his hands for a moment as if still trying to comprehend his new self. "It's strange. As Leo, I could get to lion form, but not eagle or gryphon, for obvious reasons. As Arden I could get to eagle, but not gryphon or lion. So, I guess combining what I learned while I was two halves, as whole, I can be any of my incarnations. I just think myself into the shift and I come out as planned. I…we never imagined it would be possible, but I think I like it."

"You think you do… I get to have three men in one and then some." Jill reached out and tugged on Leonard's arm, bringing him closer.

"If it hadn't been for the hovering threat of death, I would've happily remained separate just so I could still completely surround you, fill you, take you, making you mine in every way imaginable." His hands skimmed over her flesh, claiming her with every touch.

"I'll take you anyway I can have you. As one or two." She kissed him, startled when the lips she was kissing morphed and two mouths began loving her flesh. "This is going to take some getting used to," she laughed.

Then her men did as they'd promised, surrounding her, filling her, taking her, making her theirs over and over again.

Epilogue

"Trick or treat!"

Sitting in the office in the back of the house, Jill smiled as the sound of children's laughter mixed with Arden and Leo's teasing growls. The duo loved Halloween, dressing up in fur and feathers to pass out candy to the neighborhood kids. It was the one day of the year they could become their other halves for public consumption.

The rest of the year, they were hers alone.

The computer booted up smoothly and Jill clicked buttons and typed in her webmail password. It was time to introduce her mom to Leonard.

Hi Mom~

I know you've been worried about me, alone so far from home. Well, I'm not alone anymore. Someone wonderful has come into my life. His name is Leonard, and he embodies everything I've ever wanted. He's kind, honest, charming, adventurous and he loves me as much as I love him.

And yes, he's for real. ☺ He even has a really good job, running an advertising and web development company with his two brothers, Leo and Arden.

I'm really blessed, Mom. They've welcomed me into their family, just like I hope you and Dad will welcome them into ours.

Today, Leonard asked me to marry him and even though the courtship has been quick, I've said yes. I know it's right, just like you knew the first time you saw Dad that there was no one else for you. Leonard completes me.

Since I know you're going to ask, yes I'm bringing Leonard with me for Thanksgiving. I want to show off the man I love.

I love you, Mom. Give Dad a kiss for me and I'll see you in a few weeks.

XOXO,
Jill

She reread the email to make sure she hadn't slipped and spoken in plural about her men. Somehow she didn't think her mother would understand how two men could become one, let alone the fur and feathers that came with them. She clicked send, launching the email into cyberspace.

The ring on her finger sparkled in the light from the screen. She didn't know how Leo and Arden had done it, but while she was at work today, they'd found a ring that suited their relationship perfectly. Three brilliant blue sapphires formed a triangle around a larger pear-shaped diamond.

The men had bought matching bands, diamonds and sapphires embedded in platinum. Although each of them wearing wedding bands would eventually draw questions as to who exactly Jill was married to, neither Leo nor Arden were willing to part with the symbol of their attachment. They'd even practiced shifting with the bands on to see if they could take the rings with them. Fabric ripped to shreds during transformation, but metal was more durable and made it through the phasing. As Leonard, the two rings came together, forming one larger band around his finger. In their animal forms, the rings disappeared behind feathers, or embedded in the mane.

Before shutting down the computer, Jill's gaze skimmed over the subject lines of the piled up mail in her inbox. Charlene's *Top Ten Things to Avoid on Halloween* still remained unread.

She clicked it open and began to read. Her jaw dropped, then shock turned to outright laughter.

"All right, what's so funny?" Leo asked as he walked into the room. He nuzzled the back of her neck and his fake whiskers tickled, making her giggle anew.

Arden knelt next to her and she stared at his plastic beak. Her giggles turned to guffaws and she struggled to take a breath.

"Why do I feel like we're the joke here?" Arden smiled, pulling the cone-shaped beak from his face and tossing it onto the desk.

Tears dropped from Jill's eyes, and she lifted her finger, pointing out a line on the screen.

Never trust a man in costume. They wear what they know and you get what you see. So unless you like getting plundered, avoid pirates, and stay away from animals unless you have a thing for Animal Planet.

"Are we that obvious?" Leo questioned, a twinkle in his eyes as he gestured to his oversized lion suit.

Arden flapped his black wings and harrumphed. "So, if you'd read that before we met—"

"I watch *Animal Planet* religiously." She stood up, immediately finding herself surrounded.

Fake fur and plastic fell to the floor and Jill happily surrendered to the men behind the costumes.

About the author:

Sometimes two people meet, become good friends, and share a lot in common. When you're really lucky, you meet someone who understands you, who thinks like you, can finish your sentences and together, the both of you can create whole new worlds.

Ashleigh Raine is the pen name for two best friends, Jennifer and Lisa, who share a passion for strong alpha males that succumb to the women they fall in love with. These two met in junior high where they were band geeks (but they swear they really were cool…they were percussionists after all!) But love of the arts didn't end with band. By high school, the two had a small following of fans for their stories and the characters they created…characters that would become the inspiration for their Talisman Bay series. They want to thank those fans for their continued support and interest. They couldn't have done it without them!

Both Lisa and Jennifer are married to their soul mates, who are the best support and inspiration. As Ashleigh Raine, this duo has many stories to tell, as their collective mind never stops creating fantasies that must be written down. They write larger than life stories, with adventures, hot sex, peril, hot sex, mystery, and more hot sex…but most assuredly they have a happy ending, usually with hot sex. Watch for many titles coming soon from this duo who are glad to have found their niche in writing erotic romances.

Ashleigh Raine welcomes mail from readers. You can write c/o Ellora's Cave Publishing at 1056 Home Ave. Akron, Oh 44310-3502.

Also by Ashleigh Raine:

Acting On Impulse
Angel In Moonlight
Forsaken Talisman
Lover's Talisman
Mesmerized anthology
Ellora's Cavemen: Legendary Tails IV

Enjoy this excerpt from
Things That Go Bump In The Night III

Prologue

"Fuck." Miznari Anderson whipped a thick blue penis out of her backpack. "I forgot to buy batteries for my vibrator."

Natalie Capella choked on the gulp of wine she'd just swallowed. Merlot shot up her nose. Her throat burned and her eyes watered as she tried to hold back her laughter.

"Put that thing away!" Kerry Perry's face turned as red as the checkered tablecloth. After a quick glance around the crowded Italian restaurant, she added, "Hurry, before someone sees it."

Natalie could only shake her head, her deep wine-red hair spilling over her shoulders as she dabbed her nose with a cloth napkin. Every time the three friends managed to get-together, Miz would find some way to embarrass the hell out of Kerry. Earlier that morning, when Nat had flown to Virginia from her home in New York City, she'd wondered what Miz was going to come up with this time.

"Don't you like it?" Miz's brown eyes went wide, her face the picture of innocence as she extended the vibrator across the table toward Kerry. "See how realistic the rubber is? Feels like a cock. A good ten inches, and it even glows in the dark."

Kerry shrank away from the dildo, her hazel gaze narrowing behind the prim wire frames of her glasses. In her decidedly schoolteacher voice, she commanded, "Put that in your backpack, *now*."

"I've read your erotic romances, Ker." Miz drew back, encircled the blue cock with her fingers and moved her hand up and down the penis from base to head. "You may dress like Miss Marple. Hell, you may even act like Miss Manners. But on the inside, sweetie, you're *Debbie Does Dallas*." She put the cock to her lips and swirled her tongue over the head. Miz never wore a bra and her nipples were obviously hard, poking through the thin material of her blouse.

"Miz Anderson," Kerry hissed the 's' like a snake on steroids. "Put that damn thing away before I shove it up your — your — "

"Ass?" With a grin, Miz tucked the vibrator into her pack. "Now there's a thought."

Pursing her lips, Kerry straightened the jacket of her brown herringbone suit. "You're such a shit."

"Did our Miss Perry just say *shit*?" Miz turned her mischievous brown gaze on Natalie. "Who'd've thunk it?"

"You *are* a shit." Natalie laughed and pushed away her half-eaten plate of manicotti. "But that's why we love you," she added as the waiter left the dinner bill and cleared the plates.

Kerry dug in her purse and pulled out her wallet. "Humph."

Smells of garlic bread and lasagna permeated the restaurant, along with the hum of voices, clinking of plates and Italian music in the background. Natalie absently rubbed the star tattoo that surrounded her bellybutton and the gold piercing. The tattoo she'd gotten after losing a dare to Miz in college, the piercing just because she'd felt like it. The tattoo was a unique star pattern that matched the birthmark behind her left earlobe.

Natalie shifted in her seat, her jean skirt feeling a bit snug and her thong underwear riding up her butt. It was Halloween night, and the three former college roommates had managed to squeeze in time for dinner before the "Out of this World" fantasy and sci-fi convention they were all attending that evening — the stupid convention Miz had coerced Natalie into patronizing. Miz was a cover artist and costume designer, actively involved with the convention. She insisted, on threat of public dildo use, that Nat participate in one of the exhibits Miz's friend was running.

"So, Nat." Miz flipped her short dark hair out of her eyes. "Looking forward to tonight's little experiment?"

It was all Natalie could do to hold back a groan. "I don't know how I let you talk me into these things."

"It'll be a kick-ass night." Miz grabbed the bottle of merlot and drained what little was left into her own glass. "From what Rod told me, this virtual reality machine is so realistic you'll feel like you're actually in a fantasy world. Like being in a fairytale."

"Fantasy. Riiiiight." Natalie took a sip of her merlot, enjoying the warmth flowing down her throat. She'd need several bottles of wine before she started believing in fairytales. She returned the glass to the table and trailed her fingers up and down the stem. "The only fantasies I believe in are the ones I have when I'm riding the purple bunny."

"Bunny?" Kerry paused, a twenty dollar bill in hand for the waiter, and glanced from Natalie to Miz. "What purple bunny and what does it have to do with fantasy?"

"For writing romantic erotica, you sure are naïve." Miz leaned forward, her small breasts pressed against the table. In a loud voice she said, "Nat's talking about a vibrator that has little bunny ears. The ears stimulate the clit."

Kerry's face went redder than her auburn hair as she tossed the twenty on the table and pushed out her chair. "It's time to go." She grabbed her leather briefcase, stood, and raised her chin in the air. "I need to check in at the convention center and have time to go over my presentation."

"You know what you need to loosen up, Kerry?" Miz rifled through her backpack, dug out some cash and tossed it on top of the twenty. "You need a good fuck."

Sucking in her breath, Kerry clutched her briefcase to her chest. Her eyes darted to Natalie in an apparent plea for support.

"She's right." Natalie plunked down her share of the bill and grabbed her jacket off the back of her chair. "You need to get laid."

With a resigned sigh, Kerry patted her severe bun and adjusted her glasses. "You may be right."

Miz cracked up with laughter and Natalie grinned.

The women headed out of the restaurant to the nearby Williamsburg convention center that housed the "Out of this World" convention. It was a short walk, and Natalie enjoyed the feel of the crisp fall Virginia air against her cheeks and the cool breeze stirring her wine-red hair around her shoulders. A harvest moon, perfect for Halloween night, was just rising over the Atlantic.

"What the hell is that?" Miz gestured toward a light in the distance.

Natalie squinted, watching the white glowing object float through the night sky and then vanish behind a grove of trees. "No clue."

"Probably something to do with Halloween." Kerry picked up her pace. "Let's hurry, ladies. I don't want to be late."

An eerie sensation trailed down Natalie's spine. She shivered and slid her hands into the pockets of her jacket. If she had been the slightest bit superstitious, she would have turned around and headed straight back to her apartment in New York City and to that purple bunny waiting in her lingerie drawer.

COMING TO A BOOKSTORE NEAR YOU!

ELLORA'S CAVE
2005

BEST SELLING AUTHORS TOUR

Why an electronic book?

We live in the Information Age—an exciting time in the history of human civilization in which technology rules supreme and continues to progress in leaps and bounds every minute of every hour of every day. For a multitude of reasons, more and more avid literary fans are opting to purchase e-books instead of paperbacks. The question to those not yet initiated to the world of electronic reading is simply: *why?*

1. *Price.* An electronic title at Ellora's Cave Publishing and Cerridwen Press runs anywhere from 40-75% less than the cover price of the <u>exact same title</u> in paperback format. Why? Cold mathematics. It is less expensive to publish an e-book than it is to publish a paperback, so the savings are passed along to the consumer.

2. *Space.* Running out of room to house your paperback books? That is one worry you will never have with electronic novels. For a low one-time cost, you can purchase a handheld computer designed specifically for e-reading purposes. Many e-readers are larger than the average handheld, giving you plenty of screen room. Better yet, hundreds of titles can be stored within your new library—a single microchip. (Please note that Ellora's Cave and Cerridwen Press does not endorse any specific brands. You can check our website at www.ellorascave.com or

www.cerridwenpress.com for customer recommendations we make available to new consumers.)

3. *Mobility.* Because your new library now consists of only a microchip, your entire cache of books can be taken with you wherever you go.

4. *Personal preferences are accounted for.* Are the words you are currently reading too small? Too large? Too…**ANNOYING**? Paperback books cannot be modified according to personal preferences, but e-books can.

5. *Instant gratification.* Is it the middle of the night and all the bookstores are closed? Are you tired of waiting days—sometimes weeks—for online and offline bookstores to ship the novels you bought? Ellora's Cave Publishing sells instantaneous downloads 24 hours a day, 7 days a week, 365 days a year. Our e-book delivery system is 100% automated, meaning your order is filled as soon as you pay for it.

Those are a few of the top reasons why electronic novels are displacing paperbacks for many an avid reader. As always, Ellora's Cave and Cerridwen Press welcomes your questions and comments. We invite you to email us at service@ellorascave.com, service@cerridwenpress.com or write to us directly at: 1056 Home Ave. Akron OH 44310-3502.

Discover for yourself why readers can't get enough of the multiple award-winning publisher Ellora's Cave. Whether you prefer e-books or paperbacks, be sure to visit EC on the web at www.ellorascave.com for an erotic reading experience that will leave you breathless.

www.EllorasCave.com